CW01371548

Books by Ivan Scott

Redhead in a Blue Convertible

The Redhead and the Ghostwriter

A Redhead in Tottenham

The Redhead Who Loves Hemingway

A Redhead In Brooklyn

Ivan Scott

Copyright © 2024 Ivan Scott
All rights reserved.
ISBN: 9798875603792

For the Brooklyn Dodger players and fans. I hope I captured a magical time and place that no longer exists with charm and respect. May you relive those days while reading this story

I hope everyone who has an unfulfilled dream will be inspired by the words in this book, and find the courage to follow their heart.

And for my Redhead, who is my dreams every day.

one

Sam Murdock rolled over in bed and looked out the window at the tangy orange sky. As the colors soothed him, he knew that would be the best he'd feel for the rest of the day.

He watched the light slicing through the buildings, which offered a welcomed distraction from what lay ahead. He knew once he moved, the spears of pain surging through his body, which had become a constant companion over the years, would be back to say good morning.

Sam looked at his elbow, which was now an elegant shade of purple. When he moved his arm to see how far the purple had taken it over, his shoulder sent a painful reminder of what happened the previous evening.

He dreaded rolling out of bed, since he wasn't sure if his legs would support him. To defer having to deal with that adversity, he took a few moments longer than usual to stare at the ceiling. If he lay still enough, there would be no pain for as long as he could stay in that position.

Tempting fate, he rotated his head to find the clock. When he saw the time, his head returned to the middle of his shoulders, and eyes to the ceiling. *It's time to get to work.*

He exhaled, then allowed himself a few more moments of peace.

After debating when to make his next move, Sam took a deep breath, closed his eyes, and told his body at the count of three he would place his feet on the floor. At the count of two, he jumped the gun and swung his legs through the sheets and to the carpet, hoping to catch the pain off guard.

There was a momentary numbness, then the pain washed over him as it had for so many years. *So much for catching it off guard.* Sam couldn't remember the last morning when he felt nothing but the carpet under his toes.

He wobbled on painful knees to the window. In the distance, he saw the place where all the hurting took place. As the morning hue illuminated his face, he smiled. *I'm the luckiest man in the world. I get to play baseball today.*

Sam pulled up his baseball pants, buckled his belt, and sat down in front of his locker to put his spikes on. As he put his left spike on first, he enjoyed the banter between the players. "Hey, Jacobs," a player yelled over. "Next time, can you throw the ball in the same area code as where my glove is?"

The players laughed.

Jacobs answered. "Sure, sweetheart. Want me to gift wrap it for you too?"

Sam laughed, then brought his leg up to put on his other

spike. He winced when his leg caught the side of his knee. "Ow," he said, looking down at where the pain came from. He slid his foot inside and laced it up. He was ready to go.

As the laughter died down, manager Mike Backman walked in from his office. "Anyone seen Harrington?"

Sam looked over at the locker next to his. It was empty.

He's late again, Sam thought to himself. *Better cover for him.* "Yeah, I saw him down by the batting cages earlier."

Backman nodded. "Tell him I need to see him."

"Will do."

Sam covered for Jeremy Harrington more than once. He saw the talent on the first day they met and took him under his wing. When he looked at Harrington, he saw himself from years ago. The difference was Harrington was late for many things, and forgetful of others and didn't take his career seriously. Sam took on the role of mentor.

As was the drill, Sam took Harrington's uniform, hat, and socks into the restroom. He tossed them into the last stall, then walked down the hallway to the player's entrance, hoping to intercept Harrington before Backman did.

On cue, the door opened. "Where have you been?" Sam asked.

Harrington took off his sunglasses. "I'm sorry, Sam. I got in late last night and slept through my alarm clock."

Sam looked him over. "Your eyes look like two stop signs. How hungover are you?"

Harrington rubbed the bridge of his nose with his fingers. "My head is playing the 'Bells of St. Marys.'"

"What did I tell you about staying out all night before an afternoon game? And setting more than one alarm clock? Damn it, this is your career."

"I know, I know."

"Oh, and here's some breaking news. Backman wants to see you in his office. I told him you were in the batting cage."

Harrington exhaled.

Sam shook his head. "If I didn't like you, and if you weren't the best player in the League, I would keep my mouth shut and watch you roll right down the drain."

Harrington nodded.

"Don't disrespect the game or yourself. You're better than this."

"I won't. Promise," Harrington assured him. When the kid looked over at Sam, he asked, "You love the game, don't you?"

Sam smiled. "Yeah, I do. For me, baseball is life. Everything else is waiting. You should feel the same."

"I'll remember that. Thanks, Sam."

"You're welcome. You know what to do, right?"

"Last stall?"

"Yes. Get inside and get dressed. Then go see Backman."

"What if he asks about my eyes?"

Sam thought for a moment. "Tell him you saw 'Field of Dreams' and got emotional when Costner played catch with his father at the end. He'll understand."

Sam brushed unidentified crumbs off Harrington's shirt. "Splash some water on your face so it will look like you've been

A Redhead in Brooklyn

sweating from the batting cage."

"I will."

"And use the water from the sink. Not from the toilet like you did last time."

"Okay, Sam," he said with a laugh.

Sam looked him over, then shook his head as he limped back to the lockers. "You have to stay on top of these guys every minute of the day."

Sam removed his cap, wiped his sweaty forehead, then placed the bill lower to shield his eyes. Even though he applied eye black to keep the sun from blinding him, the suffocating August haze was famous for tricking an outfielder.

He crouched in left field, ignoring the slicing pain in his right knee, and the dull ache in the left, and focused on the infield.

Sam chewed on a fresh piece of gum, then blew a bubble as he looked at the batter. It was a ritual from his little league days to drop a new piece of gum in his mouth before every inning, then before the pitch, blow a bubble.

The white blur out of the pitcher's hand heading to the batter became a loud crack, echoing through the stadium. A new blur arched into the sky, altering Sam to move. He ignored what his knees told him, turned, and ran to the wall.

No way you are going over my head, Sam thought as he ran full speed to where he thought the ball would land. He ran as fast as his sore knees permitted, then looked up for the ball. When he heard the crunchy warning track under his spikes, he was out of room.

Sam instinctively looked for the wall and, seeing he still had a few more steps, turned back and looked for the ball. He lost it in the clouds, so he put his glove up to where he thought it would come down.

To his horror, a white flash sailed over his glove, bounced on the warning track, and caromed off the wall and into the air. In his haste to get the ball back to the infield, he didn't hear the collective groan of the home crowd.

Sam gathered the ball in, turned, and threw it back into the infield. He watched the shortstop catch the ball, then wheeled and threw it to third base. When the runner slid head first and the umpire flapped his arms like a bird, Sam knew the runner was safe.

He dropped an F-bomb, then doubled over as the pain in both knees reached crippling levels.

"You okay, Sam?" The center fielder asked as he trotted over.

Sam limped a few steps, then gathered himself. "Yeah, I'm fine. I got a lousy jump on the ball. I'll get the next one."

"You saved the game for us last night. Don't worry about it."

The next batter struck out to end the inning. Sam trotted to the dugout, masking the gripping pain with each step. He entered to the farthest side so Backman couldn't see him limping.

From behind the dugout, a man wearing a fedora watched with interest.

Sam finished showering, and returned to his locker. He winced as he walked, measuring each step to lessen the intense pain in each knee. He found his stool, then finished drying off. He looked at the

A Redhead in Brooklyn

locker next to him. Harrington wasn't there.

Sam shook his head, then it hit him. *Did Backman figure out what happened earlier?*

As he dressed, Sam clowned with a few of his teammates who celebrated the victory. He told the pitcher who gave up the triple, "Why do you make me run across the state to catch those balls?"

That got a laugh out of the group. "Murdock," the pitcher replied as he put his watch over his wrist, "You run like a wounded turtle. Do they time you with a sundial?"

That got a larger laugh. Sam laughed the loudest.

One of the other players asked, "Was Babe Ruth a teammate of yours?"

Laughter echoed off the lockers. "Nah, I'm not that old. But my last birthday cake I couldn't blow out the candles," he told them. The players looked at him, waiting for the answer. Sam pulled his shirt off the hanger, then looked back at them. "The heat drove me back."

That broke everyone up. A few of the players extended their fists for Sam to bump. The pitcher from earlier told him, "You might be old, but I'd stick you in the outfield anytime I'm pitching."

Sam smiled and nodded. "Appreciate that."

As he buttoned his shirt, one of the clubhouse boys came over and handed him a note. "Thanks, Bobby," he told him as the kid walked away.

He opened it and read:

Dear Sam:

I'm sorry I didn't get to say goodbye in person. Backman told me I was being promoted to the majors, so I had to catch the next flight to Tampa.

One of the first things I'm going to do when I get there is buy another alarm clock. I promise to give everything I have since I owe that, not only to myself, but to you as well. I'll also remember everything you told me about respecting the game and being the best player and teammate I can be.

This is your victory as much as it is mine. I know you'll get promoted soon. I can't wait to fight the rest of the American League together.

Thank you for everything, Sam. Good luck in Durham. I'll see you here soon!

Jeremy

Sam smiled, then folded the letter and placed it in his locker.

"Hey, we're all heading to the Acme for a beer," one of his teammates told him. "Why don't you charge up that wheelchair of yours and meet us down there?"

Sam smiled. "The last time I met you guys, everyone was wasted by the time I got there, and the owner kicked you guys out and I had to drive everyone home. Never got a beer that night."

"Aw, we'll wait for you," they assured him.

Sam watched as they waved goodbye and walked out of the clubhouse. He pulled his jacket off the hanger and slid it on as a voice from the corner of the locker room called out. "Murdock? Can I see you for a minute?"

Sam looked over and saw Backman standing outside his office, motioning him to come into the office.

"Coach's pet," one of his teammates called out as the rest razzed him.

Sam smiled and shook his head. "Yeah. Backman must have a thing for wounded turtles.".

After a few steps in that direction, it came to him. *Am I on my way to Tampa too? I'm having a good season, so why not? Maybe all the perseverance was worth it.*

As Sam got to the door, his heartbeat accelerated, and he didn't feel the pain in his knees. He walked through the open door. "Hey, Mike. What's up?"

Backman stood in front of his desk and pointed to a chair. "Close the door, Sam. Have a seat."

Sam bit his lip as he walked into the office to mask the pain and plopped into a chair to take the weight off his knees. "Sorry about that one I couldn't get to in the sixth. I missed it by a step."

Backman didn't answer. His stone face looked at the floor, then exhaled. "Sam, I," he began, then stopped.

"What?"

Backman's eyes finally found Sam. "I'm sorry, but the organization wants to make a change. We are releasing you from your contract."

Sam stared at him, seeing the lost look in his eyes. As he stared, Backman looked away. His heartbeat continued pumping, but instead of hope, it was the dull thud of loss. The dream he carried for years now lay shattered on the ground in a million jagged pieces. There would be no healing.

Sam looked away, knowing nothing would change the decision. His eyes turned to his swollen knees, and instead of fighting the verdict, chose to have closure. "So what was it? My knees? Is that why they gave up on me?" He asked, unable to look Backman in the eyes.

"Yeah, Sam, I'm afraid that's it. You're not the same player as you were a few years ago. There's a kid at Asheville who is hitting the hell out of the ball, and they want to bring him up."

Sam was on autopilot. "I guess that's best for the team."

Backman gave him a sad grin. "I wish the rest of the players had your attitude. Hell, I wish some of them would at least show up on time. What I would give for some of these guys to care half as much as you do about the game. And about this team. I wish I could keep you and release the guys who don't have your work ethic."

Sam continued looking at the floor.

"I'm going to miss you. If you need anything, you have my number. I'll do whatever I can to help you." He exhaled and said, " I didn't want things to end this way."

"I understand," Sam said without thinking as his vision blurred. At the moment, he understood nothing. As his mind dropped into an abyss, he wouldn't remember limping back to his locker.

Luckily, he had the entire clubhouse to himself. Knowing time was running out on being a professional athlete, Sam savored the last moments of the life he knew. *I guess since I'm not one of the boys any longer, I won't be heading to the Acme for a beer.*

Sam cleaned out his locker, tossing what was his in a plastic bin. The last thing he took off the wall of his locker was a picture of him and his father during happier times. He stared at the photo and said, "I'm sorry, dad."

He placed the bin in his car and then returned to the clubhouse. He found the clubhouse boys and gave them all a hundred dollars as a token of his gratitude.

Sam looked around the clubhouse for the last time. With all the boxes checked, he turned and walked away from his life.

A Redhead in Brooklyn

Jeremy Harrington was the first to call, then several of his former teammates and friends. Among the calls was one from his former head coach at Clemson, Steve Wilson, who offered him a job as the hitting coach.

Sam wanted to play, not coach, so he told Wilson he'd think about it. He stalled for time since, in the deepest recesses of his mind, he hoped for a miracle. *Maybe another team will claim me off the scrap heap?*

As the days passed, and the phone didn't ring, Sam retreated further into his shell. He stayed in Durham for a few days to get all his loose ends tied up, then drove home to Kiawah Island on the South Carolina coast.

His father, Bunker Murdock, left Sam his beach house when he passed, and now, instead of living there in the off-season, it would be his permanent home.

Sam spent hours on the couch, staring at a spot to the right of the flat-screen television as one day flowed into the next. When it appeared its darkest, his agent called to tell him the Braves asked if he'd like to come to Spring Training. He'd be a non-roster invitee, but at least it was something. "I have to level with you, Sam," his agent told him. "They told me you'd be a long shot to make the active roster."

Since Sam was out of options to make good on the promise he made to his father to become a major league player, he told his agent he'd be there in February.

His life, which seemed happy and secure, was now nothing

but a large question mark, wrapped in a mysterious box tied off with a black ribbon.

I broke my promise. What do I do now?

Sam returned from a late night walk on the beach, hoping the waves would wash away memories of Durham, and also, a broken promise.

A vibration in his pocket broke him from the memory, so he reached inside and pulled out his phone. *Did someone from another team inquire about me?*

Sam looked at the screen, but it was only a text message reminding him that the medication he ordered for his knees was ready at the drugstore.

Serves me right for being an optimist.

He walked outside to the deck. Underneath the sound of the waves crashing to the shore, he stared into the night.

As he thought about how his life changed, another memory of his father came to him.

Sam listened as his father told him another story about his favorite baseball team, the Brooklyn Dodgers. On this night, his father sniffled as he told him about the Dodgers leaving Brooklyn for Los Angeles, and how he never got over it.

"When you're sixteen, and your favorite team leaves town, that's when reality hits you and, without knowing it, you're no longer a child. Only you never know it until years later when you look back and say, 'That's when my life changed forever.'"

When he thought about the words, Sam nodded. "This is the

moment he was talking about."

From the beach, a man wearing a fedora looked on.

two

Before sunrise, Sam packed his bat bag and took the short walk to his alma mater, Kiawah High School. He wanted to stay in shape since February would be here before he knew it, and he wanted to be ready for Spring Training.

As the dusky glow of the sky turned orange, he knew there was at least another hour before anyone would be around. Sam did his work then, since he didn't want anyone to see the once star baseball player of Kiawah High School was now an unemployed failure.

He walked to the power box, unlocked it with the key the groundskeeper gave him, then turned on the lights. Another key unlocked an equipment room. Waiting for him were the pitching machine and buckets of balls. He looked into the bucket and looking back at him were the dirty balls with red stitches. The sight gave him a smile he hadn't had in weeks.

As the balls whizzed at him, Sam swung at each one, sending streaks of white light across the field. A few of the balls cleared the fence, with plenty of room to spare.

A Redhead in Brooklyn

Sam shook his head. *Those would have cleared the fence in a major league ballpark.* He filled the hatred of his circumstances with anger, and it showed by the sneer on his face as he attacked each pitch, daring to come at him.

As the sweat poured from his face, he ignored the pain in both knees. He stopped when a jagged spike ripped through the ligament in his right knee, and he stumbled at home plate. He rose and told himself, "You're not hurt. Get your ass back up."

The anger dulled the pain as he swung and sent the next pitch deep into the orange sky floating in the distance.

"You put a charge into that one," a voice from the dugout called out.

Sam stopped watching the ball and snapped his head around. "Who's there?"

A man moved from the shadows of the dugout and walked onto the field.

Sam wasn't sure who the man was, so he faced the voice with his bat ready in case of trouble.

"That one might have made it into the ocean."

Sam watched as the man walked closer. A brown fedora rested over his head. His eyes and square jaw made him handsome and distinguished.

Sam lowered his bat, but kept it ready. "Thank you," he replied curtly. When the stranger nodded, Sam asked, "Who are you?"

"Nobody. I'm just passing through."

"Passing through?"

The stranger replied, "Yeah. I saw the lights on and thought I would see who was working so early in the morning."

Sam looked him over. The fedora and suit didn't mesh with the Kiawah Island vibe. "I didn't know there was a Jimmy Stewart film festival going on."

The man looked down at his clothes, then looked at Sam and smiled. "Yeah, I look like I stepped off the MGM lot." Then the stranger went into a bad Jimmy Stewart imitation.

After a few sentences, Sam gave him a disapproving stare.

The man stopped. "Sorry. I was being facetious."

Sam sighed. "I wish you were getting to the point of what you're doing here."

"You and I need to talk, and this is as good a time as any."

"What's on your mind?"

"I know this is awkward, Sam, but—"

Sam took a step back as he brought the bat up. "How do you know my name?" He focused through the glow of the sunrise, then a smile came to him. "Oh, you're from the Braves, right? Trust me, my knees have never felt better."

"Well, I'm not from the Braves. My name is Saint Christopher, the Patron Saint of Travelers. I know that's quite a mouthful to say, so we can dispense with the formalities and you can call me Chris." He paused, then added, "I'm here to help you."

Sam squinted, then brought his bat closer. "How much have you had to drink?"

Chris laughed. "None at the moment. But the day is young so I like my chances," he told him.

A Redhead in Brooklyn

Sam never wavered as he stared at the man.

Chris told him, "Sorry if I've scared you. After all these years, I should come up with a better introduction. It tends to leave people speechless.

"Sam nodded. "Ya think?"

"Well, since the cat is already out of the bag, I guess I'll continue. Like I mentioned, brace yourself, since this is going to sound a little crazy."

"I'm not worried."

"You're not?"

"Nah. I'm sure whatever hospital you escaped from will be happy to have you back before breakfast." He lowered his bat and asked, "You need a ride? Or do they send a bus?"

Chris ignored him and continued with his presentation. "I am one of several registered Saints who work for Saint Jude, in the Lost Causes section of Heaven. Given the way things have gone for you lately, I thought you'd be happy to see me since, well, your cause couldn't be more lost."

"How do you know how things have been going for me lately?" He asked, his voice edgy.

"I know it's hard to believe, but you have to trust me."

Sam shook his head. "Trust you? Yeah. I'll get right on that."

Chris smiled. "I've been on the job for a short time, oh roughly about seventy years, so cut me some slack."

Sam gave the stranger a blank stare. "A Saint from Heaven, huh? And my name is Mother Teresa. Sorry I got home late, but I had to stack Bibles after church," he said with a shake of his head.

"Oh, and judging by your face, you don't look seventy. I'd say you're about half that old." Chris was about to speak, but Sam beat him to it. "By the way, what was all this Heaven stuff? Wait, let me guess. You were at the Kiawah Bourbon Club, right? I have to hand it to you. You aren't slurring and are keeping your balance well. Nice work, my friend."

Chris smiled. "Sam, who I am is not important, but the reason I'm here is."

"Whatever. Look, I know my calendar is wide open these days, but I'd like to get back to batting practice."

"Sam, believe it or not, and judging by the look on your face you don't, I'm here because as a Saint, we have certain powers."

Sam looked at his visitor in disbelief.

"I'm a full-time accredited doer of good deeds. A registered Saint, here to grant you, Sam Murdock, a way out of your troubles."

"Yeah, right," he said. "Where were you yesterday when the Beach Club Diner ran out of blueberry bagels during breakfast? I could have used your magical powers then."

Chris stared at him, the smile vanishing from his face. "What if I told you I was looking at the starting left fielder for the 1955 Brooklyn Dodgers?"

"I'd ask if you're seeing a whole hospital of psychiatrists."

"They assigned me to a real comedian this time."

"Thanks. The crowd around the Kiawah Beach Club thought so too. Come back later. I'm doing a 4:30 show." As Chris smirked, Sam asked, "Who are they?"

"Details, Sam, details," he said as his hand rose to calm the

A Redhead in Brooklyn

words. "Here's the deal. I can fix it so you are in Brooklyn tomorrow. You'll be the starting left fielder for the entire season."

"Well, Chuck, I can see you're not big into baseball history."

Chris put his index finger up. "Um, my name is Chris."

Sam stopped, then furrowed his brow. "The team you want me to play for left Brooklyn for Los Angeles after the 1957 season. They tore Ebbets Field down in 1960. Are you short-staffed in the fact-checking department?"

Chris smiled, "Ye of little faith. I suppose it's my job to convince you. I figured by offering you a chance to play baseball again, you would jump at it without question."

Sam's eyes sharpened. "Wait a second. How do you know I don't play baseball any longer?"

"Because I know all about you, Samuel Robert Murdock. You were born in Greenville, South Carolina on April 15th. Parents are Bunker and Leslie Murdock. Both deceased." He paused, then removed his fedora. "I'm very sorry."

Before Sam asked how he knew where and when he was born, he focused on Chris and the empathetic look on his face. After a respectful nod, Sam returned the gesture.

Chris put his hat back on. "You followed their footsteps and graduated from Clemson University. You played baseball and were an All-American. One of my favorite stories was the time you and your teammates went out to a bar after a game. You were, shall we say, engaged with a few of the coeds, and realizing it was close to curfew, sprinted back to your dorm. But in your condition, you didn't see a low-hanging branch and ended up knocked on your butt. Your forehead swelled so much you couldn't put your ball cap on for a week."

"How did you—"

"Oh, and there was the time making out with Dean's daughter on top of the Chemistry building. Sounds like the chemistry was right that night."

Sam's face was ashen. "Wait a second. Who told you–"

"Current relationship status is single." Chris smiled and said, "I figure you'd have fallen in love with someone by now."

Sam shook his head. "I'm in love with being a baseball player. I don't have time for anything else." He stopped then looked down. Eventually, he looked at Chris. "Well, since the game broke my heart, maybe I have time for other things now."

"Speaking of breaking, I have more breaking news. I know your father was a Dodger fan. And he told you stories about Ebbets Field. Haven't you wondered what it would be like to play a game there?"

Sam stared at him. "This has to be some kind of joke."

"I assure you, this is no joke," Chris said. "Besides, I've been doing better when it comes to researching my trips. On my first assignment, I had a guy who wanted to play football for Vince Lombardi and the Green Bay Packers. He ended up in Greenland on a whale-watching excursion. Needless to say, he was not happy with me."

Sam shook his head. "How did you get that mixed up?"

"Aw, Sam. Green Bay, Greenland. What's the difference?"

"My confidence in you is surging as we speak."

"I've gotten better since then, so don't give it a second

thought. So? What do you think? Do you want to go back in time to Brooklyn? 1955 was a pretty cool year."

Sam gave him a long look. Finally, he said, "Are you sure we'd end up there? For all I know, I'll end up in Bora Bora making mustache brushes."

"Bora Bora sounds great, especially at this time of the year. But I assure you we'll be at Ebbets Field in Brooklyn."

Sam didn't speak. He looked down at the grass, saturated with the morning dew. After a few seconds, he turned to the outfield, lost in the sunrise. "Maybe I've thought about Ebbets Field before." Then he looked at Chris. "But even if I took you up on this fantasy, how would you make this happen? I told you the Dodgers are no longer in Brooklyn."

"I took care of it."

"You took care of it? Even if the Dodgers were still in Brooklyn, it's September. The season begins in April, so you are a few months behind schedule. Oh, wait. Do you need a few months to rebuild Ebbets Field? Let me know if you need help hauling the bricks." Sam laughed. He was sure he had the stranger now. "You'll need a miracle to pull this off."

"When you deal in the business of miracles, Sam, the word impossible doesn't exist."

"Look, Clem–"

"Um...Chris."

"Look, Chris, the Hollywood ending you laid on me has my heart all aflutter. Please make sure to roll the credits while I clean up the field. I'm sure the images of me picking up wet baseballs with the sunrise as a backdrop will leave your audience teary-eyed. I know I get weepy thinking about it."

Sam picked up an empty bucket. "If you really want to help me, you can either gather up the balls and toss them into this bucket, or roll the pitching machine to the equipment room. If I were you, I'd do the pitching machine. When the bucket gets full, the handle kills the palm of your hand."

"You still don't believe me?"

Sam walked with a slight limp behind home plate. "Nope," he said without looking, then picked up a few balls and dropped them into the bucket. "I guess you get the pitching machine, you lucky dog."

Chris grinned. "Fine. Before I go, union regulations require me to say what I came here to say. I promise, after I've said my piece, you can go back to doing," he paused, looking around the field, "Whatever it is you've been doing."

Sam bent over and tossed a ball into the bucket, then stood straight and looked at Chris. "Well, we wouldn't want you to get in trouble with the union. You know, they still haven't found Jimmy Hoffa," he told him, then bent over and scooped up a couple of baseballs.

Chris didn't smile. "Sometimes in life, there are sublime moments, tiny flickers of light that burn into our souls and live on forever. Those moments don't come around every day. But when they do, it's what makes life worth living."

Sam stopped, then rose and looked at him. "I don't have a life any longer. Since you know everything about me, I'd figure that would be at the top of your list. Whoever is putting together my bio sheet needs to be fired. Trust me. I know what that feels like."

A Redhead in Brooklyn

After walking to another set of balls resting in the infield dirt, Sam picked a ball up and held it in his hands. "When my career died, that was the last hope I had of-" he stopped, then looked out to the sunrise. He tossed the ball into the bucket. Then he looked at Chris. "I'll never forgive myself for not making it to the major leagues."

"Don't you see?" Chris replied as he took a step toward him. "This is your chance to make it right. Sam Murdock, the new left fielder for the 1955 Brooklyn Dodgers. This is the miracle you've been hoping for."

"What miracle? You're talking about a place and team that no longer exists. Stop talking about it as if it does."

Chris smiled. "I've pulled off some amazing things in my time as a Saint."

"Yeah? I'm sure the guy who you took to Greenland thought the same thing. He must of had a whale of a time." Sam raised his eyebrows, and when Chris didn't respond, he joked, "See what I did there?"

Chris ignored the pun. "Gather ye rosebuds while ye may. And this same flower that smiles today, tomorrow will be dying."

Sam squinted. "What are you talking about? I wanted to be a major league baseball player. Not a florist."

"It's something I've learned about life."

"What do rosebuds have to do with being a baseball player?"

"Sam, we all have an expiration date. And when opportunities come that change our lives, we have to follow where it leads us, even if we don't understand the path. One day, if you don't grasp it with everything you have, it can slip away forever, and then it's too late."

"It's already too late."

Chris shook his head. "People are so disillusioned. Worn down by the reality of life. But there are miracles. They happen every day. And you have to keep your eyes and heart open to the possibilities. That's the difference between the people who have a pity party and those who do things that last forever. Those are the ones who believe in miracles. And when you believe, I mean really believe, then courage takes over and makes it possible to enter the realm of magic. It allows you to see what lies beyond the veil of reality. And once you've seen it, nothing can stop you."

Sam's eyes locked on his. "Your passion is inspiring. It makes me want to believe you."

Chris smiled. "I'm a helluva salesman."

Sam looked down, then shook his head. "Fine. Tell me all about what glorious plans you have for me. I won't believe a word of it. But I could use a good laugh."

"Here's the way it will play out. The Dodgers starting left fielder, Sandy Amoros, breaks his ankle in the last game of spring training. You hit .346 at the Dodgers top farm league team in Montreal last season, so you are the only option the Dodgers have. The papers say you could be the next superstar. You become a Brooklyn Dodger, you play in Ebbets Field and you finally get to be a major league baseball player. It would only be for the 1955 season, but what would it matter? You would get to live your dream. And in this world, not everyone gets to do that. I'm giving you the chance of a lifetime, but as chances go, you must decide now. As powerful as I am, even I cannot bring the fantasy to life a second time."

"I have to admit, your presentation was well done. You did all of that without using a whiteboard."

Chris smiled. "Good thing. I forgot to bring my dry erase

markers," he joked.

Sam smirked. "For the sake of argument, how could I disappear back to Brooklyn for an entire season? My agent tells me the Braves are kicking my tires. What if they call? And if they didn't, wouldn't someone around here miss me?"

"The trip back in time would begin on April 13th and conclude on October 5th. But in actual time, you'd be back here right this moment. Well, give or take a few seconds, depending on the traffic."

"Traffic? Are we carpooling with the guy who wants to be there for the reading of the Gettysburg Address? I'm cool with us dropping him off on our way back."

Chris rolled his eyes.

"Just to be clear, I'd return to Kiawah at this exact moment? That's a little strange."

Chris nodded. "I admit it's a pretty neat trick. But it's nothing to worry about. Leave everything to me."

"That gives me a warm feeling."

"Look, that Greenland thing was years ago, so forget I even mentioned it. I'll be with you the whole way, so don't worry about being alone. I'm what you would call an official escort."

"Can I bring anything back with me? A real Brooklyn ball cap? A first-edition Hemingway book? A photograph?"

Chris shook his head. "You may venture into the past but not remove anything from it."

Sam asked, "Why not?"

"Because it's the rules. Understand?"

Sam shrugged. "I guess so."

An orange sphere rose out of the water. Sam looked at the sky, then back to Chris. "Let me get this straight. I can go with you, be a Brooklyn Dodger for a season, and when it's over I can come back here and it will be right now? I will not have lost any time, right?"

Chris nodded. "Correct."

"And there is no danger of me ending up getting lost in some strange hyperspace and ending up as a waiter at the Last Supper?"

"I can arrange it if you like," he joked.

Sam looked back at him. "I'll pass. I hate goodbyes anyway." He kicked at the dirt, then asked, "How long do I have to decide?"

"Soon. Think carefully, Sam Murdock. I'll be waiting for your answer."

Sam shook his head. "Yeah. You do that," he said, then reached down and grabbed a few balls and tossed them into the bucket. "This is crazy," he said, then reached for two more. He was going to ask another question, but when he looked over, Chris wasn't there.

Sam looked around the field. The silence was the only thing staring back at him. "What was his name? Um...Mr...Mr. Saint Dude?" He called out.

When nothing but the birds answered, he resumed walking around the field, picking up the balls. "At least he could have rolled the pitching machine off the field before he left."

Sam dropped the last ball into the bucket, then winced as the weight of all the baseballs made the handle dig into the palm of his hand. He set the bucket inside the dugout, then walked to the pitching machine.

A Redhead in Brooklyn

As he got to it, the memory of sitting in Backman's office replayed in his mind. It then sliced downward and cut up what was left of his heart. "Forget it. I don't need this any longer," he said as he unplugged the pitching machine from the extension cord.

After winding the cord, he looked around the field. *I remember playing before thousands of cheering fans in double-decker stadiums. Banks of lights that turned night into day. And a jumbo scoreboard that was clearer than my TV at home. Now, all I see are a few rows of empty aluminum bleachers. Lights attached to crooked wooden poles. And a tiny scoreboard that needed a paint job. Quite the fall from grace.*

The longing for the old times when his career was in front of him, and his body was free from pain, urged him not to throw away an opportunity. Even if it was as far-fetched as this one.

He knew if he went, he'd only have one season there. At least that was one of the terms of the deal. But what did it matter? Where he stood this morning, there were no more seasons. There was everything to gain. Nothing to lose. A chance to live without regret.

An emotional tug of war gripped him. Pride fought against what was left of his heart. Finally, he gave a resigned shake of his head. "Damn it."

As the silence became deafening, he placed the rolled-up cord on top of the machine. "Mr. Saint guy? Fine. You win. Let's do that thing with the roses."

Sam gave it a minute. He looked around the field, waiting for something to pluck him off the field and hurl him into a time travel blur. When nothing happened, he laughed. "Yeah. Back to Brooklyn. Some of his madness must have rubbed off on me. At least he could have left me some of whatever he was drinking."

After Sam rolled the pitching machine into the equipment room, he locked the door, then walked over to the power box and turned off the stadium lights. He walked across the field under the glow of the coming day and said to himself, "There are no more miracles."

A few seconds later, the sun rose over the scoreboard. It ascended into the sky and within seconds, the field was a blinding blur of golden orange. The birds stopped their conversation as the field went silent.

"Wow, that's a sunrise," Sam said as he shielded his eyes from the light. After a few more steps, the light poured over him, and he couldn't see a thing. He was about to speak, but before he could say a word, the wind picked up and within seconds, he was no longer in Kiawah.

three

When Sam felt his feet on the ground, the light subsided, and he opened his eyes to see what lay in front of him.

Gone was the Kiawah calm of beach life. Replacing it was the controlled chaos of a maze of humanity surrounding him.

Sam's mouth dropped open as the scene roared to life.

He stood in the middle of what seemed like a swirling whirlpool of faces moving in and out of the slivers of light above. Sam looked up to find several tall, arched windows letting in the morning light and illuminating the smoke ascending to the ceiling. The faces looked familiar, but it was the suits, hats, and dresses that threw off his compass. "Where am I? And who are these people?"

As his eyes lowered, he found an antique four-sided brass clock. The hands told him it was a little past eight-thirty. Below the clock was a round kiosk where people stood. From above, a loudspeaker told passengers where their trains were. "Trains?" Sam asked, looking around, "Where are all these trains?"

"Hey there, rookie," a voice called out from behind. "I'm glad you took me up on the offer."

Sam spun to the voice. The fedora and eyes he'd seen recently, but it wasn't in this place, so he tried to piece together why his worlds were colliding. In the dull audio of the crowd, he put it together. "You're...um...It's a C name...Conrad, right?"

"Um, it's Chris. You never get that right."

"Sorry. I'm a little confused at the moment." Sam's eyes widened as he watched the people pass. As he stared at their attire, a paralyzing thought overtook him. *What am I wearing?*

His eyes shot downward, and as he raised his arms, saw a tweed jacket. Then he looked at his legs to see them inside a pair of khakis, which draped over a shiny pair of penny loafers. After seeing his new attire, he exhaled, then looked at Chris. "How did you do that?"

"How many times do I need to tell you? I got this. The suitcase next to you has a few other things, so you'll fit in. And whatever you don't have, I'll get for you."

Sam shook his head. "What suitcase?"

Chris looked at his feet. Sam followed his eyes and found a brown leather suitcase on the marble floor next to him.

"I'll be damned," Sam said after locating the suitcase.

"I hope you won't, but if it happens, I'll see what I can do to get you out of it," he said with a grin.

Sam nodded, then continued looking at the crowd. "What's this, a fedora contest?" He asked, then looked at Chris, who wore a navy blue fedora, "Don't worry, I'll vote for you."

Chris laughed. "Thanks. I've been practicing all week." He paused, then told Sam, "Let's get going."

A Redhead in Brooklyn

As they moved through the crowd, Sam asked, "Why is everyone wearing a dress?"

Chris squinted and looked around. "Even the men?"

Sam gave him a sarcastic nod. "Funny."

"Sam, this is 1955. That's the way people dress. Don't worry, you'll get used to it."

As Sam looked around, he asked, "This doesn't look like Ebbets Field to me. Did you screw up and give me the Thomas the Tank Engine fantasy?"

Chris nodded. "Oh. You were serious about playing baseball for the Dodgers?"

As Sam looked at him stone-faced, Chris laughed. "We are in the beautiful Grand Central Terminal," he told him, looking up at the Celestial Ceiling, then around the massive space. "This place is the gateway to the dreams and aspirations of millions of people who grace this concourse. I'd say you fall under that heading, so I thought it was fitting we began your journey here."

Sam exhaled. "I never thought it would be like this."

"Like what?"

Sam continued looking around. "I'm not only in a different place, but in a different time. I don't know anything about living in 1955. What am I supposed to do?"

"Don't worry about it. I told you I'll look after you."

As Sam followed Chris through the crowd, he squinted, then stopped and looked at his legs. He furrowed his brow and continued staring.

"What's wrong?" Chris asked.

"Nothing. It's—" he said, then felt his pants. "My knees. The pain is gone. How did you do that?"

"The union doesn't permit me to divulge company secrets," he said with a laugh, then continued walking.

Sam didn't move as his perplexed gaze wouldn't allow him another step. He felt his knees again, then smiled and followed Chris through the crowd.

They eventually walked out of the Terminal and onto Forty-Second Street under the Pershing Square Bridge. The stiff breeze and gray flannel skies greeted them as they walked along the sidewalk. The breeze caused Sam to shiver, so he pulled up the collar of his jacket. "Where are we going?"

"A rookie's first day on the job should start with a nice breakfast," Chris smiled. "I know a place close by."

After crossing the street, Chris stopped at a newsstand and bought a newspaper. While he paid, Sam looked around. He shook his head, as his apprehensions about being in a new world heightened.

Gone were the sleek cars from his world. What he saw looked like bubbles on wheels, taking up most of the road as they rumbled down the street. Even the street signs were in different shapes and colors as they stood tall over the pavement. Horns reminded the well-dressed pedestrians to pay attention to the crosswalk.

"Different, isn't it?" Chris said as he walked up.

"Very," Sam said as his eyes continued watching the people walking along the sidewalk.

"Come on. The place is close by," Chris told him.

After walking a couple of blocks, Chris led Sam underneath

an awning. He opened the door and said, "After you."

Sam walked inside to the warm smell of eggs and bacon. The place also smelled of smoke, but not the kind he liked when he thought of breakfast.

He slid into a red leather padded booth and looked around the diner. As before, everyone looked like they were going to church. Sam scrunched up his nose, then waved his hand. "Kinda smoky in here. The Terminal smelled the same way."

Chris placed the newspaper on the table, slid it across from him, and looked around. "Yeah. In 1955, they didn't care about secondhand smoke. Don't worry, we'll be on our way to Brooklyn before you know it. And after this adventure is over, you'll thank me."

"Thank you? We'll see about that."

"Believe it or not, we have a lot in common. More than you realize."

A waitress with strands of hair escaping from a barrette walked over with pen and pad in hand. "What can I get for you two?"

Chris told her, "Coffee for me, and a blueberry bagel for my friend."

She wrote the order on the pad, then scurried away.

Sam's eyes widened. "How did you know I liked blueberry bagels?"

"It was in your bio," Chris winked.

Sam nodded. "I'm scared to ask what else was in there." After looking around the diner, he asked Chris, "How is this going to work?"

"How is what going to work?"

"Me being a player for the Brooklyn Dodgers. Before I walk into Ebbets Field, I need to get a few things straight."

"Such as?"

"You need to refresh me on the backstory you mentioned in Kiawah."

Chris grabbed the newspaper, unfolded it, and slid it over to Sam. "If you turn to the back page, you'll find what you're looking for."

Sam looked at it, then flipped it over. Eager to solve the mystery, he scanned the text. The date was the first thing he saw: April 13, 1955.

He stared at the page for a few seconds, then exhaled. His eyes looked down and found what he was looking for.

YANKEES AND DODGERS OPEN TODAY, with a smaller headline underneath. GAMES RAINED OUT YESTERDAY. TODAY SENATORS AT YANKEE STADIUM. PIRATES AT EBBETS FIELD.

Sam glanced to the bottom right corner of the paper and smiled. The bold type caught his eye. MURDOCK IN LINEUP, and, in smaller print, ALSTON HOPES ROOKIE IS ANSWER TO LEFT FIELD PROBLEM.

"They're writing about me. How'd you do this?"

Chris folded his arms. "Look, this is your moment, and I have the power to make a lot of things happen. Will you stop worrying?"

Sam looked at Chris, then nodded.

BROOKLYN--Sam Murdock, star outfielder of the Dodgers triple-A team in Montreal, hopes to be the answer to

A Redhead in Brooklyn

manager Walter Alston's outfield problem. Sandy Amoros' broken ankle means the Dodgers have a need in the outfield. What could be on Sam Murdock's mind before he suits up for his first game for the Dodgers?

"I'm happy to be here and hope I can help the ball club."

Sam looked at Chris. "Hope I can help the ball club? That's an original answer."

Chris threw up his hands. "Don't worry. We'll work on your interview skills."

Sam shook his head. "Oh goodie. With an answer like that, the fans are going to be lining up for miles to hear what I have to say next."

After they finished breakfast, they walked outside to the cool, misty morning. Chris hailed a cab, then opened the door, and the two got in.

Sam wondered how much time they had before the game started, so he looked down at his watch. To his surprise, a dull bronze watch with a square face, old-looking numbers, and copper hands looked back at him.

He gave it a quick double-take, then relaxed as his mind was now conditioned to accept any surprises. The face on the ancient watch told him it was almost ten o'clock.

"Where to, youse guys?" The cabby asked.

"Ebbets Field," Chris told him.

"Kinda early to be getting to Ebbets Field. Youse two are

going to be early birds," the cabbie replied in a thick New York accent.

Chris spoke up as the cab rolled away from the curb. "The reason we're getting an early start is because my friend here is playing his first game for the Dodgers. Batting practice is at eleven. We can't have our rookie left fielder late for his first day on the job."

Sam blushed and motioned for Chris to keep quiet.

"Right, mistah. As soon as I drop you two jokers off, I'm due at da Daily Planet so I can change from a mild-mannered taxi driver into da man of steel," he chuckled.

Sam sank back into the brown leather seat of the cab and stared out the window at the New York skyline. He ignored the smell of smoke, most likely left by the previous passenger, then rolled down the window to get some fresh air. Despite the cool morning, he would rather freeze than get black lung. Through the chilly breeze slipping through the open window, he recognized the Chrysler Building, then the Empire State Building in the distance. A few minutes later, the Brooklyn Bridge appeared on the horizon.

"This may sound stupid, but are you looking forward to seeing me play?"

"Are you kidding? My money's on the Pirates today," he said with a wink.

As they crossed the Brooklyn Bridge, Sam looked through the cables at the East River. As a million tiny waves jumped out of the water, he thought, *I'm a long way from home.*

A Redhead in Brooklyn

The trip ended with a few twists and turns through the streets of Brooklyn. As the cab rolled along Flatbush Avenue, Sam's eyes widened, and he sat up in the leather seat. Through the drizzle, it became visible in the distance. White letters shining atop a brick building spelling out, EBBETS FIELD.

"There it is," Sam said to Chris. "It's real, and it's in front of me to look at as long as I want."

"I thought you'd like that," Chris told him.

"Oh, I do. But, it's..."

"It's what?" Chris asked.

Sam took a few seconds, then told him, "I've seen pictures, and my dad told me all about it. But seeing it alive right before my eyes is...it's...more beautiful than I ever imagined."

Indeed, it was there, growing larger with each passing block. As Sam took it all in, what caught him first was how simple Ebbets Field looked. It was spectacular in its simplicity.

The cab pulled over to the curb and stopped. Sam stayed in the cab, staring out of the window.

Chris paid the driver, then exited. He walked around to Sam's side and opened the door. "You know, Sam, if you are ever going to be a real Dodger, the first step toward it would be to get out of the cab. If your legs will cooperate."

"I know, I know. Give me a second. I'm feeling a little overwhelmed right now."

"By the sight of this place?"

"Yep," Sam answered, continuing to look at the brick walls.

A few seconds later, Sam exited the cab. As they walked along the sidewalk, Sam veered to the brick wall. He stopped, reached his hand out, then pulled it back. Finally, he placed it on the wall and raked his fingers over the course, ketchup-colored brick.

Chris smiled. "Didn't believe me, did you?"

Sam continued looking at the wall. "I did, but—" he stopped, soaking in what lay before him. "I never thought it would be like this."

Sam followed Chris to the front entrance. As they turned the corner, Sam met a blur in a white dress coming from the other direction.

They stopped inches short of each other, then both backed away. "Oh, I'm sorry," Sam said.

The blur came into focus. As Sam gathered it in, the gloss of her cinnamon hair flowing out from her royal blue hat caught his eye first and didn't allow it to escape. It cascaded in slow motion and fell to her shoulders.

Next were freckles on her bright cheeks. A smile exposed two rows of ivory and set the stage for the crushing blow to his composure. Her sparkling forest green eyes.

It was those eyes that mesmerized him. He'd never seen anything like it before, but today was a new day in a new world. Sam allowed the newness to blur everything around her. The only thing heard was the accelerated beat of his heart as her eyes peered into his soul.

For the first time in months, there was a sereneness to the world. No longer did he feel fear or pain. He reveled in the calmness of her eyes.

Chris watched them. He raised an eyebrow.

A Redhead in Brooklyn

Sam moved to the right to let her pass, as she did the same. They repeated the motion to the left, then both laughed. "Shall we dance?" He asked.

The woman smiled. "I'm sorry, Fred Astaire. Maybe another time."

She scurried past him into the entrance to Ebbets Field, then disappeared into the bowels of the rotunda.

He continued looking at her, even though she vanished. When Chris walked over, Sam asked, "What was that?"

Chris smiled. "I'm not sure, but I think that's what you'd call a girl."

"A...A girl?" Sam asked, his voice slow and unsure.

"Yeah. A girl? As in boy meets redheaded girl? Boy is smitten by redheaded girl? You should brush up on your Charlie Brown. He had a thing for redheads too."

Sam's eyes never moved. "I...um...have never seen a girl like that before." As he shook his head to lift the ginger fog, he muttered, "Add that to the list of things that's different in 1955."

Chris grinned. "Come on. Let's get you inside."

They walked through the rotunda and into a portal to see the playing field. Sam watched as the ground crew set up the nets for batting practice. He wondered if they got bonuses for keeping the place immaculate.

Sam savored the aroma of the Kelly green grass, as it almost suffocated him. His father told many stories about the Ebbets Field grass and how there wasn't a color named for it. Sam now understood what he was talking about.

Interlocked inside the grass was the infield dirt. The color reminded him of winter days when he'd scoop cocoa from a jar and dump it into a cup so he'd have something warm to drink.

As they walked further into the grandstand, the stadium lights illuminated the gray morning. Sam took in the blue of the seats surrounded by red bars designating the box seats as they glistened in the stadium lights.

Sam's mouth stayed open as he looked around. "They should declare this place a national landmark. It is so beautiful."

"Yes it is, Sam. It's a shame this place is less than five years away from the wrecking ball."

Sam nodded. "Yeah, I almost forgot. If I had my way, I'd leave this place up forever."

"I agree. You know, Sam, I've lived a long time and seen many things on my travels. No matter how much time passes, I never get over the fact things change. What gets us through the hard days of loss are the memories of what once was. As long as you have memories, my friend, the things you love don't go away. You'll have them forever."

Sam looked at Chris. "You put that very well."

"Thanks," Chris said with a smile. "I've been practicing it all week. How'd I sound? Not too anxious, right?"

"You were perfect."

Sam gazed at the outfield walls with the advertisements for things he'd never heard of painted on them. The double-decked bleachers ended in center field. From there, the focal point of the right field wall was the large scoreboard.

A Redhead in Brooklyn

There were no modern-day LED lights or video screens in it. Someone manually slid square numbers into the spaces to show the score under each inning. It also listed the batting order, umpires, and other game information. Under the inning-by-inning score of the Dodger game were the out-of-town scores, which must have seemed like it was ahead of its time. This was doable since there were only eight teams in each league in 1955.

On top of the scoreboard was a giant Schaefer Beer logo. Sam remembered his father telling him that after the official scorer made his decision on a borderline play, the scoreboard would illuminate the "h" for a hit and an "e" for an error in the logo.

Lining the top of the scoreboard were colorful flags of each team in the National League, in order of where they were in the standings. Since today was opening day, the pennants lined up in alphabetical order.

Sam gave the park one last stare, then looked at his watch. "I better get going,"

"Sam, before you go, there is something you need to understand. Even though you know the fate of the 1955 Brooklyn Dodgers, once you walk into the clubhouse, you won't know the outcome of this season. If you did, it could alter the course of history and that cannot happen. You will remember everything else. Who you are, where you came from and what you're doing, but that's it. Understand?"

Sam thought about the words, then nodded. "I guess it would be more exciting if I didn't know how things were going to play out."

Chris smiled. "Good. Now get going."

Sam took a step, looked around, then stopped. "Where do I go?"

"Walk down the stairs to the dugout on the first base side. Inside the dugout, find the tunnel leading down the long walkway underneath the Stadium. You'll come to a blue door with the words 'Dodgers Clubhouse' painted on it."

Chris pointed where to go, then turned to leave.

Sam asked, "Where are you going?"

"It's part of this Saint gig. I need a reason to hang around, so I'll find a job that requires me to be here. I'll be with you every step of the way, so don't worry about seeing me. Now get going, I can't hold your hand forever. Between us, I wouldn't want to," he smiled.

"Chris?"

"You're going to make me late and by the time I get down there, all the fun jobs will be gone. I'll be wiping toilets, for God's sake. If it ever gets out, the guys in the Lost Causes section would never let me live it down." He shook his head, then asked, "What is it?"

Sam smiled. "Thanks."

Chris stared at him, then gave Sam a wry grin. "You're welcome. Now will you go? All this tearful goodbye crap I have to put up with," he joked.

Sam smiled as he watched Chris ascend the stairs and disappear through the portal. After Chris left, Sam took one last look at the field, then headed for the clubhouse.

Chris walked back from the portal and spied Sam walking down the steps, onto the field, and into the dugout. "In all the years I've been doing this, nobody ever thanked me like that. This trip could be interesting."

Sam walked through the musty, dark corridor thinking how the other ballparks he played in didn't smell this way. It had been over seven months since the Dodgers closed the 1954 season, so he understood if the place had an odor to it.

After the walk underneath the concrete stands, he saw a blue door with ivory letters reading, "Dodgers Clubhouse." He reached for the knob, but the door came open before he grasped it. Filling the door was a blur in a familiar white dress and royal blue hat who stopped when she saw him, then jerked back.

The two stared at each other. Sam grinned. "Well, Ginger Rogers. Fancy running into you again. Literally."

The woman shook her head. "Well, if it isn't Fred Astaire. Tell me something. Are you following me, or is there a dance contest after the game I don't know about?"

"I wouldn't know. I just got here."

"Well, if you see Benny Goodman roaming the place, let me know and I'll be sure to slip on my dancing shoes."

"Benny Goodman? Does he play for the Dodgers?"

The woman gave him a double take, then smiled. "Sorry, I have to run. See ya around the bandstand."

Before Sam could speak, the woman escaped into the tunnel. *Who is that girl?*

four

The first person Sam saw when he walked into the clubhouse was the legendary Jackie Robinson. Jackie gave him a nonchalant glance, then continued talking with a reporter.

He looks more impressive in person, Sam thought to himself.

Sam walked along the row of lockers. He'd performed this feat on the many teams he played on, so he knew the drill. Over the white lockers were nameplates, so he knew one of them had his name on it.

The first locker he saw had a captain's chair in front of it instead of a stool like the others. Above it was the name, 1 PEE WEE REESE. Since Reese was his father's favorite player, and was told many times that Reese was the captain of the team, it made sense. Sam stared at his nameplate, then exhaled as he stood in front of his locker and would meet him soon. "Wow," he whispered.

He walked a little further and saw 4 DUKE SNIDER, then 14 GIL HODGES, and finally 17 CARL ERSKINE.

Sam was in the middle of a bunch of Hall of Fame players. As his knees shook, he reminded himself he was one of them now and deserved to be in the clubhouse with them.

A Redhead in Brooklyn

Then it occurred to him he better find his locker. He walked further into the clubhouse, looking for his name. With each passing one, his anxiety built until he found it.

9 SAM MURDOCK.

He stared at the nameplate for a few seconds. Then he looked around to see if anyone noticed him staring. Luckily, nobody had. Sam wanted to take another peek, but he figured he'd better get dressed.

As he pulled off his jacket, he found a few items hanging on the silver bar. He pried them apart, and there it was: the official Brooklyn Dodgers jersey. The blue script letters sewn onto an ivory jersey took his breath away. Sam smiled, then exhaled. *Oh wow.*

Instinctively, he checked the sizes of everything from his jersey to the pants. His grin expanded as each size was correct. *Chris is good, I'll give him that.*

Sam spied a royal blue cap with a white "B" stitched into it on the top shelf of the locker. He pulled it off the shelf and checked it. As with his clothes, it was the correct size. He placed the cap atop his head, then looked into a mirror mounted on the corner wall of his locker. The ballplayer looking back at him smiled.

"Good to see you made it," a gruff voice said from behind.

Sam turned, then did a double take as a chubby man stood before him wearing a large, battered top hat and a stretched t-shirt over his flabby torso. His belt buckle rested under his breast, which made it look like his legs extended to his chest. A cigar anchored in the corner of his mouth. "I'm John Griffin, the emperor of the clubhouse."

Sam smiled. "Emperor? Should I bow, or can we just shake

hands?" He asked with a smile.

Griffin laughed, then they shook hands. "Does everything fit?"

Sam looked back into the locker, then back to Griffin. "Yeah, I think so."

Griffin nodded, with the cigar still crammed into the side of his mouth. "Good. See me if ya need anything."

Sam looked at Griffin's battered top hat and said, "Looks like there must have been a heck of a brawl at the formal."

"Ya oughta to see the other guy," he quipped, then smiled and walked away.

After putting on his uniform, his spikes were next. As he reached for them, he braced for the usual pain he felt when he bent his knees. He instinctively stopped and winced, but dropped his eyebrows in wonder since he felt nothing but thick muscle and bone. As he flexed his knee, he waited for the pain to arrive, but it never did. He said in a whisper. "I guess I'm still good from the train station."

Other players arrived, placing items into their lockers.

On Sam's right was Johnny Podres, a slender, left-handed pitcher. On his left was Hall of Fame catcher Roy Campanella.

Sam looked at them, then turned to his locker. *What a way to begin a day in the big leagues.*

"Hey, Podres," Campanella called over. "This must be the rookie we've heard so much about."

"Yeah, he sure doesn't look like much. Let's hope he doesn't soil his pants when they throw at his head," Podres said, looking straight ahead.

"I hear the Pirates hate rookies who get their names in the paper," Campanella laughed.

"Looks as if I'm in for a long afternoon," Sam said.

"Yeah, but don't worry, kid. That's why Griffin puts two pairs of pants in your locker, so you can change between innings," Campanella smiled.

"Thanks for the warning."

Campanella extended his hand. "I hear you can hit."

Sam looked at Campanella's hand and hesitated.

"I ain't gonna bite, kid," he laughed.

Sam smiled, then reached out and shook it. He smiled to mask his awkwardness. "I'm sorry. It was a long train ride from Montreal," he ad-libbed.

Campanella shook his head and laughed. "Damn rookies."

Sam reached for his spikes, making sure he put the left shoe on first since he followed a ritual. His father told him it was always good luck to put your left shoe on first, then the right one. He remembered him saying it's always best to finish what you do the right way, hence the superstition.

Campanella grabbed two bats from his locker, then looked over. "Let's see what you can do."

After tying the last lace, Sam told his new teammate, "I'm ready."

Campanella led him through the clubhouse and back the way Sam came earlier. When they got to the opening of the dugout, Sam felt the damp spring breeze blowing into the entrance. He ascended the stairs, walked into the dugout and over to the bat rack. After looking at several models, then taking a few practice swings, he settled on one, then walked onto Ebbets Field for the first time.

As his polished black spikes dug into the crunchy dirt around the dugout, the first thing he noticed was the size of the crowd and its makeup. With all the hats, suits, dresses and gloves, he felt as if he were walking into church rather than a ballpark. *Did everyone from the train station follow me here?*

The sights, smells, and sounds intrigued him. He heard the hot dog vendors slamming the lids of the square iron boxes. "Get your red hots here," as well as the greasy smell of hot dogs and the sweet odor of popcorn. The steam mixed with the hazy smoke from the cigarettes and cigars as the cloud floated around the ballpark.

From the seats, he could see a heavyset woman ringing a cowbell and cheering for the Dodgers. He loved her energy and enthusiasm, especially since the game hadn't started yet. His father showed him pictures of a woman named Hilda Chester, a fanatical Dodger fan who rang a cowbell to urge on the Dodgers. *That must be Hilda. Seeing her in person is more fun.*

Sam heard shouts from the crowd, but the thick Brooklyn accents threw him off. "Hey Dook," for Duke Snider. "Atta boy Oisk," for Carl Erskine. "Moider the ball Campy," for Roy Campanella.

The park itself held only thirty-two thousand fans, but appeared massive. The minor league parks Sam played in weren't near as large. And yes, it was larger than Kiawah High School's field.

Sam soaked in every unique sight while loosening up. As he took in his new surroundings, he saw a group of players around the batting cage waiting for their turn to hit. He walked toward them, hearing the intermittent crack of the bat as the players took their

A Redhead in Brooklyn

swings in the cage. Sam hid his anxiety by looking out at the batting practice pitcher.

When he got there, team captain Pee Wee Reese walked over and extended his hand. "So you're the new man in town," he kidded as he reached out to shake Sam's hand.

Sam's eyes widened. Standing before him, full of life, and not from a story, was his father's favorite player. "Nice to meet you, Mr. Reese." He smiled, then shook his hand.

"Damn, rookie. You make me feel old. You can call me Pee Wee."

Sam smiled. "Sure. Um, yeah, I can do that."

He remembered Bunker telling him how Pee Wee got his nickname, so Sam thought it would be a great way to break the ice. "My father told me you got your nickname from your days growing up in Louisville."

Pee Wee smiled. "When we played marbles, I used a Peewee marble and ended up winning the city marble championship. From then on, everyone called me Pee Wee and I guess it kinda stuck. Nobody's called me Harold in a long time." After Sam nodded, Pee Wee asked, "How were things in Montreal?"

"Not bad. Very Canadian," Sam said, not meaning to make a joke. He laughed nervously, hoping there wouldn't be a follow-up question since he'd never been to Montreal.

Where the hell is Chris when I need him?

Sam exhaled when Pee Wee laughed. "If you need anything, my locker is the one with the captain's chair in front of it."

"Yeah, I noticed that," Sam told him with a grin. "Will do."

The crack of the bat echoed throughout the park, so Sam turned and saw Gil Hodges walking out of the cage. "Tell Zimmer to look next time before he runs. I almost took his head off," Hodges yelled as he walked out of the batting cage, then saw Sam. "I'm Gil. I hear you're behind me in the lineup today."

"Yeah," he said, shaking Gil's enormous hand. Sam didn't know where he was in the batting order, so he took Gil's word for it.

"Give this old man plenty of space. Don't run me over."

Pee Wee shouted, "Murdock. Get in there." Since Pee Wee was the captain, Sam followed the order without worrying whose turn it was to hit.

Sam moved into the cage, making sure he moved with purpose to cover his shaking legs. He dug into the thick dirt around home plate, adjusted the bill of his cap, then looked out to the pitching mound. Due to the suddenness of Pee Wee's order, Sam didn't have time to think about what he was doing.

He took a few practice swings, came set and waited for the first pitch. His eyes widened as the ball came in on a line, so he swung at it. The ball rocketed off his bat, high into the gloomy sky, and landed ten rows back into the left-field seats.

"Not bad for a rookie," Hodges said as he looked over to Pee Wee.

Next pitch, same result as the ball caromed high off the fair pole and landed back on the field. Of the next eight pitches, none left the yard, but Sam crushed every one.

His last swing sent a whistling line drive to right field. It hit under the Bulova Clock mounted atop the scoreboard.

"Hey, Rook," Hodges called out. "You break the clock, you

pay for it," he smiled. Then he nudged right fielder Carl Furillo, who joined them at the batting cage.

Furillo added, "And on a rookie's salary, you might have to wash dishes on the side to make up the rest of the loot."

Pee Wee walked over to the cage. "Out of there, Murdock."

When Sam walked out, Pee Wee told him, "Congratulations, you passed round one. It's a good sign when Furillo jokes with you." Pee Wee laughed, then trotted out to take infield practice.

Sam exhaled. *Glad to see I can still hit.*

He walked to the dugout, wanting to catch his breath after the stress of his first appearance was history. Before he got there, he heard his name called from the railing, so he looked over and found a group of kids at the dugout looking at him. *How'd they know who I am?*

Then it hit him that he was a ballplayer again, and a major league player at that, so they must want his autograph. He walked closer and found several children lined up with pens, baseballs, and scorecards.

"Hey there," he told the kids as he met them at the railing. He took a baseball from a freckle-faced kid and signed it. "How are you doing today?"

"Fine, Mr. Murdock," he replied as he looked up at him with big brown eyes.

"Call me Sam."

Sam smiled and handed it back to him, then more items appeared in their little hands. He signed everything put in front of him, unaware of a woman walking closer to the group of kids.

He kept signing autographs, then heard her voice. This got

his attention.

"I'm sure he will sign everything," she told the kids. "Make sure to say please and thank you."

Sam looked to find a face matching the voice, then squinted. As he groped for something to say, the woman smiled. "How's it going, Fred? Did you and Benny Goodman get to hang out around the batting cage?" She joked.

"Ah, Ginger Rogers. We meet again. Which one of these kids are yours?" He joked.

"All of them," she said.

Sam reached for the next item to sign and scribbled his name on it. He looked to see if there was a ring on her finger, but white gloves covered her hands. "You and your husband must have an enormous house."

"I'm not married," she responded.

Sam smiled.

"This is a program the Dodgers offer to underprivileged children. I'm filling in for the girl who usually escorts them around the stadium today since she called in sick."

"So this makes three times we've seen each other," Sam told her.

"Well, you know what they say about threes in baseball."

Her comment wobbled him, but he masked it with a smile. *Three strikes and three outs. That's not what I was hoping for.* "What do you do for the Dodgers when you're not watching the kids?"

"I'm a statistician. Anytime anyone needs to know a batting average, how many fastballs a pitcher throws, or how many runners are left in scoring position, they ask me."

"Impressive. By the way, I didn't get a chance to introduce myself earlier. I'm Sam Murdock."

"I know."

"You do?"

"Yeah. After Amoros broke his ankle, I completed your bio, so the press knew who the new guy was."

He reached for a ball behind a wall of hands and signed it. "What did you learn about me?"

She flashed a wry grin. "You are six feet three, have brown eyes, brown hair and are right-handed."

"What's my favorite beverage?" Sam joked.

"Working on it," she replied with a smile.

"So, what else did you find out about me?"

"Today is your first game. Don't wet your pants when they throw at your head."

Great. Even the girl who does stats knows what's coming.

"Thanks for the warning. Do you have a name, or should I call you Ginger? Judging by your hair, I'm sure you've heard that before."

She giggled. "Brooklynn Kelly."

"Brooklyn Kelly?" He asked with a slight turn of his head. "Well, you can call me Kiawah Island Sam."

"Brooklynn is my first name. Kelly is my last name." She shook her head. "I've heard them all before, Mr. Murdock."

"Sorry. I was trying to be charming."

"Needs work," she quipped as she folded her arms across her chest.

"Brooklynn," Sam said with a grin. "Beautiful name. It suits you. Especially being here."

She nodded. "Thanks. But it's tough sometimes trying to fill out paperwork in this town. By the way, Fred suits you better."

"Well then, Fred it is. And I'll continue calling you Ginger. It suits you too."

After the two laughed, Brooklyn asked, "Are you nervous?"

"Nervous? No," he told her as he signed another ball. "I rarely get nervous talking to a beautiful woman."

Brooklynn blushed. "There you go trying to be charming again. Gee, I hope you don't hit like you flirt. If that's the case, they will release you by the fourth inning."

Sam grinned. "Well, I plan on being in Brooklyn for the entire season."

"Sorry I won't be here to see it. I'm going on a season-long vacation starting tomorrow," she said with a laugh. "Why don't you go over and flirt with Hilda Chester? If you figure out how to do it right, she'll let you ring her cowbell."

Sam's grin broadened. "She's next on my list," he told her, then winked.

Brooklynn smirked and shook her head. "What I was trying to ask you, before you went all James Dean on me, was if you were nervous playing in your first major league game."

"Not so much nervous, but excited. You wouldn't believe how much I've looked forward to this day."

A Redhead in Brooklyn

"Here's a tip for you. Max Surkont usually starts every batter with a fastball. He'll get ahead in the count and when you think a curve is coming, he'll bust you inside with the slider. In 1954, he did that to fifty-six percent of the batters in the first inning."

Sam grinned at the way Brooklynn spit out the information. "How'd you know that?"

"They don't hand out these jobs to people walking down Bedford Avenue."

"I'm sure they don't. Who's favored to win the National League this year?"

"The Giants will be tough, especially after winning last year's World Series. I project they will win the National League and the Dodgers and Braves will fight it out for second."

Sam raised his eyebrows. "I hope you're wrong." After she explained why she came to that conclusion, he soaked her in. "You know baseball. I'm impressed."

He continued signing for the children until there was nothing left to sign. "Thanks, Mr. Murdock," the kids said as they began walking away to find their seats.

"It's Sam," he told them, then flashed a quick smile to Brooklynn.

She walked closer and extended her hand. "Thank you, Mr. Murdock. It's nice when the players take time with them."

Sam shook her hand with a firm grip. When he released it, he said, "I'm glad to help. Oh, the same rule goes for you as for the kids."

She shook her head. "What rule?"

"You can call me Sam too," he said with a grin.

"Well, Mr. Murdock," she smiled. "It was…um…interesting meeting you."

"You're pretty interesting yourself, Ginger."

Brooklynn exhaled. "Well, I better get going." She turned and was about to walk away when she had to stop and let the kids walk up the aisle.

Sam figured he better make his move now because he wasn't sure when he would see her again. "Would you like to grab a cheeseburger after the game?" He figured it would be an acceptable 50's pickup line.

She told the kids to hold up for a second, then turned and walked closer to the rail. "I'm sorry, Fred. I don't date ballplayers."

Sam pivoted to Plan B. He wasn't sure what Plan B was, so he figured he would make it up as he went along and hope for the best. "Well, we're going to be seeing each other around Ebbets Field, so you wouldn't have to date me. Since I'm new in town, maybe you can show me around?"

"Oh, of course," she smiled. "I'd be happy to do that."

Sam's face lit up.

She pointed over his shoulder. "That's the scoreboard. Over there is the visiting team dugout. And if you look to your left, you'll see the place where your soon-to-be girlfriend rings her cowbell and yells insults at the other team. Oh, and also certain Dodgers when they aren't playing well. You better bring your A-game."

"I can see that already," he said with a wink and a smile, making sure she got the message. A grin and sway of her head let him know, mission accomplished. "I'm sure I'll need more pointers as the season goes on, so I hope I'll run into you again."

A Redhead in Brooklyn

She stared at him for a few seconds, then snapped out of it and went back on the offensive. "With any luck, I'll see you first and avoid the collision," she replied, then turned toward the grandstand to help the kids find their seats.

Sam shook his head and walked back to the dugout and into the clubhouse.

As he got to his locker, he looked around for his glove. Underneath the hanging jerseys and his clothes was a tiny brown leather glove. It reminded him of a small brown couch pillow. *How am I going to catch anything with this?*

Next to the glove, he found a small stack of papers stapled together. It wasn't there when he left for batting practice, so Sam looked through it to see whom it belonged to.

As he turned the pages, he saw the names of every pitcher on the Pirates. Listed were their strengths, weaknesses and the percentages of what pitches they threw in certain situations. As he flipped through the pages, he noticed Johnny Podres returned.

"Murdock, they ain't released you yet?"

As a rookie, he knew he'd get razzing from his teammates. He smiled and shot back, "They figured they'd release us at the same time to get a group rate."

"Hilarious, Murdock," he smiled. "Are you reading up on who you're going to see in this series?"

Sam nodded. "Yeah. Did you put this here?"

Podres shook his head. "Nah. The dame who does stats for the Dodgers leaves the scouting report in each player's locker before every series."

Sam squinted his eyes, then looked at the pages again. "This must be what Brooklynn was talking about."

Podres buttoned up his jersey, then grabbed his glove. "Have a good game," he told him, then tapped his shoulder with his glove as he passed.

"Thanks, Johnny," he called out as Podres disappeared down the row of lockers.

Sam studied the pages for a while, then saw a group of men in suits and fedoras heading his way. Within seconds, the questions flew at him like a batting practice fastball.

"How do you think you'll do against big league pitching?"

"Are you excited to play in Ebbets Field?"

Sam answered every question, making sure not to give the same boring answers Chris showed him in the newspaper. When there was silence, a familiar voice asked, "Is it true you are seeing Ingrid Bergman?"

He wasn't sure who asked the question, but as he looked closer, the face was familiar.

Sam smiled. "No, not at the moment, but tell her she can call me anytime if she'd like to come to a game."

The group of reporters laughed, then left to get quotes from other players. Chris waited for the group to leave, then walked over to Sam, sporting a press badge pinned to his jacket pocket.

It read, *Chris Saint - New York Daily News*. Chris smiled. "Nice response to my question. I guess we can cancel the interview skills class I signed you up for."

Sam laughed, then looked at the badge. "I didn't know your last name was Saint. That's ironic."

Chris smiled, "I figured I'd need a last name if I were going to pull this off. Besides, it was this gig or follow the elephants during the opening day parade with a shovel, if you know what I mean. I made a wise choice, don't you think?"

"I don't know. I thought you were full of shit when I first met you," he joked.

Chris smiled. "You know, I thought the same thing about you."

"You did?"

"Because your eyes are brown. I figured the extra ended up there."

As they laughed, Chris asked, "How do you like Ebbets Field and 1955 Brooklyn?"

Sam looked around the clubhouse, then back to Chris. "So far, its been amazing. I hope it continues."

"Don't worry, Sam, it will. Focus on the game, and I'll focus on everything else."

Sam looked around the clubhouse. "By the way, since you're focusing on everything, do you know where they keep the bubble gum?"

Chris looked over Sam's shoulder and nodded.

Sam turned and looked up. On the top shelf of his locker was a box with the words "Bubble Gum" written on the front.

"You have enough to get you through the first few weeks," Chris said with a smile.

Sam turned and reached inside to open the box. After seeing what was inside, he smiled. "Yeah. You're right." He grabbed a handful of wrapped pieces, then placed them in his back pocket.

"So, what happened with the redhead you were speaking with after batting practice? Is that the same woman you almost knocked over when we got here this morning?"

Sam squinted. "How did you know about that?"

"I see things. By the way, that's twice in one day."

Sam shook his head. "It's been three times since I almost ran into her walking into the clubhouse."

"Three times? Is destiny trying to tell you something?"

Sam smiled and shook his head. "Oh yeah. It's telling me to leave the girl alone since she has no interest in me."

Chris nodded. "Aw, you know as well as I do, a game goes nine innings. This was only batting practice. Keep swinging."

"It's time to move on to other things. Like being a real major league baseball player and trying to help my team win."

"The team means that much to you, doesn't it?"

"Yeah, it does. Especially now, since this is the only chance I'll ever have to play in the majors. Either way, once October comes, I'm back home in Kiawah wondering what I'm going to do with my life. I should savor these days. I finally made it to the big leagues," he said as his face lit up. "Wow. After all these years. I finally made it."

Chris smiled and nodded. He looked at Sam's face, seeing the joy. Then it melted into loss as he looked away. "What's wrong?"

Sam's face gazed into nothing, his body the only thing tangible in the Ebbets Field clubhouse. When Sam didn't answer, Chris asked, "Sam?"

Sam continued looking into a memory. Finally, his voice

spoke, but it wasn't to Chris. "I met Pee Wee today. He was my father's favorite player."

After a pause, Chris stayed quiet and waited for him to speak.

"I wish Dad were—" he said, then his voice trailed off, and he fell back into the abyss of memory.

Chris watched as Sam's eyes glistened. He didn't speak for a few seconds, watching the scene unfold before him.

Sam continued staring, then came back to the present. He picked up a towel and wiped his face. When he dropped the towel next to his stool, he smiled, and his moment of vulnerability was over.

"You okay, Sam?"

Sam sniffled as his smile grew. "Me? Oh yeah, I'm fine. You know how the spring is hell on allergies. Mine are bad right now."

Chris nodded and let him have his dignity. "Yeah. Mine are bad too." He paused, then said, "You know, Sam, baseball is full of memories shared between fathers and sons. Thanks for sharing one of yours with me."

Sam nodded. "You're welcome." He paused, then looked around the clubhouse, then back to Chris. "Look, um, that allergy thing. You aren't going to tell anyone about that, are you?"

"Unless I can find you an endorsement deal for allergy meds, I think we can keep that one between us. But it's okay to feel that way about things. I used to..." He said, then smiled and shook his head. "Aw, this is your day. Let me stop babbling on and get out of here so you can enjoy it. I'll see you on the field." Chris winked, then turned and walked out of the clubhouse.

Sam watched him walk out, then he rose and turned to face

his locker. He took another look at himself in the mirror and when the face looked back at him, he smiled. *I deserve to be here. This is my time and nobody can ever take it away from me.*

Sam nodded, then turned and took the last steps over the threshold of everything he always wanted to be.

five

The umpires began their walk through the Dodger dugout and onto the field.

As customary, team captain Pee Wee stood at the top step and waited for the Dodger theme song to end. When it did, he motioned for the rest of the Dodgers to run onto the field, and they did to the loud cheers of the fans welcoming them back from a seven month hiatus.

Sam put a fresh piece of bubble gum in his mouth, then hopped up the steps, careful not to trip over them on his way out, and dashed into his heaven. He wasn't sure his feet were touching the grass as he trotted out to his position in left field.

As he waited for the first batter, he looked around the old ballpark. The color, smells and sound of the crowd left him in awe, and a tingle went through him. Sam waited years to play in a big league ballpark and today was the day. He couldn't control the smile on his face as he took everything in.

Carl Erskine set down the Pirates in order. Sam didn't have to make a play, so it gave him a chance to settle down from the surge of emotion washing over his body.

P.A. Announcer Tex Rickards told the crowd, "Leading off for the Dodgers, second baseman, Junior Gilliam." The Dodger faithful let out a cheer.

Pirates pitcher Max Surkont, who would go on to led the National League in Earned Run Average and win fourteen games in 1955, looked like a rookie in the first inning as the Dodger offense came out on fire.

Sam walked to the end of the dugout. After looking around for a few seconds, he asked the bat boy, "Where are all the batting helmets?"

Veteran bat boy, Charlie "The Brow" DiGiovanna, gave him a puzzled look, then told him, "Only a few of the fellas wear a batting helmet."

"Wait? You mean the Dodgers don't wear batting helmets?"

Charlie raised his eyebrows. "Um, yeah. Pretty much everyone in baseball doesn't either, but I can get you one if you want it."

Sam wanted to focus on the upcoming at bat, so he dismissed the question. "No, that's okay." As he walked away, Charlie gave him a perplexed look.

He ignored the urgent pleas to protect his head, popped up the dugout steps and walked over to the bat rack to find the bat he used in batting practice. He slid it out of the rack, then took his place in the on-deck circle.

As he applied pine tar to help with the grip on the bat, he heard his name. Well, he thought he heard it. "Hey, Moordock! We're wit ya rookie," a thickly accented Brooklyn fan shouted to him.

While looking out to see what Surkont was throwing,

A Redhead in Brooklyn

Charlie returned from collecting a discarded bat and kneeled next to him. "Guaren-damn-tee you get one under the chin first pitch, so be ready for it," he warned. "Sure you don't want that batting helmet?" He said with a laugh, then rose and walked back to the dugout.

"I'm so screwed," Sam said under his breath, then took a few practice swings while kneeling in the circle.

After Gil Hodges made the first out on a line drive, it was Sam's turn to hit. From above, Rickards' voice boomed again, "Now batting, number nine, left fielder, Sam Murdock."

The roar through the stadium sent chills down his spine because he never heard such an ovation during a game. Then again, this was the major leagues. He walked with purpose to the batter's box, focusing on getting there in a straight line, since the emotion of the moment caused his vision to blur. The roar only intensified.

Everything cleared up when Sam got to the batter's box. He looked at home plate, and as he focused on setting his feet inside the box, he heard umpire Lee Ballenfont ask the Pirates catcher, Chris Shepard, "Why is the crowd going crazy? It's only the first inning."

"It's his first major league at-bat," the catcher replied.

"It is, huh?"

Ballenfont got between Sam and home plate. "Back away for a second, and enjoy the moment kid. It only happens once in a lifetime," he told him as he walked to the front of home plate. He pulled out his brush, then took his time as he bent over and dusted it off. Sam looked at Ballenfont, not sure what was going on.

Ballenfont made sure Sam wasn't going to get cheated. He rose, then took his time adjusting the straps on his mask.

As Sam waited, the applause grew louder. He looked around,

then at Shepard. "They're cheering for you, rookie," he told him.

Sam blushed and looked down at his spikes. The crowd roared. Finally, he raised his head, then tipped his hat to them. Somehow, the crowd got even louder.

A redhead in the press box smiled as she watched the events unfolding inside Ebbets Field.

When Ballenfont walked behind the plate and put his mask on, Sam scooped up some Ebbets Field dirt, rubbed it in his hands, then dug in.

He took a few practice swings, then stared out at the pitcher's mound. *Oh my God, I am about to take my first swings as a big-league player.*

Surkont looked in for a sign, his eyes laser-focused. He came set, gave a quick look at the runners, then fired home. A flash of white light flew at Sam's head.

"Damn," Sam said as he dropped his head down and away.

An ominous hissing grew louder as he ducked and hoped the next millisecond wouldn't feature the splitting pain of being hit in the head. As he crashed to the ground, he heard the loud pop of the ball snacking into the padded leather of Sheppard's mitt.

As he lay in the dirt, the only pain came from his pride. Sam looked up as Sheppard told him, "Lucky for you, he didn't throw his fastball."

Sam shook his head, then rose and refused to dust himself off. *I guess that was the first time being knocked on my ass in the major leagues.*

Ballenfont had to dust off the plate again. When he finished, he looked at Sam and smiled. "Welcome to the big leagues, rookie."

Sam got back into the batter's box. He ignored the noise

from the crowd and the encouragement from his teammates and focused on his inner dialogue. *The first pitch was at my head. The next one will be outside, probably a curve ball on the outer half. Let it come to you. Hit it where it's pitched. All right. Deep breath. You can do this.*

Surkont got the sign from Sheppard, went into his stretch, and threw home. The spin of the red laces rotating away told him it was a curve, and it headed outside.

Sam adjusted his body. Acting on instinct and preparation, he moved across the plate and swung at where he knew the ball was going to be. He trusted his eyes and hands, allowed the bat to do the work as it connected with the ball, and sent it on a line toward the right of the Pirate infield. Second baseman Curt Roberts fielded the ball on one hop, saw he had no chance to get Pee Wee streaking home, so he threw to first base to get Sam by a step.

He made a quick right turn and headed for the Dodger dugout to the ovation of the fans for getting the run home. The cheering wiped away Sam's disappointment for not getting a hit in his first at-bat.

The first to greet him at the top step of the dugout was his new friend, Johnny Podres. "Way to get the runner in, Murdock," he said as he extended his hand. Sam said thanks as he shook it.

After his first at-bat, things fell into place. His confidence grew, and before he knew it, this was just another game.

In the fourth inning, Sam took his position in left field. As he put another piece of bubble gum in his mouth, he heard the sounds of a band mixed in with the crowd. *A band? In a ballpark?*

Walking around the park was a band of ragtag musicians who didn't play music, only made a lot of noise. Sam heard them as he warmed up, and after seeing them interact with the crowd, he couldn't help but laugh. *Geeze. These guys are awful.* Then he remembered this must have been the band his father told him about.

It was the Dodger Sym-Phony. Emphasis on the phony. They walked up and down the aisles, playing music and getting the crowd excited. The joke around the park was if you wanted to locate either Hilda or the Sym-Phony, they were in Section Eight. The joke came from the military term for being mentally unstable. And no, that wasn't a coincidence.

As he watched them move around the grandstand and the crowd's reaction, he shook his head. *Well, I'm not in Durham any longer.*

In the eighth inning, Sam got his first major league hit, a double to center field. Even though it was a fantasy, and would never be in any history book, he didn't care. All that mattered was it happened, and he'd remember it forever, since this was something history could never take away.

Tex Rickards' voice came over the loudspeaker. "Double by Murdock is his first major league hit," which prompted a standing ovation from the crowd.

Sam stood with his muddy black spike on the dirty white base and bowed his head. He took a glance around the park, then tipped his hat to them for the second time today. He wasn't good at basking in the spotlight, so he hoped the moment would pass soon.

Brooklynn raised an eyebrow as she watched him standing with his foot on the base.

As tradition, when a player gets their first hit in the major leagues, the umpire called time and made sure the player got to keep the ball. "Gimme the ball," growled the umpire. He then wheeled

A Redhead in Brooklyn

and threw it toward the Dodger dugout, where Charlie retrieved it. "I'd keep my eye on the ball if I were you," the umpire smiled.

Carl Erskine went the distance in the 6-1 Dodger victory. In the victorious Dodger locker room, the reporters gathered around Erskine to get the story. They eventually made their way to Sam's locker to get his reaction.

"How does it feel to get your first major league hit?" Someone asked.

Sam looked up from unlacing his spikes. He smiled. "Feels great. I hope there's a lot more."

After the other reporters asked their questions, they all moved on to the other players, so Chris walked over. "Didn't I say you would be fine?"

Sam unbuttoned his jersey. "I guess you were right," he replied, then tossed it into a laundry bin sitting in the middle of the row of lockers. "But this is only game one. We still have 161 to go."

Chris informed him, "Um, in 1955, they play 154 games, so you have only 153 to go. Well, unless the Dodgers make the Series. Then it could be more."

Sam smiled. "I hope so. Anything to lengthen my stay, right?"

"The way you played today, it's a possibility." When Sam smiled and raised his eyebrows, Chris shook his head. "No, I'm not going to let the cat out of the bag."

"Oh well, it was a thought."

"What do you say to a couple of cheeseburgers at the

Plymouth Café? Just make sure you shower and shave, will ya?" He joked.

Sam grabbed a towel from his locker. "Have you ever considered being my mother instead of my escort?"

Chris smiled. "What's the difference?"

six

After ordering dinner, Sam had a question for his new friend. "I've been meaning to ask you something."

"What?"

"Why am I here?"

Chris unrolled his napkin. "What do you mean?"

Sam took a sip of water, then asked, "Why did you pick me to come back in time? I'm sure there are more important people who deserve to have their dreams come true."

"Well, why not you?"

"I haven't done anything extra special lately. I've said my prayers and tried to be a good guy. Why am I the one who gets the opportunity for redemption?"

"Sam, the reason you've been saying your prayers is so you can have this inner turmoil that is tearing you up inside."

"What inner turmoil? I have no inner turmoil," Sam said, then looked away.

"You can't lie to me. Don't forget, I know everything about you. The only thing you've ever loved tossed you to the side. And you feel guilty about it. If it were me, I'd feel the same way."

Sam loosened up to his friend. "Maybe I'm still a little messed up inside, but that still doesn't explain why I'm here."

Chris looked around the restaurant. Finally, he looked back at Sam. "You're here because you are supposed to find something. I can't say if you'll find it, because that part rests with you. But I'm here to help. You're in good hands with me."

"What are you, Saint Allstate?"

"Cute, Sam, real cute. By the way, did you know I've won Saint of the Month two months in a row?"

"Congrats. I'll bet you're enjoying the free set of steak knives. Or do they give you a toaster?"

"You are a riot, Murdock."

Sam got back to the task at hand. "What is this about me finding something? What's that about?"

"All I know is, I can take you only so far, then it's up to you."

"What's up to me? What am I supposed to find?"

"Whatever it is, when you find it, your inner turmoil will vanish. Remember, in matters such as this, the journey to find happiness can be as rewarding as the final destination."

Sam thought about the words. "Maybe you're right."

"I usually am," Chris laughed. "Now, stop asking so many questions, and finish your cheeseburger."

"I should have asked you this earlier, but where am I staying?"

"The Hotel Bossert. It's the nicest, most luxurious hotel in Brooklyn, so you'll be comfortable there."

A Redhead in Brooklyn

"Who's paying for all this luxury?"

Chris smiled. "I can cover you for the first night, but after that..." he said, then asked, "Have you ever thought about getting a side gig washing dishes?" He teased.

Sam shook his head. "Oh great. I'll be the only player in the National League with dishpan hands."

After dinner, it was time to get Sam settled at the hotel. Chris put his fedora on as they walked to the curb to catch a cab.

"It's gotten colder," Sam said as he saw his breath in front of his face in a white puff that floated into the night and evaporated. "By the way, are you going to our game tomorrow?"

Chris smiled, "Yeah, I should be there unless I'm assigned to someone else for telling you what's going on."

"They wouldn't take you off this assignment, would they? You're the Saint of the Month two times running."

"Believe it or not, I have my regrets."

"Regrets? What regrets?"

Chris looked away, and his words tripped over each other. "Nothing...it was nothing. I...Um...It was something that happened a long time ago. We'll discuss it later," he said, then dismissed it with a laugh.

Sam looked at Chris, who turned and looked off into the night but did not ask another question. However, he put the incident in the back of his mind as a point to ponder on the mysterious past of his new friend. "Don't worry about what I know," Sam assured him. "I'll play dumb."

Chris turned back and smiled. "Should be easy for you."

Sam laughed, then watched as his new friend continued looking into the night.

After finding a cab, they traveled down Flatbush Avenue. Sam asked, "What's it like being a saint?"

Chris kept looking out of the window. "It beats being a garbage collector," he laughed. "Why do you want to know?"

"I'm curious. What do you get out of this?"

"I get the satisfaction of knowing I brought joy and fulfillment into the lives of others."

"Thanks for the employee handbook answer. Now tell me the real reason," Sam prodded.

"What can I say?" Chris's stone face replied.

"You can answer the question," Sam replied directly.

When Chris remained mute, Sam knew there would be no answer coming. "All right, Chris, you'll have to tell me someday."

Chris gave him a curious smile. Sam squinted his eyes, wondering what lay behind it. Whatever it was, he was sure what lay behind the smile would shed some light on the dark side of Chris.

As the cab rolled along Montague Street, Sam shook his head. "Man, I'm in another world. How am I going to function here, let alone try to play baseball?"

"You'll get used to it. With every new experience, there is an adjustment period. But don't worry, it will come," Chris assured him.

"What if it doesn't?"

A Redhead in Brooklyn

Chris smiled. "Then you're going to have a long summer."

Sam shook his head. "Great. So, why did you bring me here again?"

"Oh, there are reasons, believe me."

seven

As the second week of May came to Brooklyn, the Dodgers were sailing along with a 21-2 record. So far through the first month of the season, they looked unbeatable.

Sam did his part as he tore up National League pitching and played well in left field. But as the spring faded, and summer was on the horizon, Sam's batting average also faded from the top of the National League standings.

The Dodgers returned from their first western trip of the season, winning seven of the twelve games. Brooklyn opened a brief, three-game home stand by losing to the Phillies 5-3. Sam failed to reach base in the game and struck out twice on high fastballs. The last one with the bases loaded in the ninth inning.

After the game, Chris walked over to Sam's locker. "What's up with the high fastball?"

"Don't remind me. I hate striking out. Especially when the game is on the line."

"You look off balance on some of your swings. Are you stepping into the bucket?"

A Redhead in Brooklyn

Sam thought about it for a few seconds. "Nah."

"It looks like it."

"It has to be something else. I need more batting practice so I can figure it out."

Chris asked, "Speaking of batting practice, whatever happened to your redhead?"

"Who? Brooklynn?"

"Oh," he said, raising an eyebrow. "I thought you weren't good at remembering names?"

Sam shook his head. "She's the only woman I've met so far here. Plus, it's the same name as where I'm playing, so it makes it easy to remember." He stared into the clubhouse and smiled.

"Thinking about what's her name, aren't you?" Chris smiled.

"She's not interested in me, but it's fine. I have baseball back in my life, so I'm good. No use getting distracted now."

"As pretty as that one was, Sam, I would try again if I were you."

"I've got more important things to worry about."

Chris smiled. "When was the last time you smiled like that and it didn't have to do with the game?"

Sam dismissed the comment with a wave of his hand. "Look, I'm in the middle of one of the worst batting slumps in the history of the National League."

Chris smiled. "I'd say the American League too."

"Oh, that's funny," Sam smirked. "Tell you what. While you are lining up your next joke, how about helping me?"

"How?"

"This time, you grab the bucket of balls, and don't worry about the pitching machine."

"Why not?"

"You'll be the one doing the pitching."

Ebbets Field said goodbye to the last of the fans and grounds crew a few hours earlier, so the echo of an empty stadium followed every crack of Sam's bat. The sound wasn't as deafening as it had been earlier in the season.

Sam dug in his spikes and looked out at Chris. He cocked his bat, then waited as Chris wound up and threw a pitch. He swung and after seeing the ball roll slowly to shortstop, shook his head.

The next swings lacked the power of earlier in the season. Most fluttered into foul territory or would have been an out in a real game.

Sam took another swing. His eyes followed a weak dribbler to the first base side of the field. He stopped, then looked down.

Chris picked up another ball. "That was your worst swing of the day so far."

"You think?"

Chris looked into the grandstand, pondering the question. "Now that you mentioned it, I'm not sure. There are plenty to choose from."

Sam walked back to the batter's box. "What am I doing wrong?"

A Redhead in Brooklyn

Chris dropped a ball into the basket behind the pitching cage. "You're opening up your hips too soon and that's throwing off your balance. Your timing and power are off because of it. Try to explode through the ball and move toward the pitcher instead of third base."

Sam looked down at the dirt, then at Chris. "How do you know about that?"

Before Chris answered, a familiar voice called out. "He's right you know."

Sam looked to where the voice came from, and within seconds, the mystery solved itself. "Ginger? What are you doing here?"

Brooklynn smiled as she approached. As she got to home plate, she turned and looked at Chris. "I don't believe I've had the pleasure."

Chris waved. "Hello. I'm Chris. Sorry I can't say a proper hello, but I'm a little sweaty at the moment."

Brooklynn giggled. "Do you work for the Dodgers?"

"No, I'm a writer for the Daily News, but I'm pulling double duty to help Sam out of this terrible slump he's gotten himself into."

Brooklynn looked at Sam. "Oh, that's right. No hits in the last, what is it now, sixteen at-bats?"

Sam glared at her. "Fifteen. What are you doing here?"

"I had some post-game stats to compile before the next series and I like to work in the grandstand since it's peaceful."

"Even with us on the field taking batting practice?"

"Especially with you taking batting practice."

Chris snorted, then concealed a smile.

Sam's glare transferred in his direction as his friend stifled a laugh. "Sorry. But that was funny," Chris said.

Sam shook his head, then turned to Brooklynn. "You've been watching me?"

"Yes, I have. And the way you've been hitting, you could take batting practice in an elevator and not hit a wall."

Chris didn't want to betray his friend, so turned to the outfield so he could laugh in private.

"It's not that bad," Sam insisted.

"If this keeps up, they are going to have a Sam Murdock Day Off in Brooklyn," she assured him.

Sam watched from behind as Chris put his hand across his face, and his body jerked back and forth, then he turned to her. "Look, I'm not in a slump. I'll break out of it tomorrow."

Brooklynn smiled and shook her head. "I won't hold my breath." She looked out at Chris and asked, "He's stubborn, isn't he?"

Chris finished his laugh, then turned. "Yep. He's as stubborn as any of them. But what can you do, ya know?"

Sam shook his head. "Fine. What's your magical suggestion?"

Brooklynn walked to the batter's box. With her white canvas sneaker, she smoothed out the dirt, then drew out a batter's box next to home plate. "Get in the batter's box and take your stance."

Sam furrowed his brow, and after a few seconds, obeyed her request.

Brooklynn watched him set up and take a few practice swings. "Okay, Chris. Throw him a fastball."

A Redhead in Brooklyn

Chris nodded, then picked up a ball from the basket, wound up, and threw it.

Sam swung and made contact. The ball fluttered into the air and landed over third base in foul territory. He watched the ball roll away, then looked at Brooklynn. "You're a tremendous help."

Brooklynn smiled and walked closer. "Look at where your front foot ended up."

Sam walked out of the batter's box. He looked down to see the divot from his spike pointed toward third base.

Brooklynn looked at Chris. "By chance, did they move the pitcher's mound to third base since the game earlier today?"

Chris shook his head. "I don't think so."

Brooklynn quipped, "Chris doesn't think they moved the pitcher's mound to third base after the game today."

Sam asked, "Are you two working on a comedy routine?" He exhaled, then looked at the spot where his foot ended up. Then he looked at her.

"You're stepping away from the pitcher and that has you off balance," she told him. "You're stepping way in the bucket."

"Wow. I wish I would have thought of that," Chris told him. A wide grin accompanied the words.

Sam glared at Chris.

Brooklynn grabbed him by the arm and led him back into the batter's box. "Okay. Setup like you usually do, but this time, move your right foot away from home plate."

Sam looked at her, then dug in as usual. This time, he moved his back foot away from home plate as Brooklynn instructed. "This feels a little strange."

"It should, but after a few swings, it will feel natural. Try it."

Sam looked at her, his face mired in uncertainty. After she nodded, he took a few practice swings, then looked out at Chris.

"Throw him a fastball," Brooklynn told him, then backed away and focused on what happened next.

Chris nodded. He wound up and threw a fastball in the middle of the plate.

Sam's eyes widened. His body uncoiled and exploded at the point of impact, sending a thunderous crack echoing off the steel girders of Ebbets Field. The ball became a whizzing white blur rocketing into the outfield that landed in front of the wall. It bounced, then hit above the padding on the metal wall with a thud and bounced back to the grass.

Sam stared at the ball as it came to a stop on the crunchy dirt of the warning track. "I'll be damned."

Brooklynn smiled. "Told ya."

He looked at Brooklynn. "How did you—"

Brooklynn ignored him. "Chris. Throw him another."

Chris repeated the motion.

The ominous crack of the bat echoed as before. The ball landed in the upper deck of the left field seats.

This time, Sam didn't look at Brooklynn. Instead, he looked at Chris. "Throw some more."

For the next five minutes, Sam took out a month's frustration on the baseballs. Brooklynn watched the hitting display with a grin.

When it was over, Sam walked out of the batter's box.

A Redhead in Brooklyn

"What just happened?"

Brooklynn smiled. "Simple positioning, my dear Watson. You're stepping away from the ball, which leaves you off-balanced, and therefore there is no power behind the swing since your bat is not in the right path to meet the ball squarely, nor is your timing at it's apex when you connect with the ball. . But now, with your back foot away from the plate, your front foot will still swing out, but now it will swing forward and the ball and pitcher are in front of you."

Sam thought about her explanation. "You're right. Wow, that was so simple."

Brooklynn nodded. "I hope it helps."

Sam smiled. "Yeah. I think it will."

Brooklynn asked, "By the way, do you read the pre-series notes I prepare for the team? I put them in all the lockers."

"Um. The notes. Yeah...I...I have to do that."

Brooklynn shook her head with a disapproving frown. "I can only do so much for you, Mr. Murdock. If this keeps up, sports companies are going to pay you not to endorse their products."

"Gee, thanks for the vote of confidence."

She looked out at Chris. "Bye, Chris," then turned to Sam. "Have a great afternoon," she said, then headed toward the grandstand.

Sam looked at Chris. When Chris nodded, Sam took his cue, then turned to Brooklynn. "Um, Ginger?"

Brooklynn stopped and turned.

"Would you like to get that cheeseburger I mentioned when we spoke on opening day?"

"Sorry, but I've done my good deed for the day. Besides, if I were to perform two miracles in one afternoon, the Saints would ask me to start coming to their meetings."

Sam looked out at Chris and raised his eyebrows. Chris replied with a wink.

Brooklynn looked at them, then asked, "What was that about?"

"Oh nothing," Sam told her.

She stared at Chris, then looked at Sam. "Goodbye, Mr. Murdock."

"I told you on opening day you can call me Sam."

"Yeah. I heard you the first time," she said with a smile, then turned and walked into the grandstand.

"Um, Ginger–" he paused. He looked around, then at her, and took a deep breath. "Thanks for helping me."

Brooklynn smiled back. "You're welcome. Look, if you don't start hitting, we can kiss our chances of playing in the World Series goodbye. It's important the Dodgers play in the Series this year."

Sam asked, "Why? You have money on us or something?"

Brooklynn smiled. "You wouldn't believe me if I told you, Mr. Murdock."

Sam watched as she walked up the steps, then disappeared through the portal. Then he turned to Chris. "Why does she call you by your first name, but doesn't do that with me?"

Chris grinned. "I'm not the one who's gone hitless in his last sixteen at-bats."

Sam snarled. "How many times do I have to tell you? Fifteen."

A Redhead in Brooklyn

"Funny, it seems like a lot more."

A few days later, Sam and a few of the Dodger players headed to Steeplechase Park inside Coney Island for an autograph event.

Sam sat behind a table and signed autographs while chatting with the fans. From the side, he heard a cowbell, and when he looked over, it was super fan Hilda Chester.

"There's Sam Mooordock, da best playah in the National League."

Sam looked over and saw her walking over to the table. "And there's Hilda Chester, the best fan in the National League."

Hilda swooned. "Ah, Moordock, look at dat handsome mug of yours. If I didn't have every joe in Flatbush chasin' me, I'd be chasin' ya every day."

Sam blushed. "Well, thank goodness for that."

They both laughed, then Hilda placed a sheet on the table. It was her iconic sign reading, "Hilda is Here," which she posted on the railing of the grandstand. However, with her voice, fans didn't need a sign to know where she was. "Moordock, will you sign dis for me?"

"It would be a pleasure," he told her as he took the cap off his marker and signed his name. "Want me to sign your cowbell too?"

Hilda smiled. "You know me, Hilda, wit da bell."

Sam signed her bell next.

"We gonna win da whole thing this year?" She asked.

"I hope so. We're off to a good start, so far."

Hilda nodded. "Good. When we win the Series, I'm gonna stand in the middle of Flatbush Avenue and tell every Giant and Yankee fan, 'Eatcha heart out, ya bum.'"

After Sam finished with her bell, he handed the items back to her. Hilda responded by leaning over and kissing him on the cheek. The photographers were there to get the money shot, and the flashbulbs popped.

It took a few seconds for the flash of light to vanish. As Sam regained his eyesight, he found a familiar face standing next to the photographer. Through the subsiding haze, and a freckled-faced grin, the voice said, "I see you made good on your promise to flirt with Hilda. I'd say that's your best work since you've been in Brooklyn," she joked.

Chris walked over and stood next to her. "Ain't he a cutie?"

Brooklynn laughed. "He is. But he's not near as cute when he strikes out."

Sam smirked, then greeted the next fan, who asked him to sign a ball. He signed, then posed for a picture. After he said goodbye, he looked at Brooklynn. "What are you doing here?"

"I needed a break from crunching numbers, so I thought I'd get out of the office and see how the autograph event was going."

As another fan walked over and handed Sam a Dodgers pennant, Chris looked at Brooklynn. "After the love fest with our friend here, we should all walk over to get lunch at Nathans. I don't believe Sam has had the pleasure of a Nathan's hot dog."

Brooklynn grinned. "Well then. I guess it's up to us to educate him. As much as we've had to babysit him lately, I'm beginning to think it's a career."

A Redhead in Brooklyn

Sam listened to their conversation and rolled his eyes.

Chris smiled. "Great. We have reservations for three."

Sam watched the scene unfold. As he did, he dropped his pen, and it rolled out from under the table.

Brooklynn picked it up and walked around the table to hand it to him. As she did, the photographer said, "Smile."

The request caught them off guard. Sam looked at Brooklynn with raised eyebrows. She shrugged her shoulders.

Brooklynn leaned in close, and when Sam brought his head closer, they smiled at the camera.

After the autograph event, the trio walked through the crowd and stopped at the corner of Surf and Stillwell Avenue.

As they stood in line, Brooklynn looked at Sam and raised an eyebrow. "So, how long has this thing been going on with you and Hilda?"

"Since opening day. I took you up on your suggestion since I have a thing for cowbells."

"Well, the world is a twisted place," she replied with a giggle.

After a few minutes, they got close enough to see the signs with the prices. Sam looked up, then asked, "Five cents for a hot dog? Five cents for a soda? And six cents for a milkshake? Where was this place when I needed it in Clemson? I would have cleaned up at the Esso Club."

"Clemson?" Brooklynn asked, eyebrows raised. "The Esso Club?"

Sam looked at her with a surprised grin. "What about the Esso Club?"

"I'm from Charleston. I've been there with some friends of mine that went to Clemson."

Sam raised an eyebrow. "You're impressive, Miss Kelly."

She winked. "I've heard that before."

After receiving their hot dogs and sodas, they walked to a table in the shadow of the Wonder Wheel. With the sounds of carnival music blanketing Coney Island, they sat in the cool sunshine of the late spring afternoon.

Brooklynn looked across the table. "You're swing is much better the last few games. But you've had a problem with the high fastball. Russ Meyer struck you out twice on high fastballs in the Phillies series."

Sam took a sip of his soda through the paper straw. "Those balls weren't high. The plate was low," he said with a grin as he looked away.

"When the ball almost hits the umpire in the mask," Chris told him, "Those balls are high. Didn't they teach you the strike zone at Clemson?"

"You know, it never came up. But they did teach us when we were in the presence of a pain in the--" Sam was about to finish his sentence when Chris raised his eyebrows and nodded at Brooklynn.

Brooklynn laughed. "I don't mind," she said with a giggle, then nudged Chris.

Sam bit into his hot dog. As he bit down, he heard a pop, then the taste of juicy beef filling his mouth. After swallowing, he told Chris, "Wow, that's good. The casing around the hot dog holds

A Redhead in Brooklyn

in the flavor."

Chris nodded. "Nathan's makes a good hot dog."

"The best I've ever had," Brooklynn said, then took a bite. After swallowing, she told him, "At batting practice, have the pitcher throw high fastballs and don't swing at them. Also, you might want to study my notes a little closer."

Chris nodded as he placed his paper cup on the table. "She's right."

"Oh great. Not only do I have to take on the whole National League, but I have you two to contend with," Sam told them.

Chris smiled as he looked at Brooklynn. "I told you he was stubborn."

Sam exhaled. "Okay, fine. I'll study the notes a little closer."

Brooklynn placed her hot dog on a napkin. "Good idea. If you had read what I put together, you'd know Meyer throws more breaking balls in the later innings because he gets fatigued. When he goes to his fastball, a lot of them are high because he's tired."

Sam looked at Chris, who nodded. He looked back at Brooklynn. "How did you know that?"

"I'm not just another pretty face," she said with a grin.

"I'm sure that list is rather short," Chris told her with a grin.

"Oh, how I appreciate a gentleman," she said as the freckles on her cheeks moved with her grin.

When Chris gave her an "Aw," Sam scowled. "Wait a sec. You call Chris by his first name? And you call him a gentleman too?"

Brooklynn grinned. "He doesn't have a thing for cowbells."

Sam looked at Chris and threw up his hands. Chris replied, "Well, I don't."

Brooklynn and Chris winked at each other, then she turned to Sam. "Look, Mr. Murdock, I can't keep giving you these free lessons on hitting. Pretty soon, I'm going to have to start charging you."

Chris told him, "She's right. When a pitcher gets tired, his pitches are higher since he doesn't follow through."

Sam looked at Brooklynn, who raised her eyebrows. After staring at each other, smiles broke out between them.

Chris watched the scene unfold with a smile of his own.

When they finished lunch, Chris rose and gathered his trash. "Sorry to leave you crazy kids, but I have to get back to work. You'll be okay without me, right?"

Sam looked at Brooklynn and smiled. "I think so."

"More like, I hope so," Brooklynn joked.

"Have fun," Chris said, then disappeared into the crowd.

As they walked around Coney Island, the smell of cotton candy and funnel cakes floating around them, Brooklynn looked over. "Six hits in your last eight at-bats. The adjustment is working."

Sam raised an eyebrow. "Oh. You've been watching me."

"Don't get too excited. I like to watch dumpster fires too."

Sam looked at the Wonder Wheel, then back at Brooklynn. "So, we have the rest of the afternoon in front of us. Since I'm taken, you want to spend it with Hilda Chester's boyfriend?"

Brooklynn laughed. "I'm sorry. I planned on visiting the Brooklyn Museum after the event today. There is an Impressionist exhibit I wanted to see."

"Oh yes. Impressionists. I like Impressionists."

"You do? Who are your favorites?"

"Well, Rich Little is pretty good."

"Rich Little? What's he painted?"

"Painted?"

Brooklynn shook her head. "Yes. Painted? As in Monet? Renoir? Degas?"

Sam stared at her, then smiled and gave her a confident nod. "Oh, those guys. They're much better than Rich Little." He had no idea who those guys were, but figured he covered himself. *Did my quick thinking work?*

Brooklynn shook her head. Before she could shoot him down, Sam pounced on his tiny window of opportunity. "Since you're teaching me about hitting, I'd also love a free lesson on Impressionists."

She laughed, then stopped. "Wait. What's today?"

Sam thought for a moment. "Monday."

Brooklynn shook her head and frowned. "I forgot. The museum is closed on Monday. I guess I'll have to go another day."

"Well, since we're both free, would you like to show me around Coney Island?"

Brooklynn looked ahead, her face stone.

Sam kept the momentum going. "I respect the fact you don't date ballplayers, but this isn't an official date. It's an official team function that went over the allotted time. I'm sure you can understand that."

She grinned. "My, you're tenacious, aren't you?"

"It's one of my endearing qualities," he said, then grinned. "What do you say?" When nothing came out of her mouth, Sam grinned. "Can't think of a reason to say no, can you?"

"At the moment, no. But give me time."

Sam's grin almost split his face. "Well, take as long as you like while you're showing me around."

Brooklynn shook her head. "Fine. Mr. Murdock. You win this time."

Sam grinned. "This time, huh? That implies that there will be another time."

Brooklynn shook her head. "Don't count on it. You know what they say about counting your chickens before they hatch?"

"Oh yeah. Do it quick because chickens run all over the place and that makes them impossible to count them accurately." When Brooklynn shook her head, he added, "I told you I had some endearing qualities."

"I'll let you know when I find one," she said with a wry grin.

As they walked, Sam asked, "Nice call on Nathan's. That was the best hot dog I have ever had."

Brooklynn nodded. "It is. When I first came to Brooklyn, my roommate Margaret brought me here and introdeued me to Nathans."

"What are your favorite things to do here?"

Brooklynn looked around. "I like the bumper cars. the

A Redhead in Brooklyn

parachute jump and the Wonder Wheel."

"The Wonder Wheel?" Sam asked.

Brooklynn pointed to the large Ferris Wheel ahead. "There it is."

Sam looked up and saw the giant wheel with its colorful cars swinging back and forth. "Well, let's start there."

eight

As they ascended into the sky, Sam looked out of the car.

"It's beautiful up here," he said as he looked over her shoulder at the skyline. "I'm glad we got one of the outside cars, so we have an unobstructed view. The cars in the middle of the wheel can't see out like we can."

Brooklynn raised her eyebrows and grinned.

"What was that devilish grin for?"

"Oh, you'll see."

As the Wonder Wheel rotated upward, Sam looked out to see what lay in the distance. "There's Manhattan. And we can see everything on Coney Island. This view is amazing."

"Come over to this side. You can see better," Brooklynn told him.

Sam sat next to her. When Brooklynn scooted a few inches away, he told her, "I won't bite."

"Good. But if you try to get any closer, I will," she said, then laughed.

As the Wheel continued rotating, Sam looked over at a blue

car in the middle of the wheel. "All I can see is a blue car behind us. It's blocking the view."

Brooklynn watched Sam. The evil grin returned. "It'll move out of the way."

A few seconds later, Sam watched as the blue car rolled toward him, then gained speed and wasn't stopping.

Sam's eyes widened. "Ginger," he shouted. "That car is coming right at us."

He grabbed her and moved them to the other end of the car. He braced for the collision, then looked out and saw the blue car roll over them, swinging on rails.

As Brooklynn sat on his lap, he held her, then looked up and saw the car above them. The car rolled back to its original position, still swinging. The people in the car above looked down and laughed at Sam.

Brooklynn joined them. "Thank you for saving my life. There are so many fatalities from the Wonder Wheel these days," she joked, then got off his lap and sat on the other side of the car.

Sam blushed as he looked around. "Um. Sorry about that."

Brooklynn shook her head. "I've seen some awful schemes to get close to a woman in my time, but that was pretty bad, Sam."

"No, really. I thought the car was crashing into us." He stopped, then squinted his eyes. "Wait a second. You called me Sam."

Brooklynn thought for a moment, then she looked away and waved her hand. "Minor lapse in judgment, since we were about to be crushed by a runaway Wonder Wheel car," she joked.

Sam's Cheshire Cat grin illuminated the space. Brooklyn

squinted, then told him, "Don't get used to it." After a few seconds, she asked, "Were you really trying to protect me?"

Sam nodded. "This is the first time I've ever been on the Wonder Wheel. I had no idea about the middle cars."

Brooklynn stared at him, then smiled and shook her head.

After finishing on the Wonder Wheel, they walked around the boardwalk, taking in the carnival-like atmosphere as the breeze and ragtime music accompanied them. Sam bought them ice cream, and they talked about the team and how the season was going.

Brooklynn wanted to ride the bumper cars, so Sam indulged her and they had fun crashing into each other. After finishing the demolition derby, Sam looked at his watch. "Are you good on time?"

Brooklynn nodded. "I'd like to ride the parachute Jump."

"Sure. Let's go."

After they took their seats on the padded bench and the security bar was locked in place, they ascended up the tall tower. As they settled in, Sam looked out over Coney Island. "Wow, we are up high."

"Yeah," Brooklyn told him. "Two hundred and fifty feet above the ground. Nice view, huh?"

As they sat, Sam asked, "When do we drop?"

Brooklyn looked up, then around. They remained high above Coney Island, swaying in the breeze coming off the ocean. "Well, we should have dropped already. We must be stuck."

"Really?" Sam asked.

"Yes. I think—" she said, then the car dropped, and the chute deployed, slowing their descent.

A Redhead in Brooklyn

Brooklynn screamed as she lunged at Sam and grabbed his arm. As their descent slowed once they got closer to the ground, she let it go, then scooted to her side of the bench.

Sam shook his head. "You know, Brooklynn, I've seen some awful schemes to get close to a man in my time, but that was pretty bad."

Brooklynn looked at him and was about to speak. Sam stopped her. "There are so many fatalities from the Parachute Drop these days. Good thing I was here to protect you." He gave her his sexiest grin and finalized the deal with a wink.

She glared at him, then a slight grin came to her lips.

After spending the day protecting each other from certain death, they walked to the street corner to find a cab. As they waited, Sam asked, "Are you hungry? I know cheating death always gives me an appetite."

Brooklynn giggled. "Yeah. I could eat. There's a place across from the Brooklyn Botanical Garden that's pretty good."

"Lead the way."

Brooklynn told the driver an address, and the cab headed north. It passed Prospect Park and slowed when it came to an address across from the Brooklyn Botanical Garden.

The pair exited the cab, then Brooklynn led Sam to a brick building. When he saw the door, he opened it for her and they walked inside. Once they got to a table, Sam pulled a chair out for her.

She stopped and looked at him. "You're going to pull it from under me after that crack about the Wonder Wheel, aren't you?"

"Nah, I wouldn't do that. At least not today," he said with a grin.

After she sat, Sam scooted her chair in, then walked over, picked up the napkin, and sat down. As they settled into their seats, he got an even better look at his new friend.

Her emerald eyes sparkled in the flickering light of the candle placed in the middle of the table. She smiled, looked around, then removed her white hat and placed it next to her. After coyly tucking a cinnamon strand of hair behind her ear, a server walked over and handed them two menus. "Hello, Brooklynn. Glad to have you back."

"Good to be back, Pete."

Pete looked at her and smiled. "The usual?"

"Please."

"And what can I get for--" he was about to ask, then a hint of recognition came over him. "You're Sam Murdock."

Sam smiled and nodded.

"Brooklynn didn't tell me she knew you."

Brooklynn grinned. "I'm not sure I want to know him yet."

Pete laughed. "She's a tough one, Mr. Murdock."

"I'm beginning to understand that," he replied, then told Pete. "Please call me Sam."

Pete smiled. "What can I get for you, Sam?"

Sam looked at Brooklynn. "What's your usual?"

"PBR in an ice-cold bottle. No glass."

Sam smiled at her description. "PBR works for me too."

Brooklynn grinned. "Good choice, Mr. Murdock."

After Pete left, Sam asked, "Pabst Blue Ribbon? I figured you'd be a wine or martini kind of girl."

Brooklynn smiled. "I'm not what you would call your typical girly girl. I like beer, dancing in hole-in-the-wall bars, going to the ballgame instead of some stuffy party with a bunch of squares. It bores me when I'm stuck listening to a bunch of jerks worried about how much money they make. Oh, and I'm not bashful about speaking my mind."

Sam raised an eyebrow. "Funny, I would have never thought that about you."

After Pete brought their bottles, Sam raised his. When the bottles met, he said, "To baseball and the Dodgers. Could this be the year we finally win the World Series?"

Brooklynn nodded, then they clinked bottles, gazed at each other for a few seconds, and sipped their beer.

"I saw the Schaefer beer sign on top of the scoreboard in Ebbets Field. I figure if you work for the Dodgers, you'd be drinking that."

Brooklyn smiled, then looked down at the bottle. "Yeah, but to tell you the truth," she said, then looked up at him, "I never liked the taste of it. I've tried Schlitz, Falstaff and I'll have a Reingold sometimes, but PBR is my go-to."

Sam placed his bottle down. "I'll have to remember that." When she nodded, he asked, "So, you're a long way from Charleston."

"And you from Clemson," she counter-punched.

Sam nodded. "You're correct. I live in Kiawah Island and graduated from Clemson." After he took a sip of his beer, Sam asked, "You don't sound like you're from Charleston."

Brooklynn laughed. "We moved to Charleston when I was ten, so I didn't have time to pick up an accent. But now and then I will say 'y'all,' or something southern, so people figure out where I'm from."

Pete walked over and placed a bowl of shelled peanuts on the table. After he left, Brooklynn grinned. "What are a pair of southerners doing in Yankee country? If I'd have known we were from the same state, I would have cut you some slack."

"Would you have said yes to a date with me?"

Brooklynn smiled. "Nah, we won't go that far."

"Oh well. You can't win them all."

Brooklynn took another sip, then stood. "Pardon me, but I need to powder my nose."

Sam pushed his chair out and stood.

Brooklynn watched him, then smiled. "Oh. A gentleman. You are full of surprises, Mr. Murdock."

"Wait until you get to know me better."

"Your optimism is admirable," she joked, then walked through the restaurant.

Sam returned to his seat. He looked through the window, watching the cars and people going by. Then he exhaled. For the first time since he arrived in Brooklyn, the fear he carried for how he would make it in this new world vanished. A sereneness washed over him, causing a grin. *This feels safe. I can do this.*

A Redhead in Brooklyn

A few minutes later, Brooklynn returned. When Sam saw her, he stood and waited for her to sit down. Once she did, she took another sip of her beer. "Where were we?" She asked.

"You were going to cut me a little slack since we are both from South Carolina."

Brooklynn nodded. "Oh, that's right. So, what do you miss about Clemson?"

Sam nodded as he took in what her question meant. "Knowing it's home. Every time I'm back on campus, I'm twenty-one again, and life is in front of me. When I see the same buildings, streets, and even the baseball stadium, it reminds me of how things used to be." He paused, then smiled. "I guess being home makes you feel safe."

Brooklynn gazed at him as the words flowed in her direction. "Nice answer."

"But being here somehow gives me the same feeling. I know I haven't been here for long, but this place grows on you."

Brooklynn took another sip, then nodded. "Yes. It does."

While Sam picked out a peanut and broke open its shell, Brooklynn asked, "I'm curious. Do you have any superstitions? Most ballplayers do."

Sam thought for a moment. "Well, I always chew a fresh piece of gum before I take my position in the outfield."

She asked with a grin. "Why?"

"I figure it's best to go into a new situation with fresh optimism."

Brooklynn nodded.

"I also have a ritual about putting on my spikes."

"Do tell."

"My father taught me a long time ago to put my right shoe on last since you want to finish doing things the right way. I guess I've never forgotten that one."

"I'll have to try it sometime."

Sam saw the flicker of the candle in the freckles around her rosy face as she sipped her beer. "What do you miss about Charleston?" He asked.

Brooklynn placed the bottle down and thought about it for a few seconds. "I miss the breeze coming off the Atlantic Ocean blowing through the Palmetto trees. It's kind of a spooky city and that adds to its beauty and charm. It's small so you don't feel crowded like being in Brooklyn. I also miss the beach and the sound of the waves when they crash to the shore. It's funny, but when you aren't around it, you regret taking it for granted."

"What's your favorite spooky part of Charleston?"

"My favorite scary place to visit is the oldest building in the city called the Powder Magazine. It's haunted by the ghost of a female pirate."

Sam nodded. "I can see why you'd like that."

"Why?"

"If you weren't a statistician for the Dodgers, I could see you swashbuckling on a pirate ship somewhere."

She looked down, then back to Sam. "She wasn't looking for a pirate. All she wanted was a sword."

Sam raised his eyebrows. "A Brooklynn Kelly original?"

A Redhead in Brooklyn

Brooklynn giggled. "Yeah, something like that."

The warm, golden-hued afternoon became a cool navy blue evening. Because they weren't too far from her house, Brooklynn suggested they walk back instead of taking a cab.

She shivered when a stiff breeze sliced through her, so Sam removed his jacket and draped it over her shoulders. She brought the jacket closed with her hands. "Thanks. I guess you got lucky with the weather."

"I'm sorry?"

"If it was any warmer tonight, I'd tell you to keep it. You must have said your prayers earlier."

Sam looked up. *Thanks, Chris.*

They walked along Bedford Avenue and passed Ebbets Field. As they walked, Sam glanced at Brooklynn, then looked away. As they arrived at the intersection of Bedford Avenue and Sullivan Place, they looked at each other, then looked straight ahead.

With Ebbets Field looming behind them in the darkness, they crossed the street and turned left. Within seconds, they arrived at the first of a row of houses, so Brooklynn stopped and faced him. "Well, here I am."

Sam looked at her, then turned to see Ebbets Field across the street. He looked back at her and asked, "You live here?"

"No, Sam. I live in Queens. I just didn't feel like hanging out with you any longer," she joked. "Yes, I live here. It cuts down on the commute, don't you think?"

Sam nodded. "I'd say so." He turned and looked again at Ebbets Field, then back to her house. "Wow, this is perfect."

Brooklynn nodded. "I'd invite you in, but it would break our agreement. This is only an autograph event that went long, right?"

Sam looked at his watch. "Yeah. About six hours long."

She removed his jacket and handed it to him. "Even so, it's not a date."

He took the jacket from her. "Oh, I agree 100%," he said with a smile. "Good night, Ginger. See you when we get back from the road trip."

"There's that optimism again. I have to admit, it's kinda cute."

"I thought so," he assured her. "Aw, I have a feeling we'll both be at Ebbets Field, so we'll cross paths eventually. Call it a hunch."

Brooklynn grinned and shook her head, then turned and headed along the narrow walkway and up the brick steps to her front door.

Sam watched her walk inside, then shut the door. When he knew she was safe, he turned and began his journey back to his hotel.

As he walked, Brooklynn's scent rose from his jacket and drifted into his face. A grin came to him, and it left him with a whistle on his lips and a spring in his step.

nine

June came to Brooklyn as the Dodgers finished a home series with St. Louis, winning four of five games from the Cardinals.

After the game, Sam dressed in front of his locker. Chris walked over and asked if he wanted to join him for dinner. "Sure," he replied.

As they walked along Bedford Avenue, a group of young boys approached and asked Sam for his autograph.

Sam stopped and signed for everyone until the last child walked away. He watched as the kids laughed and showed each other their autographed items. "After this is over, I'll miss that."

Chris nodded. "Yep. It's nice to be in demand."

"Where are we going?"

"You like Chinese food?" Chris asked.

"Sure."

"Well, too bad. We're having Italian."

Sam shook his head. "Do you know how much you wear me out?"

Chris continued walking. "No. But if you hum a few bars, maybe I'll remember."

Eventually, they walked under a green awning with the words, "Luigis," written in white script. Chris turned left and opened the door for Sam. When Sam entered, the aroma of tomato paste, garlic, and fresh bread wrapped around his face. The noise of patrons in the middle of conversations and a waiter walking by with a tray of dishes made Sam adjust from the sounds of traffic to the sounds of a restaurant.

A short man in a tuxedo with shiny, jet-black hair and thick mustache walked up to Chris. "Paisan, it's great to see you," the man called out in an Italian accent.

"Luigi, how've you been?" He responded with a hug.

"Never better."

He gave Chris a warm smile, then looked to his right. "And you must be Sam Murdock. I've heard a lot about you."

Sam smiled and extended his hand. "I hope it was all good."

"Nice home run today," Luigi said as he shook his hand. "I cooked an extra special batch of lasagna for you to celebrate. Come. I get you a table."

Between the sounds of stacking dishes and white noise from the various conversations, Sam heard the whispers from the tables. "He plays for the Dodgers," and "That's Sam Murdock."

Sam smiled, knowing this kind of recognition was fleeting, especially given his situation.

Luigi led them up a flight of wide, creaky, golden brown stairs. On the second level, they walked through a door to an outside patio with a view of the Brooklyn skyline. "Here you are," Luigi told

A Redhead in Brooklyn

them as he pulled a chair out for Sam and one for Chris.

After ordering salads, they exchanged small talk. Sam took a sip of water, then looked at the city as it spread over the landscape. As his eyes panned to the right, they stopped when a woman sitting alone came into view. He blinked a few times to make sure he wasn't seeing things, and when his eyes focused, he knew who she was.

Sam blurted out, "What's Brooklynn doing here?"

"Where?" He asked, then turned in several directions to locate her.

"Stop being obvious," Sam told him. "She's over there by the railing."

After Chris located her, he turned back and asked, "So? What are you still doing sitting here?"

"I'm having dinner with you."

Chris shook his head. "That's sweet," he joked. "But you should have dinner with her."

"Who are you going to eat with?"

"The coat check girl was giving me the big eye earlier."

"That's not what I meant."

Chris took a sip of water. "Don't worry about me. Walk over and have some fun. The last thing I want is for you to spend tonight complaining about being stuck with me when you could have had dinner with a pretty redhead."

"She is kinda pretty, isn't she?"

Chris looked at him, then shook his head and exhaled. "Oh boy. Is this going to be one of those Charlie Brown things with the little redhead girl and the teeth marks on the pencil? Give me a break. I'd like to keep my dinner down."

"Charlie Brown? Oh, yeah. You mentioned him before. Don't worry, I did my homework this time. I know all about the teeth marks."

"Great. I'll alert all the dental schools that you'll be sending out applications after your baseball career is over. But for tonight, do everyone a favor and walk over there. With any luck, you'll get lucky and she'll leave her teeth marks on you."

Sam looked at her, then back at Chris. "It's not that I don't want to have dinner with you. It's..." Then he looked over at Brooklynn, who surveyed a tall menu.

Chris saw where Sam's eyes focused, then he smiled. "You see me every day. How many times do you get to see her?"

As Sam watched her sitting in the early summer glow of dusk, a boyish grin came to his face. When he came back to reality, he saw Chris looking up at him with a grin of his own. "What?"

Chris teased him. "I'm not sure. It looks like...Like...Someone has a case of puppy love?"

Sam shook his head. "Can't be. I left all my dog treats in my other suit."

Chris nodded in Brooklynn's direction. "Go over there and do your best. If you crash and burn, I'll send over a bucket of ice water to douse the flames."

"That's a comforting thought."

Chris flicked his hand at him. "Shooo."

Sam sat for a few seconds, then placed his napkin on the table, rose, and walked across the deck. His heart thumped with every step across the rooftop, and when he got to her table, he took a breath to calm himself. "Good evening, Miss Kelly."

Brooklynn continued looking at the menu. "How's it goin', Alfonse? Say, could you bring me a beer? And if you get it here within the next thirty seconds, I'll slip ya a fin. Under the table, of course, so you won't have to share it."

Sam smiled. "No, it's not Alfonse."

Brooklynn looked up. When she saw it wasn't Alfonse, her eyes widened as she inhaled and sat back, then regained her composure, cocked her head and smiled. "Well, Mr. Murdock. Funny seeing you here. You making extra money waiting tables? If you have another slump, this might be a great second career for you."

Sam didn't skip a beat. "Have you ever wanted one of those relationships where you just sit with someone and not have to talk?"

Brooklynn nodded, "Sure."

"That's what I aspire for us one day."

Brooklynn's smile elevated to a giggle. "What are you doing here?"

"Well, I heard this place has the best bratwurst in the city," he joked.

Brooklyn furrowed her brow. "This is an Italian restaurant."

Sam looked around, then at Brooklynn. "Really? Nobody tells me anything." He flashed a coy smile, then asked, "Isn't it crazy we keep running into each other?"

Brooklynn threw up her hands. "Crazy is right. I was about to call Bellvue and see if I could get us a reservation for later."

"I love trying out new places," he told her with a wink.

Before she could reply, a man walked up. He looked at Brooklynn, then at Sam. After a double take, the man smiled. "Are you...You..." he said, startled at seeing Sam.

Brooklynn smiled. "Yes, Alfonse, that's who you think it is."

Sam smiled and shook his hand. "Yes, I'm Sam Murdock. Nice to meet you, Alfonse."

"Nice to meet you too. I made a novena for you earlier in the season when you were in a slump. I'm glad you're back to hitting the ball so well."

"A novena?"

Brooklynn told him, "A novena is a prayer a Catholic says over several days. At the end of the rosary, you get to ask for a special intention."

Alfonse nodded. "So I used my last prayer to ask that you get a few hits and break out of your slump."

Sam grinned. "Wow. Thank you, Alfonse. I'm sure that was the thing that got me back on track," he said, then looked at Brooklynn and raised his eyebrows.

Brooklynn rolled her eyes.

Sam reached into his pocket, pulled out a five-dollar bill, and handed it to him. "By the way, Miss Kelly wanted to know if you could bring her a PBR and have it back within the next thirty seconds. If so, this is for you."

Alfonse smiled and nodded. "Of course. What can I get for you?"

Sam looked at Brooklynn. "I'd like the same."

Alfonse nodded, took the bill, then moved so fast he became

A Redhead in Brooklyn

a ghostlike image before evaporating.

Sam smiled. "Dining by yourself tonight?"

"Yeah. Are you flying solo tonight too?"

Sam looked over at his table. "I'm with Chris."

Brooklynn looked over. "Oh yeah," she said, then waved.

Chris raised his glass, then nodded at them.

"Tell him he looks good in a fedora."

Sam smirked. "Yeah. I'll get right on that. Mind if I join you?"

"What about Chris?"

Sam shook his head. "He dumped me for the coat check girl."

"I don't blame him. I'm sure she has better legs than you." She giggled, then pointed to the empty chair across from her.

Sam sat, then looked around the rooftop at the other patrons, then the sunset falling behind the buildings. "This place is beautiful."

"It's my favorite restaurant in Brooklyn," she said as a slight breeze blew through her hair. "Whenever I need a night away from everything, I'll call Luigi, and he'll reserve this table for me. The lasagna is the best in the city."

Alfonse walked over and placed their beers in front of them. He backed away from the table. "I know what you want, Miss Kelly," he said, then looked at Sam. "What can I get for you, Mr. Murdock?"

"Please call me Sam. So, Alfonse," he said, then looked at the menu. "I don't see a Bratwurst Parmesan, so I'll try the lasagna."

After Alfonse retreated, Sam gave her a wry grin. "Can I ask a question?"

"Sure. Whether you get an answer is another story."

"Well, I like to live dangerously." He settled into his seat, then asked, "Were you always interested in baseball and tracking player stats?"

"Yes, ever since I was little. Since I can't play the game, I did the next best thing and analyze why games are won or lost. Or, why players do well in some spots, and not so well in others."

"Where did you go to college?" He asked, then took a sip of his beer.

Brooklynn picked her bottle up and replied, "I stayed home and graduated from the College of Charleston. It's a beautiful city. So beautiful, my parents came to visit one weekend, and decided to move there. Talk about losing your buffer zone," she joked.

Sam nodded. "Are your parents still in Charleston?"

Brooklynn's lips came together and disappeared for a second, then came back out. "No. They died a few years ago. Dad went first, and then mom."

Sam's face mirrored Brooklynn's. "I'm sorry."

"It's okay. I got over it, but there are times I miss them. Especially my father's wisdom, his soft-spoken manner and even his silly jokes."

"Dad jokes, right?"

Brooklynn nodded.

"What about your mom?"

"She was the one who always told me I could do whatever I wanted in life. I miss her kind words and confidence. Especially when I've had a tough day and question my ability."

"She sounds like a wonderful woman," he told her, then

A Redhead in Brooklyn

asked, "You have doubts about your ability? So far, you've been dazzling. On and off the field."

Brooklynn's face lit up, then she said, "Thank you. I try." She smiled, took a sip of her beer, then continued. "I admired her strength too."

"Her strength?"

"Yeah. She grew up without a father, so when dad passed, it reopened scars she put band aids over years ago."

"That must have been tough growing up without a father. I don't know how I would have done it."

"Well, it's quite a story. My grandparents were Dodger fans, and my mom was born across town at Brooklyn Memorial Hospital. Of course, they named me Brooklynn. My grandfather was the biggest Dodger fan, according to my mom, who passed down the stories to me."

Sam's face glowed. "I can imagine what that was like."

Brooklynn continued. "Before one of the World Series in Brooklyn, he wanted to go to a game, but couldn't get tickets. So instead of going to Ebbets Field, he watched the games on television in his favorite bar with his friends. After the game, he walked back to the apartment he shared with my grandmother. A drunk driver veered off the road and ran him over. He died early the next morning."

Sam's face turned to stone. "Oh, Brooklynn. I'm so sorry."

"Yeah, what are the odds, huh? The wrong place at the wrong time. My mom always believed that if he had gotten tickets to the game, he would have been in Ebbets Field, and not walking home at the exact moment." She paused and looked into the distance. "Life is funny sometimes."

Sam saw the hurt in her eyes. *She's human.*

After dinner, Sam walked Brooklynn back to her house, under a glowing moon and a cool breeze, making the night feel comfortable.

Once again, their walk led them within the shadow of Ebbets Field as the sounds of honking cars and traffic surrounded them. Instead of it being a distraction, it added to the ambiance of the night.

Sam asked, "Do you like working for the Dodgers?"

Brooklynn nodded. "Yes, I do. It's neat unraveling the mystery of why things happen on the field. For example, in 1949, Jackie Robinson's average was under three hundred. But they moved him to the cleanup spot since he hit fifty points higher with men on base. He ended up the MVP of the National League."

"They moved him to the cleanup spot after looking at the numbers?"

Brooklynn nodded. "Want more?"

"Sure."

"Roy Campanella is one of the best hitters in the League, but he probably won't play in the Cincinnati series. Want to know why?"

"Of course."

"His lifetime batting average against the Reds is under a hundred."

"No wonder he didn't play in the last series against them."

A Redhead in Brooklyn

As they walked further, Sam asked, "What do the numbers say about me? I'm sure it's not pretty with all the strikeouts I've had recently."

"Not as bad as you think," she said with a smile. "You strike out 58% of the time in the first three innings, but that drops to 24% after the third inning. Also, your batting average and on base percentage increase as the game goes on, so that means you make in game adjustments."

Sam shook his head. "And I was worried."

Brooklynn laughed. "Nah, you're doing fine. Keep away from the high ones, focus on your balance like we worked on, and your numbers should be even better by October."

A chill went down Sam's spine. He was having so much fun and enjoying this new world he forgot he wasn't going to be in there in October. He frowned as he looked into the night.

"What's wrong?" Brooklynn asked.

Sam shook his head, then smiled. "Aw. Nothing. I was thinking about October and if we are going to make it to the World Series."

Brooklynn had the same uncertain smile on her face. "Yeah. After October, I have some decisions to make about the future."

"What do you mean?"

"I'm not sure I'll be in Brooklyn after the season. Things are complicated."

"How so?" Sam asked.

"Aw, I don't want to bore you with the details. I'll figure it out once October arrives."

Sam nodded and thought about his deal, but put it out of his mind since he didn't want to ruin their night. "For what it's worth, I enjoy hanging out with you. Let's enjoy the season and not think too much past October."

Brooklynn raised her eyebrows. "Are you suggesting a friendship?"

Sam smiled and nodded.

"Friends, huh?" Brooklynn repeated, looking into the row of homes. "Nothing more, right?"

"No strings attached. Let's have fun until we have to go our separate ways in October. What do you say?"

Brooklynn thought for a few seconds, then replied, "I can make that work. But don't get any ideas. I know not to get involved with ballplayers."

Sam looked into the distance. As the glow of the traffic light lit his face, he looked over at her. "I wouldn't get any ideas either," he laughed. "I've heard stories about how crazy female statisticians can be."

Brooklynn laughed. "All right, Mr. Murdock. You now have someone to have fun with until October."

"Good. It's nice to be with someone who knows the city and can show me around."

"Well, Sam, I'm flattered you'd say that. I have to admit, I've had fun being with you too. It's not every day you get to meet a nice guy, even if he can't lay off the high fastball," she laughed.

Sam was about to answer, then he stopped. "Wait. You called me Sam. Counting the incident on the Wonder Wheel, I'm up to two. That's progress."

A Redhead in Brooklyn

Brooklyn squinted, then waved her hand across her face. "Well, if we are going to be friends, I guess I can at least call you by your first name."

Sam smiled. "Glad we came to terms."

As Sam was about to make another comment, he looked over and saw her face in the light coming from a street lamp. As the breeze blew through her hair, it seemed as if it was all happening in slow motion.

As they walked to her house, Brooklynn faced him. "Thank you for an enjoyable evening, Sam."

"You're welcome. Maybe we can do it again when we get back from the road trip?"

Brooklynn's manner was void of the cockiness he braced for. "I'd like that," she said, the sincerity in her face evident.

"Me too." He looked at his watch. "I better get back to the hotel. We have an early train to Cincinnati tomorrow."

"Would you like me to call you a cab?"

Seeing an opportunity to spend a little more time with her, he nodded. "Sure. I'd like that."

"Okay. Ding," she pointed. "You're a cab. Get it?"

Sam shook his head, then laughed. "Did I mention how much I'm looking forward to our friendship?"

"Tell ya what, I'll let you know if the feeling is mutual," she said with a smile and wink.

In the awkward silence before a date ends, Sam moved forward. He leaned in and gave her a gentle kiss on the cheek. She didn't move and instead closed her eyes.

Sam backed away, and they faced each other. "See you when we get back," he told her.

Brooklynn smiled, then turned and walked to her door without saying goodbye. She hopped up the steps, opened the door, then walked inside and shut it behind her.

Sam took his cue. He turned and walked down the sidewalk, looking for a cab to take him to his hotel.

Brooklynn walked back to the door and cracked it open. She watched him for as long as she could before he disappeared into the night. After shutting the door, she placed her forehead against it.

Sam boarded the Monday morning train to Cincinnati. The Dodgers would be away from Ebbets Field for two weeks, beginning in Cincinnati, then games in St. Louis, Chicago and Milwaukee.

Sam found his compartment and placed his bag on the bed. He put his clothes away, then headed to the dining car for breakfast.

Chris was at a table waiting for him. "How did it go with Brooklynn last night?"

Sam smiled. "Fine. How did it go with the coat check girl?" He joked.

"I have to admit, she's a lot better kisser than you are."

After Sam laughed, Chris told him, "Speaking of kisses, nice work my friend."

Sam thought about what he meant, then his face went stone. "How did you know about that?"

"I know everything. It's one of the perks of my profession."

A Redhead in Brooklyn

"Hooray for Sainthood," he said with a mock smile.

"I see a grin on your face. You look like a split watermelon."

Sam dismissed it right away. "Aw, it's nothing. We're going to have fun until October, nothing more."

"Is that so?" Chris asked with a grin.

"Look, I've been hitting the ball again, so I'm anxious to get to Cincinnati. We're on a roll now, so I don't need any distractions."

Chris nodded. "Thirty-eight wins in the first forty-six games is pretty good."

"I hope we keep it going."

"Are you going to keep it going with Brooklynn?"

"Why are you so concerned about her?"

"I can tell a good girl when I see one."

"We'll see each other, if that's what you mean. Other than that, once October arrives, I'll never see her again."

Chris stared at him. Finally, he said, "Sam, you have to live your life. Without fear. I can see in your eyes that girl has your attention. See where it might go."

"Why would I do that?"

"What was the quote? 'Don't be sad it ended. Be happy it happened?'"

Sam looked through the window at the passing countryside. "I'm taking it one day at a time and enjoying the moment. But I'm not falling in love. There's no future in it."

Ivan Scott

Tuesday night at 124 Sullivan Place, a redheaded girl turned off the radio after listening to the final out of the Dodger game in Cincinnati.

Brooklynn walked into her bedroom, laid on the bed and gazed at her perfectly kept scorecard from the game.

She peered for the hundredth time at the name "MURDOCK 9 LF" and thought of how he played in the game, and what he might have looked like doing it. Creeping in were tiny droplets of scenes from their walk home.

It had been a long time since a man stood toe to toe with her, and didn't put up with any of her sass. She liked it.

But when October came, she wouldn't be in Brooklyn. She reminded herself of that as she turned out the light and tried to fall asleep.

ten

July bullied its way into town, bringing heat and longer days to Ebbets Field.

As the Borough warmed, the Dodgers torched the National League. Sam's slump, which worried him earlier in the season, was a thing of the past as he once again burned through the pitchers in the National League.

After taking two of three games from the Phillies, the lead on second place Milwaukee was thirteen games. People in the Borough were already thinking about ordering World Series tickets.

Before their night game in upper Manhattan against the Giants, Sam took the twenty-minute walk from the Hotel Bossert to Juniors Restaurant. Many of the Dodger players ate at Juniors and raved about their cheesecake, so he wanted to see what all the fuss was about.

When he walked in, he saw familiar faces. "Hey Guys," he said as Pee Wee sat at a table with center fielder Duke Snider and pitcher Carl Erskine. "What are you guys doing here?"

Pee Wee scooped up a piece of cheesecake with his fork. "Whenever Carl is pitching, we come here and have a slice of cheesecake for luck."

Erskine wiped his mouth and slid his plate to the middle of the table. "Yep. This is the best cheesecake in the world. I always pitch better after a slice."

"If it makes me a better hitter, I'm ordering a slice too," Sam told them.

Sam ordered a slice of cheesecake with blueberry topping. As he reached for his fork, Pee Wee told him, "You've been hitting the ball well lately. Keep it up."

"Thanks. Slumps are never easy, so I'm glad it's over."

Pee Wee leaned back in his chair. "I'd do anything to break out of a slump. I would even walk up to the plate wearing a tutu and a dunce cap if it meant I got four hits. You'd do the same thing, wouldn't you?"

Sam thought about it for a few seconds, then nodded. "Yeah, I probably would. When I was in college, I went through a similar slump. Before the conference tournament, I began sleeping with my bats."

Duke raised an eyebrow. "I hope they were pretty."

Sam laughed. "Yes, they were. I ended up being the offensive player of the tournament and we won the championship."

Pee Wee narrowed his eyes. "You haven't been bringing your bats back to your room, have you?"

Sam smiled. "Whatever it takes."

"By the way, you wanna ride with us to the Polo Grounds?" Pee Wee asked.

Sam contained his excitement. "That would be cool."

A Redhead in Brooklyn

Pee Wee drove them up the West Side Highway. On the way there, they talked about baseball.

Sam sat in the backseat next to Erskine and listened to their stories. He wished the trip was longer since he enjoyed each story.

As the car sped north, the sound of a siren blared from behind. Pee Wee looked in the rear view mirror. "Oh no."

Duke looked behind. "Someone has taken exception to your driving," he told him.

Pee Wee pulled the car off the road and stopped.

"Let's see you get out of this one, Captain," he joked.

When the officer approached the car, Pee Wee rolled down the window and looked out with a smile.

"License and registration, please."

Pee Wee flashed the officer a genuine smile. "Good afternoon, Officer. I'm Pee Wee Reese, and with me are Duke Snider, Carl Erskine and Sam Murdock. I apologize for speeding, but I didn't want us to be late for our game at the Polo Grounds."

The officer took off his sunglasses, squinted his eyes, then smiled. "Wow. That is you. And Duke and the fellas too."

The officer said hello to everyone in the car, then put his ticket book away. "I'm sorry to hold you up. Take it easy on the pedal next time, okay, Pee Wee?"

Pee Wee nodded. "Yes, sir. I'll do that. And thanks for keeping our highways safe."

After they shook hands, Pee Wee rolled up the window and

turned to Duke. "Any questions."

Duke shook his head and smirked.

The Giants starter, Jim Hearn, had the Dodgers shutout through the first four innings.

In the fifth inning, Sam walked to the on-deck circle. He picked up the sticky pine tar rag, and when he brought it close, he wrinkled his nose due to the smell. He rubbed it along the handle of his bat, then dropped it to the dirt and took a few practice swings.

He watched Gil Hodges work the pitcher to a full count, then fouled off a fastball into the seats behind their dugout.

Sam followed the flight of the ball into the crowd. As his eyes floated from the crowd back to home plate, he noticed a young lady sitting in the first row by the Dodger dugout, who looked familiar. The hat and cinnamon hair caught his eye first.

She turned toward him, her smile filled in the missing piece of the puzzle. When she gave him a seductive wink, he knew who it was.

He continued staring at her. *What's Ginger doing here?* She had his full attention as the mystery engulfed him.

With his heart beating faster, he walked toward her and was about to speak when he heard his name called. The tone of voice was not pleasant.

"You're up, Murdock," the umpire shouted. "Stop flirting with the dames in the crowd. I'm running a game, not a dance."

Sam looked over to see home plate umpire Augie Donatelli

A Redhead in Brooklyn

giving him the death stare, and the Giants catcher laughing. Then he looked at Brooklynn, who placed her gloved hand in front of her face and giggled. He walked into the batter's box, ignoring the crowd as they hooted it up. He scooped up some dirt and rubbed it on his hands, then dug in and was ready to hit. After what had happened, all the preparation for his at-bat was out the window.

Chris saw everything as he sat in the press box and shook his head. *Here comes a strikeout.*

Sam watched the first two pitches go by for strikes. On the third one, a high fastball, Sam swung but missed for strike three.

The only saving grace was Sam made the third out of the inning, so he didn't have to walk past Brooklynn to retrieve his glove. Instead, he tossed his bat toward the dugout, then trotted to his position in left field.

Among the thousands of fans in the Polo Grounds, one in particular wanted Sam's attention. "Mooordock," the female voice screamed. "Mooordock," she repeated.

Sam ignored the voice and focused on the game. It came a third time, "Mooordock, look at me when I'm talking to you."

When Sam heard a cowbell, there was no doubt who it was. "Hi ya, Hilda," he yelled up to her. "What are you doing here?"

"Never mind that. Give this to Alston."

She dropped a folded piece of paper from the first row of the left field seats. Sam walked over and picked it out of the dirt. He looked up and yelled, "No problem." He placed it in his back pocket, then turned to focus on the upcoming batter.

When the inning ended, Sam ran back to the dugout. On the way there, he saw the owner, Walter O'Malley, sitting in a box close to the dugout. "How ya doing, Sam?"

"Great, Mr. O'Malley. Don't worry, we'll pull this one out."

O'Malley nodded.

As Sam stepped down into the dugout, Alston passed by. "O'Malley giving you financial advice?" He joked.

Sam laughed. "As rich as he is, I'll take whatever he wants to give me."

Alston laughed and continued past him. Before he got too far away, Sam reached into his back pocket and got his attention. "Oh, this is for you."

He gave Alston the folded paper, then walked into the dugout.

The Dodgers scored twice in the top of the seventh to take a 2-0 lead. But it was short-lived as the Giants scored three times in the bottom of the inning.

As the eighth inning began, it appeared the Dodgers were in trouble. However, Pee Wee led off with a walk, and when Gil hit a sharp single to left field, the Dodgers had something going.

Sam walked to the plate. The thoughts in his head kept him focused on the task at hand. *Relax. You can do this. Remember, Brooklynn's scouting reports for what Hearn throws in the late innings.*

He looked out at Hearn, who rubbed the ball in his hands behind the pitcher's mound. He walked to the mound, then focused on his catcher, who gave him the sign for the next pitch.

Sam raised his bat in front of his eyes and focused on his breathing. Then he heard his father's voice, as he did for years when he coached Sam's team.

A Redhead in Brooklyn

Let the ball come to you. Hit it where it's pitched. Don't try to do anything you aren't capable of doing.

He looked down, making sure his feet were where they should be. Once they were set, he tapped his bat on the plate, then took a couple of practice swings, and looked out at the pitcher.

You can do this.

Everything around Hearn blurred. All sound ceased. There were no lights, but Sam saw Hearn perfectly.

Hearn came set, then checked the runners. When he saw they weren't too far off the bases, he wound up and threw the ball.

Sam saw the white blur. It was higher than the last set of pitches, so he let it go.

"Ball," the umpire growled.

Good job, Sam. Way to lay off the high pitch. Now, what's Hearn going to come back with next? Sam thought about Brooklynn's report. *When Hearn starts with a fastball for a ball, he will come back with a curve on the outside part of the plate.*

Hearn got the sign, kicked his leg and fired. As expected, the pitch was a curve on the outside corner and Sam let it go by.

"Strike," the umpire said with the same gruffness as with the first call.

I should have swung. Come on Sam. Get your head out of your ass. You knew what was coming. Pull the damn trigger next time. Okay. What's next? Hearn usually throws back-to-back curves, especially if he gets the first one over for a strike. Okay. One ball and one strike. Don't let him get two strikes on you. Focus. Remember what to look for. Relax. You can do this.

Hearn came back with another curve, and Sam fouled it

back for strike two. Sam called time, then backed away and knocked the dirt out of his spikes. He rubbed the dirt off the barrel of his bat, then walked back to the plate. *Why did I miss that last pitch? Okay, Sam. Forget it. It's over. Move on. Two strikes. What will he throw? Okay, Brooklynn, what do you think? Oh yeah. Brooklynn. She looks good in a hat. And those green eyes. Wow. Okay, fine. Back to business. She wrote Hearn will throw a fastball with two strikes instead of another curve or waste a pitch out of the strike zone.*

Sam set his feet and looked out at Hearn. He took a deep breath and felt his body loosen in a warm haze. He was ready and knew what he was looking for. With the Giants crowd going crazy, Sam returned to the zone. He looked out and all he saw was Hearn in front of him. The only sound was the beating of his heart and his inner dialogue. He took a few practice swings, then pointed the bat at Hearn for a split second, then cocked it behind his head.

It's you and me now. Give me your best shot. You're not going to beat me.

Hearn got the sign from the catcher, then went into his windup and fired home. As Brooklynn predicted, it was a belt-high fastball.

Damn, she's good. It's a fastball, and it's lower than the first one. He made a mistake throwing it there. I can hit that pitch. Okay, body, take over and do your thing.

Without telling his body to do anything, it spun and his bat sliced through the humid air. The next sound was of the ball rocketing off the bat, which penetrated his soundproof zone. He took a few steps toward first base as he watched the ball ascend into the black sky, heading for left field.

Whitey Lockman and Willie Mays gave chase, but they ran out of room as the ball cleared the wall and landed in the seats where

A Redhead in Brooklyn

the crowd fought for it. The Dodgers now led 5-3.

Sam kept his head down as he toured the bases. When he got to third base, he looked up and saw Alston waiting for him. He extended his hand and Sam shook it.

After touching home plate, he saw Charlie DiGiovanna waiting for him with a smile. As they shook hands, he said, "Nice shot, Sammy."

"Thanks. You think you could get the ball back for me?"

Charlie nodded. "No problem. One of the Giant fans already threw it back on the field."

"Gee. Tough crowd."

As Sam got to the steps of the dugout, he saw Brooklynn clapping, a grin on her face. He tipped his cap to her, and she responded by shaking her head at his cockiness. He was about to say something when he felt a tugging on his jersey, and before he knew it, his teammates mobbed him in the dugout.

"Why can't you hit one while I'm pitching?" Podres joked.

"Because we're so far behind when you pitch, what would it matter?" Sam responded with a smile.

Podres laughed, then hugged him.

A few minutes later, Charlie walked by and handed him the ball. Sam looked over the dirty white ball, noticing the force of the bat smeared the inky black National League logo. Sam picked up a pen lying on the top shelf of the dugout and scribbled something on it. When the inning was over, he found Charlie. "Give this to the pretty girl wearing the white hat next to the dugout."

Charlie looked into the seats. "Is that your girl, Sam? Wow, she's a looker."

Sam smiled. "Nah. She's only a friend."

After the inning ended, Brooklynn updated her scorecard. As she filled in the number of runs the Dodgers scored, an usher in a white shirt and orange bow tie approached her.

"This is for you, ma'am," he said, handing her the ball.

Brooklynn asked, "What's this?"

"It's from someone on the Dodgers. The bat boy asked me to give it to you."

She looked at the ball and noticed the writing on it.

For Ginger:

You were right. Fastball with two strikes. Want to have dinner tomorrow after the game?

Sam

She looked out to the field, noticing him blowing a bubble as he got into position for the next batter. He looked confident, bordering on cocky. She liked that.

Dodger pitcher Billy Loes retired the Giants in order in the eighth, and it looked as if he would have a chance to get a complete game victory. But, inexplicably, Alston took him out for a relief pitcher to begin the ninth inning.

With one out, Willie Mays hit a home run to close the gap to 5-4, and it looked like Alston's strategy was about to backfire as New York loaded the bases and threatened to steal the game in their last at-bat. After bringing in two more pitchers, the Dodgers escaped with the win, but it was a shaky victory.

In the Dodger clubhouse, Sam sat with his head resting on the side of his locker. He was tired after playing his best game of the year. After his strikeout, he hit a single, double, then his home run to provide the winning margin. He also dove into the seats to catch a ball, which earned him a polite ovation from the Giants fans.

After removing his spikes, he unbuttoned his jersey and looked forward to the post-game shower. However, that was going to have to wait.

From the row of lockers, John Griffin appeared. Sam couldn't miss him, since he wore a straw hat with miniature figurines clipped on it. There was also a pocket at the top to hold his Lucky Strikes, and a cup holder at the top where he kept a can of Shaefer beer.

"Nice hat, John," Sam told him.

"Thanks. Now I don't have to worry about getting thirsty," he said, then pointed to the can resting above his head.

"Always nice to have a backup."

He smiled, then told him, "Alston wants to see you in his office."

Sam looked down the row of lockers, then back to Griffin. "Sure. Tell him I'll be there in a minute." He kept his undershirt on, then rose and walked in his stocking feet across the clubhouse to the manager's office.

He opened the door and slid his head inside. "Griffin said you wanted to see me?"

Alston's face, which was already flushed, turned to crimson. He rose and shouted, "Damn you, Murdock. Don't you ever give me another note from O'Malley during a game."

Sam walked into the office and threw his hands up. "I never gave you a note from O'Malley."

"Don't lie to me," he shouted. Alston reached into his back pocket, pulled out the note from earlier, and held it up so Sam saw it. "You gave this to me during the game."

Sam looked at it, then his face relaxed. "That wasn't from O'Malley. That was from Hilda."

The crimson in Alston's face leaked out, and within seconds, it was all white. His voice lost its bite as he asked, "Hilda?"

Sam nodded.

Alston looked at the folded paper, then turned and flung it into the trash can and walked out of the office. Sam walked over, pulled it out, and unfolded it.

Get Loes out after the eighth inning. His arm won't make it through the entire game.

Sam shook his head. "Now we have Hilda making managerial decisions. This place in crazy." He exhaled, then returned to his locker.

Chris walked over and asked, "What was that about?"

"Nothing. I was passing a love note from Hilda to Alston during study hall."

Chris looked up the row of lockers to the manager's office, then back to Sam. "What?"

"Don't ask."

Chris smiled. "Speaking of hitting, you had a nice game tonight."

"Yeah, thanks."

"Your little in-game romance with freckle face strawberry was the talk of the press box. They all know who Brooklynn is, so they think you're a brave man for trying to woo her."

"I am?"

"Yeah. As a matter of fact, we have a pool going on your little romance."

"What kind of odds am I getting?"

"You don't want to know," Chris assured him.

As Sam sat and pulled his socks off, he told him, "Put me down for a sawbuck. I'm good for it."

Chris laughed, then asked, "When are you going to see her again?"

"Who?" Sam asked, feigning surprise.

"Brooklynn? Even the head usher at Ebbets Field can see what's going on here."

"The head usher? You don't think he's going to ask her out, do you?" He joked.

Chris rolled his eyes. "After the exchange today, I'm sure you've made plans to see her outside the office."

Sam grinned. "We might have dinner tomorrow."

"You might?"

"Well, I asked, but," he stopped.

"And?"

"Well, I'm not sure what her answer is."

"Why not?"

Sam looked around the clubhouse, then back to Chris.

"I gave her the home run ball today with a message asking if she wanted to have dinner after the game tomorrow."

Chris grinned, then threw his head back and laughed.

"What's so funny?" Sam asked.

"Oh, Sam. I'm calling my dentist since I now have a cavity with all the sweetness around the clubhouse. Excuse me while I go and throw up."

Sam shook his head. "Whatever. Look, I'm sure she's going to say no, so we can hang out together if you don't have any plans."

"You give up too easy."

Sam shook his head. "It ain't happening. Tell ya what, why don't we go back to Luigis? I promise I won't leave you for the coat check girl this time."

"My heart is all aflutter at that though," he joked.

He pulled a towel from the top row of his locker and was ready to walk to the showers when John Griffin handed him a slip of paper. "This is for you, Murdock."

"Don't tell me. Alston' wants me to give this to Hilda. If I'm going to be a mailman, I need more money."

Griffin laughed. "Nah. Some broad at the door asked me to give it to you."

Sam's eyes squinted, then he opened the folded paper. His eyes scanned the words. A smile came to his lips.

"Looks like a love letter. Ya think you can slip it to Hilda during third-period auto shop class?

"Oh, you're funny," Sam told him.

Chris laughed, then added, "Are there three boxes? One for

yes, one for no and another for maybe?"

Sam ignored the jokes and looked at the note again. He smiled, then said, "I have plans tomorrow."

"Good for you. I'm sure being Alston's driver for his date with Hilda will be a real knee slapper."

eleven

The cab stopped in front of 124 Sullivan Place. Sam tried to pay the driver with cash, but the cabbie would only accept an autograph. Sam obliged, then stepped out to the sidewalk, flowers in hand.

As Brooklynn opened the door, Sam smiled wide and said, "Hello, Ginger."

Brooklynn looked at her watch. "You're twenty-seven seconds late, Mr. Murdock. I was about to make other plans," she said with a coy tilt of her head.

Sam pulled the flowers from his back and handed them to her.

Brooklynn's face lit up as her eyes widened. "Well, I guess I'll excuse a little tardiness."

"Well, that's the reason I'm late," he said, then handed them to her. "I hoped you would like them," Sam told her, enjoying the look of warmth on her face.

She brought the flowers to her face and breathed them in. "They are beautiful. Thank you." After giving them a closer look, she asked, "You didn't wait around until they bloomed, did you? I know how stubborn you can be."

Sam laughed. "It's mandatory to bring a gift to a young lady when you are going to see her, so I thought flowers were a nice touch. But I had second thoughts about the flowers so they got tossed on Fourth Avenue. Then I had third thoughts when the cabbie told me I was being a jackass, so he drove me back so I could pick them up."

"Were they still there?"

"Yeah. But a little old lady grabbed them before I could, so I had to promise to hit her a home run tomorrow."

"That's all?"

"Oh. I also had to give her a kiss."

"A kiss?"

Sam nodded. "And another for her dog, Toodels. In case you were wondering, Toodels was prettier."

Brooklynn laughed. "Well, at least someone in the neighborhood wanted to kiss you," she said coyly.

As she led him inside, the smell of roast beef and potatoes hung heavy in the living room. There was also the faint but sweet smell of apple pie somewhere, and as he followed her into the kitchen, he saw it cooling on the sill of an open window.

Sam looked around, then at Brooklynn. "I thought I was taking you to dinner?"

Brooklynn grinned. "Funny how you never expect things to turn out. I thought we'd have dinner here."

Sam nodded. "I like your idea of having dinner better than mine."

"Nice game today. That's two in a row over the Giants."

"Yeah. It puts us up eleven and a half games on the Braves, and fifteen and a half over the Giants, so it's looking good."

From behind, they heard the door creak open, and the sounds of footsteps walking inside, then the door closed. The footsteps got louder, then stopped in the hallway. "Brooklynn?" The female voice called out.

"In here," she called out.

A few seconds later, a brunette walked in, and after looking at Brooklynn, she turned to Sam with a grin. "Well, hello. You must be the ballplayer Brooklynn's been telling me about."

"I hope I'm him," he laughed, then walked over and shook her hand. "I'm Sam Murdock. It's a pleasure to meet you."

"I'm Margaret. Nice to meet you too. I hear you aren't able to lay off the high fastball."

Sam shot Brooklynn a glare. "Tattletale."

After they laughed, Margaret asked, "By the way, did we get any mail today?"

Brooklynn looked at the opening to the living room, then said, "Oh, I'm sorry, I forgot. Do me a favor and watch the meat. I'll check the mailbox."

They watched Brooklynn walk out of the kitchen, then heard the screen door open and close. This gave the pair a chance to talk.

"This is interesting," Margaret told him. "Usually Brooklynn saves roast for people she likes."

"Really?"

Margaret nodded, then asked, "How was it you two met?"

"We met at Ebbets Field. She was escorting children around

the park before a game."

"Oh yes, the littles. Brooklynn's a softie when it comes to children."

Sam said, "Yes, I saw that. She can be sassy sometimes."

"I think what you mean to say is she can be a pain in the ass sometimes."

"I get your point," Sam said, then grinned.

"She comes off that way, but deep down, she has a good heart."

"I've noticed," Sam said.

"Has she told you about–" Margaret stopped when they heard the sound of the screen door opening, then smacking into the frame.

Brooklynn called out, "Nothing for you, but I got a few bills," she told them.

Margaret smiled. "Well, I am off to an outdoor performance of the Brooklyn Symphony Orchestra."

"Would you like dinner before you go?" Brooklynn asked.

"No, thanks. The performance is in a half hour, so I better get over there." She turned and walked over to Sam. "It was nice meeting you. Do come around again sometime."

"If I am invited," he said as they kissed cheeks.

"If Brooklynn won't invite you, I will." She flashed him a coy smile.

I must have impressed her. That's a good sign. "You may have competition," he told Brooklynn.

Brooklynn glared at Sam, then looked at Margaret. "Get out of here, you troublemaker."

"Later, alligator," she said, then left the apartment.

After dinner, Brooklynn suggested they take a walk. It was a warm evening, and it felt better to be outside than in a stuffy house. The streets were alive with the sounds of jazz music coming from the various bars around the neighborhood. The soothing breeze added to the relaxed mood as they walked.

Brooklynn said, "Nice catch in the fifth inning today."

"The one where I jumped into the wall?"

"Yes, that's the one. How did you hold on to the ball?"

"Before every game, I spray my glove with glue, so the ball will stick to it," he laughed.

She elbowed his arm as they laughed. "Do you mind if we take a little detour?"

"Not at all. Where are we going?"

She smiled and looked over at him, her hair blowing in the breeze. "It's a surprise. I think you'll like it."

Brooklynn led Sam to the Brooklyn Botanical Garden. "Here we are," she told him.

Sam looked around. "Well, I don't see a Ferris wheel, and I'm sure they don't serve PBR here, so isn't this a little out of your comfort zone?"

"It's a distinct possibility," she joked.

A Redhead in Brooklyn

Sam looked around. "This place is gorgeous. The scent from all the flowers is wonderful."

"This is one of my favorite places in Brooklyn. It's so peaceful here," she told him.

As they walked into the Garden, Brooklynn led him to a field of various colors.

Sam asked, "What's this?"

"It's the Crawford Rose Garden. There are over a thousand types of roses here."

"Do you come here often?"

"As much as I can," she said, then walked to a row of rose bushes.

The colors of golds, reds and pinks stood out in the evening hue. "Did you know," Brooklynn said as she leaned in and inhaled, "The first roses planted in the 1920s are still alive today?"

Sam walked over, leaned in, and followed her lead. "Wow. That's some fragrance." As they walked along the rows of roses, Sam took in the vivid colors stretching as far as the eye could see. "What do you like best about the rose garden?"

"That's the surprise," she told him, then motioned for Sam to follow her.

They walked along a walkway leading to a rose-covered gazebo, then down brick steps until they stepped into a small stone circle. In the middle was a bronze statue of a woman holding a bouquet of roses in one arm, and a butterfly on top of a sundial in the other.

Sam walked up to it. "She's beautiful. Who is she?"

Brooklynn joined him. "The name of the statue is Roses of Yesterday. It's also called, The Rose Maiden."

Sam walked around to see the woman's face. "She looks sad."

"Some say she's pondering the love of someone who is no longer there."

Sam nodded, then looked at the sundial. "What is this inscription?"

Brooklynn smiled as she looked at the statue. "Perennis Amor. It's Latin for endless love."

Sam saw the look in her eyes. "You like her, don't you?"

Brooklynn continued looking. Finally, she said, "Yeah. I do."

Sam looked at the woman again, this time closer. "So do I."

The daylight of the summer evening in Brooklyn seemed as if it would never end. Sam and Brooklynn wanted to enjoy every last second of it, so they decided to walk back to her house instead of taking a cab. When they arrived in the shadow of her house, Sam told her, "Thank you for dinner."

"My pleasure."

"And thank you for showing me the Rose Maiden. She was beautiful."

"I'm glad you liked her. It's one of my favorite things in Brooklyn."

"It's nice to know there are still things in the world with charm and grace."

A Redhead in Brooklyn

Brooklynn nodded. "Yeah. I agree."

Sam locked on her eyes. "I wasn't talking about her."

Brooklynn stared at him for a few seconds, then she took a step forward at the same time Sam moved to her. But before they embraced, they stopped and looked at each other.

"Um, we're supposed to be friends, remember?" Brooklynn reminded him.

Sam nodded and put his guard back up. "I was about to remind you."

"Message received. I'm glad we came to our senses," she said, then looked away.

Sam smiled. "Yes. That was almost a disaster."

They both avoided eye contact.

Finally, Sam looked at her. "I enjoyed being with you tonight. I know we said no guarantees, but there's one thing I look forward to when we're together."

"What's that?"

"That we'll have fun. I'm counting on that until you have to leave in October."

Brooklynn's smile returned. "Count on it. See you at Ebbets Field, Fred."

"Sounds like you're the one being optimistic, Ginger."

Sam began his walk back to the hotel. He wasn't thinking about the walk. He was thinking about Brooklynn.

Thoughts of seeing her for the first time tonight when she answered the door. The way she gazed at the statue. Her face in the sunset. And the way he felt when he moved closer to her. *What might have happened if we tempted fate?*

Before he knew it, he was blocks away, but never felt as if he took a step. From behind, a cab approached and slowed when it got parallel to him. Through the window, a familiar voice called out to him. "Need a ride?"

Sam leaned down and saw who was driving. "Well, as long as you're here," he grinned, then got inside.

"Best date you've had in a while, wasn't it?" Chris asked. "A trip to the Brooklyn Botanical Garden? I see you're movin' up in the world."

Sam smiled, then looked out the window. "I was about to ask how you knew about that, but I hate asking stupid questions."

"Are you going to see her tomorrow?"

Sam continued looking through the window. "Hopefully I'll run into her at the park."

Chris looked at him in the rear view mirror and said, "Hopefully, huh?"

Sam blushed. "I meant maybe."

Now it was Chris' turn to laugh. "Maybe you will? Ha, that's a laugh."

The cab drove north along Flatbush Avenue. Sam saw the Grand Army Plaza passing by. He gazed at the elliptical park with its military memorial arch and fountains. "Wow. That's beautiful."

"There's a lot of beauty in the world," Chris told him as he

A Redhead in Brooklyn

looked at Sam in the rear view mirror.

Sam stared off into the darkness. The lights from the streetlights illuminated his face as the car sped along the street to the hotel.

"Anything you want to talk about?" Chris asked.

Sam continued staring.

"Sam?"

Sam broke out of his trance. "Yeah?"

"You okay?"

"Me? Sure...I'm...sure. Never better."

Chris gave him another look, then returned his eyes to the road.

twelve

The next day, a man in a beige uniform walked up to the door at 124 Sullivan Place and rang the doorbell.

The door opened, and a smiling face filled the doorway. "Yes?"

"I have a delivery for Brooklynn Kelly," the man said.

"I'm Brooklynn Kelly."

"Sign here, please."

She signed the thin white paper attached to the clipboard and handed it back to the man. He handed her a vase with a dozen roses of various colors peering out.

After saying thank you, Brooklynn walked into the kitchen and set the vase on the table. When she opened the card and read the words, she smiled.

Dear Brooklynn:

Thank you for a wonderful evening and the surprise visit to the Botanical Garden.

I know these roses aren't as beautiful or have the legacy of the ones we saw last night, but I hope they will remind you of our time together. By the

A Redhead in Brooklyn

way, these flowers never touched the pavement and arrived without any second thoughts, or promises to kiss strange women. Or their dog.

Your Friend -

Sam

Brooklynn laughed. "Well, Mr. Murdock. You sure know how to impress a girl. And not only on the baseball field either."

The phone rang in Sam's room. "Hello?"

"It's Pee Wee."

"Pee Wee? What's up?"

"Since we've won two in a row over the Giants, and none of us like to mess with a winning streak, we drove over here to pick you up for the series finale. You don't mind riding with us again, do you?"

"No, not at all. It will save me from having to walk over to Ebbets Field to take the team bus."

"Great, I'm in the lobby now. Grab your stuff and meet us outside. It's Duke's turn to drive, so look for a baby blue and white Chevy Bel-Air."

"Will do. Give me five minutes and I'll be down."

Sam had no idea what kind of car that was, but at least Pee Wee gave him the color, so he had something to look for.

The trip to Manhattan was a carbon copy of the last few days, only it was Duke's day to drive. The stories were even better, the day was brighter and the skyline of New York glistened as they passed it by along the West Side Highway.

Something else that repeated itself was the sound of a siren. Duke looked into the rear view mirror and shook his head. Then he pulled the car over to the side of the highway and looked over at Pee Wee. "No problem. I got this."

Pee Wee grinned.

The officer approached the car. "License and registration, please." Duke smiled, then reached for his wallet. He looked at Pee Wee and winked, then back to the officer. "Here you go. By the way, you'll see on my license it reads Edwin Donald Snider. But everyone in Brooklyn calls me Duke."

The officer kept looking at the license. "Oh, so you're Duke Snider? The baseball player?"

Duke's face lit up. "Yes, I am. And with me are Pee Wee Reese, Carl Erskine and Sam Murdock. We're on our way to the Polo Grounds."

"So you are," he said with a smile. "Believe it or not, I am too. I never miss a Giants-Dodgers game."

"Really?" Duke asked.

The officer nodded. "By the way, I'd love an autograph. You think you could do that for me while I'm here?"

Duke beamed. "Of course. It would be my absolute pleasure."

The officer handed him his ticket book. "Put your autograph on this, ya bum. I'm a Giants fan."

Duke's smile faded.

After signing the speeding ticket, the officer told him, "Have a nice day. Oh, and by the way, I hope you lose tonight," then walked back to his motorcycle.

A Redhead in Brooklyn

Duke looked at the ticket and shook his head. Then he turned to a grinning Pee Wee, who suppressed a laugh. Duke snarled, "Don't you say another word for the rest of the trip."

A few weeks later, with the Dodgers in Cincinnati, Brooklynn was in the middle of slicing potatoes for dinner. After putting them on the stove, she walked into the living room and turned on the radio.

Margaret sat on the couch, reading *Hollywood Confidential*.

Brooklynn asked, "I wonder if the Dodgers game is still on? They started at two, so hopefully I didn't miss it."

Margaret smiled. "Don't you get enough of the team when they're in Brooklyn?"

"Oh, way too much. I wish they were on the road more than they are. I was only wondering how they did today." Brooklynn giggled, then looked away.

Margaret laughed as she placed her magazine down. "You could submit that performance for an Academy Award."

"I need to check on dinner. Can you find the game? Usually it's on WMGM."

"Sure," Margaret told her. She walked to the tall radio and adjusted the knobs, but all she got was static.

"What's the problem?" Brooklynn asked, leaning her head in from the kitchen.

"Oh, nothing," Margaret told her as she took a step back. She looked at the radio, sized up the situation, then slapped the top of it with her fist. Immediately, the room filled with the sounds of a baseball game. "There you go." She walked over, sat down, and picked up her magazine. "If there's no more drama, I would like to continue reading about Grace Kelly winning the Oscar for her performance in *The Country Girl*. I loved that movie."

Brooklynn walked over to the tall radio, then looked back at Margaret with a perplexed stare. When Margaret ignored her, she turned the volume knob and heard the Dodgers play-by-play announcer, Vin Scully, describing the game.

Margaret continued reading her magazine as she asked, "How's the job going?"

"Great. I knew when I came here I'd enjoy it."

Brooklynn looked at the radio, then turned to Margaret. "This might sound silly, but—" she said, then stopped.

"What?"

"Oh, forget it." She turned away, focusing on the radio.

A few minutes later, she walked to the window and saw Ebbets Field in the distance. After staring at the ballpark, she looked back at her roommate. "Do you know if they do extensions?"

"Extensions?"

"Yeah. Could I stay with the Dodgers after October?"

"All you've talked about since April is how you're off to Los Angeles once the season is over."

"I know. It's time to get on with my life." Her words lacked conviction.

Margaret raised an eyebrow. "What's going on?"

Brooklynn looked away. "Nothing."

"Nothing, huh? We've known each other long enough for me

to know that look."

"I'm good. Once the season is over, I'm heading west."

Margaret put her magazine on the table. "Is this about Sam?"

Brooklynn smiled and shook her head. "Of course not. You know I wouldn't even think about sticking around here for some stupid ballplayer."

Margaret glared at her. "My mom once told me when two people know the truth, a lie is pointless."

Brooklynn shook her head. "I'm not talking to you anymore."

Margaret laughed, then watched Brooklynn turn to the radio and listen to the end of the game.

The Dodgers finished their long road trip by losing to the Cubs. Despite being swept by Chicago, the Dodgers were still in first place by fourteen games over the Braves.

In the dining car of their train heading back to Brooklyn, Sam sat opposite Chris, then picked up his napkin and unfolded it. "What's on your mind?"

"I wanted to ask you about something. Something that's intrigued me ever since I picked you up from Brooklynn's house." Chris looked at him as he did on that first morning they talked in Kiawah. "What's going on with you?"

"Nothing." Sam said as he unfolded his napkin.

"I saw your face the other night. You're struggling with something, aren't you?"

Sam squinted his eyes. "What do you mean? For the first

time in a while, things are good. Trust me. I'm fine." He looked away and smiled.

Chris gave him a close look. "I know a little something about the world, Sam. I can tell when a man's lost his heart to something." He paused, then added, "Or to someone."

Sam looked at him. His eyes lost their will, and he looked away, then to his lap. A few seconds later, he looked up and met Chris' eyes. "The other night, it hit me. I am enjoying myself. A little too much."

"What do you mean?"

Sam looked through the window at the passing countryside. After he heard two bells and saw a train station pass, he said, "I never thought it would be this way when I signed up for this. I'm living my dream. And then I meet this woman. We have so much fun together. I've never felt that way about a woman before, so I'm not sure what I'm doing, or if I should be doing it."

"Sounds like whatever you're doing, you're doing it right. What's the problem?"

"That's it. Come October, I have to say goodbye to everything. The other night in the cab, it hit me that all this is going away at the end of summer. How can I go full speed into everything, knowing I won't be there at the end? It's not right to Brook-" He paused, then finished his sentence. "The Brooklyn Dodgers."

"It sounds like you were about to say something else."

Sam looked past Chris to the end of the dining car. "I don't know what you mean."

"Deny it all you want, Sam, but you are struggling with something. And yes, it's the Dodgers. But it's also Brooklynn."

A Redhead in Brooklyn

"I'm going to lose her and the Dodgers when October comes. I know that was the deal, but I never thought about how I'd feel about saying goodbye to this. All of this."

Chris smiled. "I know it's difficult, but you have to live, Sam. Do what makes you happy because these days will never come again. One day you'll be back in Kiawah wishing you were here. Don't leave before it's actually time to go."

Before Sam could speak, Chris added, "And I'm not talking about just the Dodgers and Ebbets Field."

Sam stared at Chris, then looked at the table. "If it were only that easy."

thirteen

The Dodgers were on the road for most of July. But August arrived, and since the team was about to begin a long home stand, Sam had time to check in on a friend.

He searched the office doors for the name of the Dodgers media and public relations manager, Irving Rudd, since he was Brooklynn's boss. Eventually, he found his office and poked his head inside.

"Hi ya, Irving."

"Sam Murdock. What brings you by today? I figured after the long road trip, you'd be asleep until our next game."

Sam smiled. "I found my second wind."

"Are you good for the autograph day at Prospect Park I mentioned earlier in the week?"

Sam nodded. "Yes. Looking forward to it."

"Good. What brings you by today?"

Sam looked around the room. "Is Brooklynn here?"

"She's here somewhere. You need some numbers crunched?"

"Yes, I do. With the Cubs coming to town, I would like to prepare for who they are going to pitch against us. I thought Brooklynn would have what I needed."

From behind, the door to the office opened, and in walked the freckle-faced smile Sam enjoyed seeing. "Well, if it isn't Ginger Rogers," he said, his grin assured.

Brooklynn stopped, then looked over. Her face lit up. "Fred Astaire. What brings you by today?"

Rudd looked at them with a furrowed brow. "You two been taking dance lessons?"

Brooklynn smiled. "I told Murdock if he didn't stop laying off the high fastball, he better start taking dance lessons, since he'd be looking for a second career." She winked at Sam.

Rudd stood. "O'Malley wants to see me about some upcoming promotions, so I'll see you both later," he said, then gave them a curious smile as he walked out of the office.

Sam spoke first. "Learned any new dance steps while I was away?"

"I wanted to learn how to tango."

"Why?"

"Well, with all the roses I received in July, the urge struck me."

Sam gave her a mock glare. "Who's been sending you roses?"

Brooklyn laughed. "You never know, Mr. Murdock."

Sam shook his head. "Roses huh? Did they have tire marks on them like the last ones?"

"Not this time. Trust me, I looked to make sure." When they

finished laughing, she said, "Thank you again, Sam. They were beautiful."

"You're welcome. Sorry about not including a sundial with the roses. They were sold out of those."

Brooklynn grinned. "You remembered the Rose Maiden. Good to see you were paying attention." She turned and walked to her desk. "I'm glad you stopped by."

Sam's eyes widened. "Really?"

"Yes," she told him, then pulled a drawer out and reached inside. 'I've been meaning to give this to you." Brooklynn pulled her hand out, clutching a square manila envelope.

"What's this?" He took the envelope from her and reached inside. He pulled out a black and white square picture of them together.

Brooklynn smiled. "It's us at Coney Island during the autograph session."

Sam's eyes lit up, and his lips curled upward. "Wow, we've come a long way since then."

"We have?"

"Sure," Sam smiled. "Now we like spending time with each other," he said, with a coy wink and smile.

"It was more of you wanting to spend time with me. And as far as wanting to spend time with you? Well..." she said, then laughed.

"Once you're done for the day, do you have plans?"

"Yeah. For the rest of the day and night actually."

Sam's smile drooped. "Oh. Sorry to hear that."

A Redhead in Brooklyn

"Well, I plan on going back to my house. Plan on having dinner. Then plan on going to bed. Did you have something you'd like to do between all my plans?"

From his jacket pocket, he pulled out an envelope and handed it to her. "These might be better than flowers."

Brooklynn walked closer, looked at his hand, then took the envelope. "Should I open it now?"

"Unless you're the Amazing Kreskin and can tell me what is inside."

Brooklynn squinted her eyes. "Who's the Amazing Kreskin?"

Sam raised his eyebrows, knowing the reference was a few decades before its time. "Oh, he's a...aw, it's nothing."

Brooklynn shook her head, then looked at the envelope. She reached inside, and when she pulled out two tickets, her eyes widened. "You got tickets for the impressionist exhibit at the Brooklyn Museum?"

"Is that what they are?" He asked, then took the tickets from her and looked at them. "Oh man, that guy on the corner gypped me. I was going to take you to the Three Stooges Film Festival at the Paramount. He must have switched envelopes when I wasn't looking."

She grinned, so Sam threw his hands up. "Oh well. I guess this is your lucky day."

Brooklynn's eyes rose from the tickets to Sam's face. The emerald glow sparkled when the sunlight from the window found her eyes.

The two spent the afternoon at the Brooklyn Museum.

Brooklynn led Sam around, showing him some of her favorite paintings. He watched as her face lit up when she described why she liked a particular artist and painting.

They approached a painting of a night scene with cars lined up on the street between two buildings. The short, choppy brush strokes came together to create a scene, and as they approached, Sam understood what they were. "Wow, that's beautiful."

Brooklynn continued looking at the painting. "It is, isn't it?"

"What do you like about it?"

Brooklynn stared at the painting, taking it all in. Finally, she spoke. "I like that it takes me to another time and place. I'm no longer standing in 1955 Brooklyn, but I'm exactly where Pissaro was, at the exact time he saw this scene and decided he wanted to capture it on canvas."

"He must have loved that street."

"I imagine he did. But-" she began but stopped.

"What?" Sam asked.

She paused as she focused on the color and scene, then looked at him. "In every work of art, whether it be painting, books, dance, whatever, the artist draws inspiration from life. I imagine Pissaro watching the street and painting what he saw. And even better, how he felt when he saw it."

Sam studied the painting. "He's captured a small piece of time that the world forgot as soon as it was over. One of a billion moments in time that nobody even thinks about that passed like all the others, but he captured it so it will live forever."

Brooklynn stared at him, then a small smile came to her face.

After spending time discussing the Monet, Renoir, and Manet paintings, Brooklynn led Sam to a painting by Degas. "I like this one."

Sam looked at what lay on the canvas. Before his eyes was a painting of three women and a horse in front of what looked like a pond. "What is this?"

"This is *Portrait de Mlle Eugénie Fiocre*. He painted this in his studio from memory after witnessing the scene during a ballet rehearsal where the performers were taking a break."

"From memory?"

"Yes. He had a little help since he sketched them by the water. But he took those sketches as a blueprint, then used his memory for how he felt about the scene and painted based on that. Quite extraordinary, if you think about it."

"It's beautiful," Sam agreed. "A moment in time nobody would think about, but he captured it, and we are talking about it today. Amazing."

Brooklynn nodded. "The funny thing about Degas was he admitted he studied the other great painters. Since he didn't know anything about painting, he took his inspiration from them and then created his own path."

Sam nodded, then told her, "I guess if we are to live our lives to the fullest, and leave something wonderful behind for the world that will live forever, we have to leave what's comfortable and forge a new path into the unknown so our greatness can come alive, and take us places we never thought we'd have the courage to go."

Brooklynn stared at him. When he looked at her, she smiled.

"I like that, Sam."

"You know, I never thought I'd be in Brooklyn and playing baseball with the Dodgers. I know it's a cliche, but it is a dream come true. Life can take unexpected turns in the path at the moment we least expect it."

"I know what you mean. I never thought I'd be here either. But we are, and I'm sure there's a reason for it."

"Any ideas why?"

"Haven't a clue," she smiled. "But as long as we are here, we should enjoy whatever is supposed to happen. Right?"

They looked at each other, speaking only with their eyes.

Sam broke the silence by clearing his throat. "I don't know about you, but I'm getting hungry and would love a plate of Luigi's lasagna. Are you hungry?"

After dinner, Sam walked Brooklynn back to her house.

"You will have your hands full with the Cubs," she told him.

"I'm sure I will. Who's pitching?"

Brooklynn continued looking into the night. "Sam Jones has excellent control, and can throw his curve ball for strikes when he needs to."

"He struck me out twice on curve balls the last time I saw him, so he has my attention."

"Then you'll see Bob Rush. He's a two-time all-star with a live fastball that moves away from a right-handed batter. He will throw that pitch with two strikes since the batter thinks it's outside,

A Redhead in Brooklyn

but it will break over the plate at the last instant."

"Point taken. What about Warren Hacker? He should go in the last game of the series."

Brooklynn nodded. "Hacker has a good fastball, but his earned run average is high, so make him throw you a strike. His control has been a little off this year, so be loose at the plate. I'd hate it if you took one in the head."

Sam raised his eyebrows. "Your concern is touching."

Brooklynn added, "If you aren't around, who's going to buy me flowers?"

"Margaret doesn't buy you flowers?"

Brooklynn laughed. "Nah. She'd rather buy me wine. One night she came home–" she said, walking off the curb at the intersection of Bedford Avenue and Sullivan Place.

Sam saw the car coming down the street, and with a green light, it wasn't going to stop, so he waited at the curb.

However, Brooklynn never saw the car and continued looking back at him as she spoke. Things moved in slow motion as Sam saw the car, where Brooklynn was, and what was about to happen.

Instinctively, he jumped into the street, reached out and grabbed her, then jumped them out of the way. The car swerved and honked its horn as it continued speeding by. She was in his arms now, too scared to speak. Sam could feel her heart thumping as he held her, the look of stunned fear on her face.

They gazed into each other's eyes as the moment of fear drifted into a moment of passion. They weren't sure what was about to happen next, but whatever it was, they welcomed it.

"I guess I've stepped up my game from the Wonder Wheel," he said with a smile.

"Yeah," Brooklynn responded, her voice soft. "You have a thing for protecting me."

As they looked at each other, Sam felt Brooklynn trembling. "Are you okay?"

She snapped out of it. Her voice was back to being strong and ready to banter. "Of course. I've never been better."

"You're shaking."

Brooklynn looked away, and they released. "I'm cold."

"It's August."

Brooklynn glared at him, and shot back, "I said I'm cold."

Sam smiled, then released her. "Am I going to have to hold your hand every time we cross the street?" He asked, flirting more than admonishing.

Looking into his huge brown eyes, her voice lost its sass. "I guess so."

They smiled at each other, then Sam extended his hand. Brooklynn looked at it.

"It's okay. I won't tell anyone."

Brooklynn smiled, then looked at his hand again. She reached for it, and their fingers interlocked.

As they walked along the sidewalk, she told him, "Don't get ideas, Fred. This is a one time moment of weakness."

Sam grinned. "Do me a huge favor, will ya, Ginger?"

A Redhead in Brooklyn

"What?" She asked, looking over to him.

"For one in your life, could you just shut the hell up and enjoy the moment?"

Brooklynn was about to speak, but nothing came out of her mouth.

Sam stopped her. "Don't speak. Words would only ruin a moment we'll both think about long after tonight."

As they walked to her house, their hands never released. From time to time, they gazed at each other with an amorous smile.

fourteen

The Dodger steamroller gained strength as the season rolled along. Before anyone knew it, fall arrived, and the Dodgers were on the threshold of a League championship. They ended their early September home stand by beating Philadelphia to put them within one game of winning the National League pennant.

During the last home game before the road trip, Sam broke the little toe on his left foot crashing into a wall to make a catch against the Phillies. The pain was unbearable, but he'd played with pain before, and this was no exception.

Pee Wee walked over to him. "Hey, rookie, are we going to wrap this thing up in Milwaukee?"

"No sweat," he said. "Who do you think is going to take it over in the other league?"

"I hope it's the Yankees. I've played in five World Series, all against them, and they've beaten us every time." Reese looked down. "How's the toe?"

"Fine. It only hurts when I walk on it," Sam joked. "I'd like to keep this quiet."

A Redhead in Brooklyn

"If it hurts too bad, get out of the lineup. I don't want you to hurt it worse before the World Series."

"You know, if I was hurt, I would ask out of the lineup," Sam smiled.

"Sure, Murdock," he told him, unconvinced.

"By the way, do we have a treadmill in the clubhouse?"

Reese gave him a curious look, then his face brightened. "Oh yeah. I've heard of those before. My doctor has one in his office, but we don't have one here. Why would you want to know that?"

"Because I need to improve my stamina. The summer heat has zapped me, and I'm getting gassed in the late innings. I need to get my body in better shape so I don't hurt the team."

Reese shook his head. "You have a broken toe. Go easy, will ya? Don't make me pull you out of the game like I did in St. Louis."

"I told you I was fine."

Reese laughed. "Right. After you ran into the wall and were unconscious for a few minutes, the first thing you asked when you came to was if you scored a touchdown. I had to have Charlie take your glove and hide it so you wouldn't try to play the next day."

Later that afternoon, with the game long over and Ebbets Field empty, Reese walked from the tunnel up to the press box to speak with legendary Dodgers radio announcer, Vin Scully. As they chatted, he looked down at the field. He squinted, then asked, "Who's running around the warning track?"

Scully looked at the field, then back to Pee Wee. "Murdock.

He has been out here for about an hour."

Reese watched him jogging. When Sam passed by the third base dugout, he stopped, then reached down and felt for his injured toe. After a few seconds, he resumed jogging, but he favored his broken toe as he limped around the field.

"Why is he limping like that?" Scully asked.

"He broke his toe, but the stubborn fool is worried he's hurting the team, so that's why he's out there putting in extra work."

Scully nodded. "Those are the kinds of players you want on your side."

Reese smiled and shook his head. "I'm going to have to kill that guy to get him out of the lineup."

"Don't be silly," Scully told him. "There'd be an investigation."

"Yeah. Good point. I wonder if I can get my deposit back from the Gambinos?" He joked.

Brooklynn sat by the radio and listened to what was happening in Milwaukee. The news was good early as the Dodgers held a 1-0 lead in their game against the Braves.

Here, Sam's bubble of secrecy burst. As he limped to home plate, trying to mask the pain in his toe, Vin Scully ratted on him.

"Coming to the plate is Sam Murdock. He's batting .314 with twenty-seven home runs and ninety-one runs batted in. During the series with the Phillies, Murdock broke his toe, but is playing tonight. I'm no doctor, but I'm sure it takes more than forty-eight hours for a broken toe to heal."

"What?" Brooklynn asked as she raised her voice, then repeated herself in a lower tone, not wanting to attract Margaret's attention.

"What's wrong?"

"Oh, nothing," she said, then went back to looking at her scorecard to write in the result of the previous batter.

Margaret raised an eyebrow. "Sam has a broken toe, huh? But you wouldn't care about that, I'm sure."

Brooklynn glanced at her, then turned away. The rest of the night, she battled mixed emotions. Half worried about his condition, and the other half angry she cared at all.

The Dodgers scored four times off Bob Buhl in the first inning, and from there never looked back. The Braves scored twice in the fourth, but the Dodgers rolled up the score in the next inning, scoring four more runs.

They took a 10-2 lead into the ninth inning. When Karl Spooner struck out Del Rice to end the game, the Dodgers were officially National League champions. It was their third pennant in the last four years.

After the last out, the Dodgers poured out of their dugout to mob pitcher Karl Spooner on the mound. Sam and Duke jumped into each other's arms in the outfield.

The champagne flowed from one end of the clubhouse to the other. Vin Scully, who outed Sam earlier, found him in the locker room. "I'm joined live in the Dodgers locker room with Sam Murdock. How does it feel?"

"It feels great Vin, I'm happy we clinched the pennant."

"The Dodgers are the only team to clinch the pennant so early in a season. What's been the secret?"

"We've been fortunate all year. The pitching has held up, the offense has been solid and we've caught the breaks at the right time. I hope we can continue the same success into the Series."

"Anything for the fans in Brooklyn?"

"Yes, thanks for the support, and we look forward to coming home to celebrate with you."

"Thanks, Sam."

"You're welcome, Vin. See you in the Series." Then he poured champagne over Scully's head.

When Sam returned from the shower, he noticed a yellow envelope on his chair with the Western Union logo printed on the front. He looked around the locker room, not sure what it was or where it came from. He opened it, pulled out the paper, then focused his eyes on the only word typed on it.

Congratulations

He had no idea what this meant. He looked at both sides of the paper, then brought the envelope up to examine it.

In the upper left-hand corner was a clue.

Brooklyn, New York

Sam smiled. *I have an idea who sent this.*

fifteen

Pee Wee got his wish as the New York Yankees won the American League. This would be the sixth time they would face each other in the World Series. Since the Dodgers were 0-5 against the Yankees, word on the street was this year wouldn't be any different.

There was one Dodger who had never played in a World Series, so he decided to get away from the cauldron of the hype and walk to Prospect Park. He figured the tranquil setting would do him a world of good, since he had a lot on his mind.

First on the list was the Series, but creeping in undetected was Brooklynn. Sam allowed himself fleeting thoughts of her and their time together. The Wonder Wheel. Luigi's. The night on Sullivan Place when he held her for the first time. They all clamored for his attention.

Sam lost himself in replaying their time together. Especially the night when he pulled her out of the way of the speeding car. He could still see Brooklynn's sparkling eyes and the way she looked at him as no other woman ever had before. He remembered the way her warm fingers interlocked in his and the way the touch of her hand tingled up his arm.

Before he knew it, those memories invaded every part of him. Once they had a hold of who he was, there was no escape. The struggle was real, and he was in the middle of a fight he knew he'd never win. As much as he tried to slow it down, his last days in 1955 would play itself out, and could not be stopped.

The pain of his broken toe subsided once he took in the serenity of the Park lying before him. The grass was inky green, and the smell of it almost suffocated him as it rolled into his nostrils. There were fathers and sons playing catch on the thick grass, and in the distance, he could see picnic blankets laid out.

The leaves blew on the trees. A few had signs of changing from the military green of summer into the bronze of autumn. Some had already fallen, and they lay beneath Sam's feet.

He found a bench looking out to the lake, so he headed in that direction. When he approached, he saw a brown fedora over a familiar face, sitting alone. He squinted his eyes to make sure he recognized the face and when he confirmed who it was, he joined him on the bench.

"Hello, Chris," he said, giving him a suspicious grin. "Funny seeing you here."

"I know. Kind of like I scripted it, huh? Once you get back to Kiawah, you can tell everyone you were in a Hallmark Movie."

Sam asked, "What's a Hallmark Movie?"

Chris rolled his eyes. "Never mind.

"I see we've upgraded our meeting places. The park is beautiful," Sam said as he looked around.

"It is," Chris agreed. "So, how are you feeling about the Series?"

A Redhead in Brooklyn

"Good. I can't wait to get on the field and play. Especially in Yankee Stadium. That's another iconic park."

Chris nodded, then asked, "Is there something else on your mind?"

Sam continued looking down, lost in thought. He heard the birds chirping in the trees and watched the leaves roll past his feet in the breeze. "I've been thinking about what's going to happen this week. It's going to be hectic, and then after it's over, I'm going home."

"Yeah. So?"

Sam told him, "It's going to be difficult."

Chris nodded, then looked out at the Park. "I can imagine." He paused, then asked, "How's Brooklynn?"

Sam looked at Chris. "Brooklynn? Why would you ask about her?"

"I'm curious."

He looked over and said, "She's great. Just like everything else here."

Chris allowed the silence to build, so his next question had some punch. "Do you love her?"

"What?" Sam asked, his face guarded.

Chris continued looking out to the Park, then over to Sam. "You heard me."

Sam stared at him, then looked down. He stared at the ground for a few seconds. Finally, he told him, "I don't know. It's kind of hard to fall in love with a girl when you know you'll never see her again."

"Sometimes, when it comes to love, it doesn't matter the obstacle. Your heart will find a way through adversity. No matter how bleak it might look."

"First, I'm going back once the Series is over. That's a biggie. And if by some chance I wasn't, Brooklynn told me she might not be here after the season ends. Makes things kind of difficult for a happy ending, wouldn't you agree?"

"Difficult. But not impossible. Remember what I told you the first morning we met? I deal in miracles."

"I know you do. But I don't know if you have one big enough in your bag of tricks for something like this." Sam leaned forward, rubbed his hands together, and exhaled. "I'm setting new standards in the how I've screwed up my life department. I'm sure even Hollywood wouldn't consider a script like this since nobody would believe it." Sam raised his eyebrows. "I can't seem to get out of my own way."

"What do you mean?"

"I came into this deal a broken man with no job and no future. Then I travel across the galaxy in a time capsule to get away from it, and I'm in more trouble now than I was before."

Chris nodded. "I know it's difficult, but where else would you rather be?"

"I know. I'd be on my couch in Kiawah wondering what is going to happen in February with the Braves. This is much more exciting. But the excitement comes at a price."

"Look, Sam, I spoke to St. Jude, and he told me there might be an option."

"Option? What do you mean, option?"

"We had a case years ago where someone decided to stay where they were, instead of returning."

Sam's face twisted in wonder.

Chris nodded. "It's up to you. If you want me to see about the possibilities, I'll look into it."

Sam looked down and considered the words. He added it all up and replied, "I don't know. Being in Brooklyn has been a dream come true, but I want to hold out for the Braves deal. I can be a real major league player, and what I do would end up in the history books."

"If you make the roster. You still have to win a job in spring training," he reminded him.

"Yeah, I know. But I'm afraid it doesn't completely solve my dilemma."

"How so?"

"I have to accept the fact that I can't play baseball forever. Even here, there will come a day when I can't play anymore. Time catches up with everyone. Even the guys who travel back in time to cheat it. What do I do when it's all over?"

"That's why Brooklynn is important."

"Brooklynn? Where does she fit in with this?"

"No matter if you stay, or if you return, you'll need someone to share your life with. All the highs and lows. There are some things we all should go through with someone. To share our passions with. And if you decide to stay, you'll need her to be there for the wins and losses. Then all the wins and losses that come after your career ends. That's when you'll really need her there."

"That's if she decides to stay."

"Well? What are you waiting for?"

Sam pulled away and looked at Chris. "What do you mean?"

"What do I mean? Do I have to give you a free lesson in living? Fight for her. Convince her to stay."

"Convince her to stay? I don't even know if I am going to stay."

Chris told him, "Fine. You know the arrangement. When the sun rises on October 5th, you will leave Brooklyn. Forever. Make your decision wisely, because, as I told you before, I cannot bring the fantasy to life a second time."

Chris looked at him, but Sam continued looking down. "You'd go back to Kiawah and leave this all behind?"

Sam paused before speaking. Finally, he looked at Chris and said, "Yeah. It's the safe play."

When Sam looked over, Chris stared at him, "I'm not talking about the Borough. Don't lose your courage at the exact moment you need it."

"Why are you doing this?" Sam asked, the irritation and fear evident in his voice.

Chris continued looking forward. "It's my job."

"Don't give me that it's your job crap. There's a reason you chose me to come here. And there's a reason you're doing this."

"I'm a Saint. What else can I tell you?"

"The first night on the way to the hotel, I asked what you get out of doing this. You pulled a Houdini on me. I'm not moving until I get a straight answer out of you." After the words hit their target,

A Redhead in Brooklyn

Sam glared at him.

Chris rubbed his hands together, continuing to look into the distance. He stared at them as they moved back and forth over each other. "There was this guy I knew years ago. He was a ballplayer, like you. I loved watching him play. He could hit, field, and played the game harder than anyone I ever saw."

"Yeah? So what?"

"He reminded me a lot of you. He was tough, hit the hell out of the ball, and loved the game more than anything. This guy was going to be one of the greats."

"Was?" Sam asked.

Chris nodded. "He never played after his first year. After Uncle Sam requested his presence at the European Theater, he went off to fight for his country. He never made it back."

"I'm sorry," Sam said. "Was he a close friend?"

"Yeah. Quite close." Chris gazed into the distance as his face turned to stone.

Sam studied the lost look in his eyes. "You?"

After a few seconds, Chris nodded.

"You were a ballplayer?"

"I was a rookie in 1941 for the same Dodgers you now play for. We won the National League but lost to the Yankees in the Series. I thought I'd have more years to play with the Dodgers and also get back to the Series and win it. I never figured that would be my only chance."

"What happened?"

"Pearl Harbor happened a few months after the end of the

1941 season. I thought there were more important things than being a baseball player, so I enlisted in the Army. I made it through D-Day and thought I had a chance to get out of that whole stupid war. During the Battle of the Bulge, I was leading a squad in the small Belgian town of Bastogne and a bullet got me. As I lay there in the snow, I looked up and thought about how I would never see Ebbets Field again. Or Yankee Stadium. Even the Polo Grounds. My dream of being a pro baseball player, although brief and promising, was over."

"So that's why you decided to take my case?"

Chris shrugged. "Yeah. Something like that." He paused and looked into the Park, then spoke. "I guess I've always had a weakness for lost causes once they're really lost. No wonder I ended up in the Lost Causes section of Heaven, helping people like you."

Sam looked at his friend. He allowed the tingles to live on for as long as they could before the next words spoken caused them to evaporate. He savored the allure, then couldn't stay silent any longer. "Why did you choose me?"

Chris smiled, then looked at him. "I see myself in you. The tenacity, the work ethic. The way you hold the game sacred. I felt that way when I was in your spikes. I carried this great longing for what I lost for the rest of my life, but when I saw you, I made peace with my past."

Sam stared at him.

"When your case came across Jude's desk, I told him this one was mine and I'd fight anyone who tried to take it. I saw the greatness that lies within you and how time and circumstances robbed you of it all, as it robbed me. I wanted to watch you do the things I didn't get the chance to do. I longed to know what this feels like." Chris paused, then looked at Sam and said, "You brought me back to the living as much as I've brought you back."

Sam raised his eyebrows. "I don't know what to say."

"You don't have to say anything. It all lies in front of you now. Rarely do things line up the way they have, but it's there. Right now. This moment is yours. This is something that will last forever, even if it will never be in a history book. You'll know what happened. And in this lifetime, that's all any of us can ever hope for. That one moment in time that nobody can take away from you."

"Is that why you're pushing me to stay here? So I can have a career in the major leagues and be with Brooklynn?"

Chris nodded. "I never had anyone to love. Like you, my career was the most important thing. One of the last things I thought about before my last breath was what would it have felt like to have someone to share my life with. That feeling. Waking up in the morning, and she'd be there."

Sam watched as Chris spoke from the heart.

"She'd be there to watch me do the one thing I could do better than anyone else. Then when the day came when I couldn't be better than anyone else, she'd be there. And it would be okay. I could walk away knowing I had everything I ever wanted."

Chris paused, then continued. "One day when it's time for you to walk away, I hope you'll have the peace of mind knowing there was nothing more you could want."

Sam watched Chris looking into the distance. He saw the regret in his face and the memory of his missed life replaying in his eyes. "I'm sorry," Sam told him. "I had no idea about any of that."

"It's okay. We all have things we have to live with. I hope the you'll cherish your past, instead of regret it."

Sam nodded, absorbing the words. Finally, he said, "I wish I knew how things are going to play out," Sam admitted.

"Do what's in your heart. You'll be fine."

Sam continued looking forward. After a few seconds of silence he wanted to cut with a knife, he asked, "You think Brooklynn is in love with me?"

Chris nodded. "I know a little about women. When you saw each other in front of Ebbets Field on the first day you arrived, I saw it in her eyes. Then when you were taking batting practice, and I was pitching. I saw the way she looked at you. Some things are so transparent that there's no doubt in my mind."

Sam smiled, then exhaled. "I don't know," he said, his voice floating over the breeze blowing through the trees. "I have a lot to think about." He looked out and watched a young woman holding a young girl in pigtails, pointing to a row of ducks swimming in the water.

As he peered over to the grass, he noticed a young couple holding hands as they walked down the sidewalk, laughing together.

Behind them was a family. The father placed a blanket under a tree, and they all sat down to a picnic lunch with the shade as their protection from the cool sun.

Sam took it all in. "I wish I knew what to do."

Margaret looked down the hallway. "Brooklynn? It's time."

When Brooklynn got to the living room, she found the

mirror. She checked the buttons on her dress, then straightened her hat. She sighed. "Okay. Let's do this."

The cab took them north along Washington Avenue, and after a left on DeKalb, they were within sight of where Brooklynn needed to go. When the cab stopped in front of the long brick building, Brooklynn gazed through the smudges on the cab's window.

"Want me to go with you?" Margaret asked.

Brooklynn continued staring. The sunlight warmed her face as she considered the request. Finally, she shook her head. "This is something I have to do alone."

She rehearsed this moment with Margaret for months. Now it lay only minutes away. Brooklynn's heart pumped harder, and her knees lacked dexterity. She went over each detail in her mind. Where she needed to be, and when. Who would she see. What she would say, and what would happen once the moment was over.

The past gave way to the present. She was now only a spectator to what fate had in mind. She left the cab, then walked inside the building.

After doing what she came to do, Brooklynn walked to a row of babies in their bassinets, focusing on the ones covered in pink blankets. Her eyes widened when she found the one she was looking for.

"There you are, little one. You don't have to worry about anything. You're going to be okay."

Brooklynn gave the baby girl a smile, then walked out of the building and rejoined Margaret in the cab.

"How did it go?" Margaret asked.

Brooklynn smiled. "Fine."

"How does it feel?"

"Like the weight of the world is off my shoulders."

"Does this mean you're ready to leave for L.A.?"

"The season isn't over until the last out of the World Series. Right?"

Margaret thought for a few seconds. "Yeah, I suppose." When the cab stopped at a red light, She asked, "What about Sam?"

Brooklynn looked through the window. When the green light flashed and the cab accelerated, she muttered, "I don't know."

sixteen

Game One of the 1955 World Series began at massive Yankee Stadium on a crystal clear autumn afternoon in the Bronx.

Sam sat with his back to the clubhouse, staring into his locker. He focused on breathing, then he visualized himself at the plate, and patrolling left field. Finally, he opened his eyes, exhaled, then turned and was ready to go out to the field.

He exited the clubhouse and across the corridor to a long sloping tunnel. His spikes clicked and scratched on the cement floor, then he reached the opening to the dugout.

Waiting for him was a creamy blue sky serving as a backdrop to the iconic ivory Frieze, hanging from the top of the stadium and circling the grandstand. Pennants of each team in baseball lined the roof and flapped in the glow of autumn. Their rich color was a spectacular contrast to the blue of the sky and the white of the facade. Red, white, and blue bunting hung along the railing on the field level, the upper deck, and on top of the dugouts.

Managers Casey Stengel and Walt Alston stood in front of the backstop. The horde of photographers clicked away as the two smiled for the cameras.

Starting pitchers Don Newcombe and Whitey Ford stood by the dugout shaking hands for the movie newsreels and the press.

Sam's legs shook as he walked onto the field, in awe of his surroundings. He looked over and saw baseball legends Mickey Mantle and Yogi Berra talking to reporters. They looked young and strong, which was in sharp contrast to the older versions Sam saw after their careers were over. The sight of them, coupled with being in Yankee Stadium, left him light-headed.

Chris walked up to him and quipped, "Sam, do I have to get the super glue so you don't fall apart?"

Sam never acknowledged him.

When Chris touched him on the sleeve of his jersey, Sam jerked back, then saw his friend. "Oh, Chris, there you are. I can't believe I'm in Yankee Stadium, about to play in the 1955 World Series. This is incredible."

"That's why they call them fantasies, my friend." Chris looked at Sam, and after seeing him frown, asked, "What's wrong?"

"I know I said it before the season began, but what I would give for Dad to be here."

Chris nodded. "I guarantee he's watching."

The Yankees won Game One, 6-5. The Dodgers took an early 2-0 lead, and it was tied 3-3 into the sixth inning, but the Yankees scored three times to put the game away. Jackie Robinson provided the highlight of the game by stealing home in the eighth inning to pull the Dodgers within a run, but the rally fell short.

A Redhead in Brooklyn

Game Two featured more excitement. Unfortunately for the Dodgers, it was the Yankees who provided the thrill for the fans. Billy Loes gave up four runs in the fourth, and Tommy Byrne became the first left-hander to go the distance against the Dodgers in 1955, as the Yankees won, 4-2.

The locker room was spooky silent as the Dodgers stared at a two games to none Series deficit. Sam sat on his stool with his head resting on the side wall of his locker. He closed his eyes and thought about what went wrong.

Chris walked in and made his way over to Sam's locker. "Hello, Sam. Tough one today."

Sam opened his eyes and brought his head forward. "It's been a couple of tough days." He exhaled, then added, "God, I hate losing."

"He knows," Chris kidded him. "You're going back to Ebbets Field tomorrow, so all's not lost."

Sam frowned. "No team has ever come back to win a World Series after losing the first two games."

"Yeah, I heard that up in the press box. Don't give up hope yet. Who's pitching?"

"Podres. Alston can't use Erskine, since his arm needs another day to rest. Podres is the only pitcher we have left."

"You'll get it done tomorrow, Sam. By the way, are you going to the League party tonight? It's at the Hotel Bossert."

Sam stood, unbuttoned his jersey, then shook his head.

"You could use a night out."

"I should get to bed early since we have to be at Ebbets in the morning. I should get to the park early and get some extra work in."

"Tell you what, why don't we go for an hour or two, sample the buffet, have a few beers, then we'll get out of there."

Sam didn't have the energy to argue. "Fine. I'll come down for a little while, then get back to my room to get a good night's sleep."

Sam met Chris at the doors to the ballroom for the post-game World Series party. This party was an annual event for members of the media, team officials and staff, and celebrities.

The plush red carpet and elegant crystal chandeliers greeted everyone. Once inside, the guests discussed everything from who would win the Series to the rumor the Dodgers were leaving Brooklyn. Their discussions went on as an orchestra played and couples danced.

Sam walked to the bar. He ordered an Old Fashioned, then did a double take and told the bartender he would love a PBR instead. After taking the bottle from the bartender, he turned and before he could walk over to where Chris stood, he found someone blocking his path.

"Hello, Fred," Brooklynn said as she gave him a warm smile. "Fancy running into you at one of these things."

"Well, hello Ginger," he said as he regained his swagger after the surprise of seeing her beautiful face stunned him. "You never know where we'll run into each other these days," he smiled.

A Redhead in Brooklyn

"After the last two days, shouldn't you be back at Ebbets Field taking extra batting practice?" She grinned.

"I said the same thing, but Chris said I needed a night out."

Chris smiled and then leaned in and kissed Brooklynn on the cheek. "Thank God you're here. Our boy needed a night out."

"I agree," she told him, then smiled at Sam.

Chris nodded. "Would you do the Dodger fans a favor and hang out with him? He needs a night to forget about the first two games."

Brooklynn looked at Sam. "The Dodgers always play better in Ebbets Field," she assured him. "You're not dead yet." She flashed him a smile that soaked into his soon-to-be crimson cheeks.

He looked at her and said, "Please don't smile at me like that. It wrecks my concentration."

Brooklynn furrowed her brow. "Really?"

Sam smiled. "I was talking to Chris."

After they all laughed, Chris told him, "If you'll both excuse me, I have some people to speak with for my column tomorrow."

Sam shook his hand, then Brooklynn hugged him. "See you tomorrow," Sam told him.

"I'll be there. And I'll try not to smile at you," he said and gave him a wry grin and a raised eyebrow.

After he left, Sam gave Brooklynn a closer look, since it had been a few days since he had the pleasure of her company.

Brooklynn's cinnamon hair lay over her shoulders, and it shone in the artificial light from the dance floor. The sparkle of the lights danced off her rosy cheeks and freckles, which seemed more colorful tonight than he remembered. As Sam looked her over, he noted she was still in work clothes. But to him, she was more beautiful than any of the glammed-up women at the party.

"Did you come from the office?" Sam asked.

"Yeah. I had to deliver press credentials to some writers for tomorrow's game." She looked at the bottle, then smiled. "Looks like I'm rubbing off on you."

Sam squinted, then looked into his hand. "Oh yeah. I figured why change horses now?"

Brooklynn nodded, then looked around the ballroom. "Even though I don't like these things, there are some interesting people here," she said, then nodded to her right. "Over there is Vice-President Nixon."

Sam looked over and saw a short, youthful man with black hair standing by a table talking to a few people, as well as a few secret service men around him. Sam grinned, knowing what lay ahead for the future president.

"And over there are Dean Martin and Frank Sinatra." She rolled her eyes and said, "They started flirting with me the moment I walked in."

Sam looked over to the other corner of the massive ballroom and saw them standing by the bar, with a group of women around them. He made eye contact with both of them and within seconds, they left the women they were speaking with and walked in his direction.

Brooklyn saw them coming. "Oh, no."

"What's wrong?" Sam asked.

"They are coming over here."

A Redhead in Brooklyn

"I'll take care of it," he smiled. He moved in front of Brooklynn and expected a confrontation. Instead, they greeted him with a smile and extended hands.

"Sam Murdock?" Dean asked as they got to them.

Sam's heartbeat accelerated as the famous Dean Martin knew him by name. Then again, this all was a fantasy. "Dean Martin," he said, shaking Sam's hand.

"Nice to meet you," Sam said.

His partner introduced himself next. "Frank Sinatra," he told him, extending his hand.

Sam grasped it.

They both looked charming and handsome, as age had not yet robbed them of their boyish good looks.

Dean asked, "Does Podres have a good game in him for tomorrow?"

"He'll be all right. Besides, tomorrow is his twenty-third birthday. As long as he doesn't start drinking early, karma is on his side," he joked.

They all laughed as the initial intimidation Sam felt faded away. "Are you both Dodgers fans?" Sam asked.

"I am," Dean told him, "But Sinatra is a Giants fan. Something to do with having a lot of friends on the team," he joked.

"They give me better seats at their games than the Dodgers do," Sinatra smiled.

As they spoke, Sam realized they gave him all their attention and never looked at Brooklynn. "Have you two met my friend Brooklynn Kelly?" He asked, then turned and pointed to her.

They smiled as they looked over at her, said a quick hello, then went back to grilling Sam. "How tough is Whitey Ford?" Dean asked.

Sam grinned as he looked at Brooklynn, then turned to them. "Whitey Ford? I couldn't hit that guy if I used a telephone pole," he joked, which got them all laughing.

Sinatra asked, "What's it like to play in Yankee Stadium?"

Sam took a sip of his beer. "What can I say? Yankee Stadium is an icon. But I like Ebbets Field since it's home."

They talked for a while about their chosen professions, then the two celebrities excused themselves.

"It was a pleasure meeting you both," Sam told them as they all shook hands.

"Good luck tomorrow," Dean told Sam.

"Have a good game, Murdock," Sinatra told him with a wink and a smile.

Dean leaned in close and said, "In my next lifetime, I want to come back as a ballplayer."

"Why is that?" Sam asked.

He looked at Brooklynn, then back to Sam and said, "You ballplayers get all the pretty girls," he grinned.

Sam winked at him, then watched as the pair walked away. Then he looked at Brooklynn. "I hated the way they slobbered all over you," he joked.

Brooklynn smiled, and shook her head.

Sam looked around the ballroom, then back to her. "What do you say we get out of here and find a couple of bottles of beer?"

A Redhead in Brooklyn

Brooklyn gave him a surprised grin. "What about getting to bed early since you have to be at Ebbets Field early tomorrow?"

Sam raised his eyebrows. "I have a feeling Ebbets Field will still be there in the morning. I'm sure you know of a place that we can go."

When he gave her a coy smile and nod, Brooklyn returned it.

Brooklynn led him to a corner bar with a sign reading "Gordon's Bar and Grille." She opened the door, and they walked inside the smoky bar to the sounds of live music.

Brooklynn found a table by the wall. "I love this place."

"Why?"

"It's a hole in the wall, but the beer is cheap, cold and I get to dance. And I don't have to worry about being all prim and proper."

A tall blonde walked over. "Brooklynn. How are you?"

"Mia. My favorite girl in the world. I've been busy with World Series stuff, so I'm taking a night off."

Mia looked at Sam for a few seconds, then smiled. "And you must be Sam Murdock."

Sam extended his hand. "I am. Nice to meet you."

"Nice to meet you too," she said, shaking his hand. "Tough couple of days in the Bronx. How's tomorrow going to go?"

Sam gave her an assured grin. "We'll come back tomorrow. You'll see."

Mia smiled. "What can I get for you, Mr. Murdock?"

"Please call me Sam," he told her, then said, "We'd like two PBRs in the bottle. No glass."

Mia grinned, then looked at Brooklynn. "You have trained him well," she joked.

When she left, Sam breathed in, then coughed and waved his hand in front of his face. "It's smoky here."

Brooklynn nodded. "Yeah, it is. That's one thing I don't like about being in bars. Too smoky. Yuck."

Sam looked at the stage. "Who's playing tonight?"

"Nobody we'd know. Some of the popular bands got their start here, so you never know who you'll see. Sometimes, they have established bands trying out new material, so we might get lucky and see someone famous."

The 50s rock-and-roll was a break from the music Sam listened to. He felt like he stepped onto the set of *Happy Days,* but he loved being in 1955, so he soaked it all in.

After Mia brought their beers, they toasted to the Dodgers, the 1955 season, and to each other. As they chatted about what might happen in Game Three, they heard the leader of the band speak into the microphone. "I know this is an old one, but we like it, so let's get everyone on the dance floor."

A few seconds later, the band broke into The Glenn Miller Band's "In the Mood." As soon as the music flooded the bar, Brooklynn stood and removed her sweater. She placed it over the chair, then told Sam, "Take off your jacket. We're dancing."

Sam's eyes widened, then he stood and removed his jacket. *I don't know how to dance in the 50s. What should I do?*

When they got to the floor, Brooklynn faced him and then

A Redhead in Brooklyn

reached for his hand. "Do you know the Lindy Hop?"

When she said the words, the weight lifted off his shoulders. "The Lindy Hop? It's been a while, but I think I can remember it." He brought her arm up and spun her around. After that, they took off. As the music raced faster, and the lights blinked in various colors to illuminate the dance floor, they swayed and jumped to the beat of the music. Before long, the other couples moved around the perimeter to watch them dance.

Sam spun her around, then threw her into the air. After coming back together, kicking their legs out, Sam grasped her hand, brought her to him, then leaned over and tossed Brooklynn around his back. She landed in front of him with a smile, much to the cheers and applause of the crowd. Their moves made the band play louder and longer since nobody wanted to see it end.

The pair lit up the dance floor as their moves could have given the real Fred and Ginger a run for their money. As much as nobody wanted it to end, especially Brooklynn and Sam, the song came to a close. And when it did, Sam brought Brooklynn to him and dipped her. She extended her arm and arched her back, then looked at the crowd with a smile. The bar erupted.

As the applause subsided, the band played another song, this one slow and somber. The lead singer approached the microphone and told the crowd, "We are going to slow it down a bit. We hope you like this one. It's appropriate for October."

The sounds of a piano took over the room. Sam looked at Brooklynn but didn't move. Brooklyn smiled, then raised her eyebrow. He moved to her and they wrapped their arms around each other's back. Brooklynn moved her head closer, and their cheeks touched. Tingles consumed Sam's body as he held her for the first time. *What am I doing? I can't fall in love with this girl. It's not right.*

With their cheeks together, the intoxicating smell of a rose garden suffocated him. It was reminiscent of the smells from their trip to the Brooklyn Botanical Garden. When he breathed it in again, he realized it was Brooklynn. The more he breathed her in, the more it calmed him. Within seconds, he closed his eyes and allowed destiny to take them wherever it wanted. *It's okay, Sam. Everything is going to be okay.*

When Sam's senses returned, he heard the lyrics. "But I miss you most of all, my darling. When autumn leaves start to fall." As the words soaked in, a razor of reality sliced through Sam's heart, so he held her tighter.

After the song ended, they looked at each other. As the seconds passed, and the blue light from above the stage illuminated Brooklynn's face, Sam's inner conflict took hold of him. They stared at each other, then once again, released at the same moment, not wanting to jinx their friendship. "I guess we need to finish our beers," she told him.

"Yeah, good idea," he assured her, then led Brooklynn off the dance floor and back to their table.

When they got to the table, Sam told her, "Wow, you can dance."

Brooklynn smiled. In the artificial light, her eyes glowed. She took a breath and replied, "You're not so bad yourself. Where did you learn how to dance like that?"

Sam took out his handkerchief and handed it to her. "I thought you might need this," he said, seeing the glow of sweat beads on her rosy cheeks. "I took a dance class years ago. It's been a while, but once we got going, it all came back to me. How about you?"

Brooklynn finished dabbing her cheeks, then told him, "My mom and dad danced like that when I was growing up, so one day I asked her to teach me how, and she gave me a few lessons. It was nice to have someone to dance with, just so I could show off my moves," she said with a grin, then handed his handkerchief back.

When Sam folded his handkerchief and placed it in his pocket, he glimpsed his watch. He gave it a second look, then brought his wrist to his face. "Oh wow, it's getting late."

Brooklynn asked, "What time is it?"

"It's almost ten. I better get you home."

Brooklynn gave him a sad smile. "Yeah, I guess you better. You have a big day tomorrow."

"Why the sad face, Ginger?"

"I...this was so much fun. Why didn't we do this in June or July?"

Sam smiled. "Well, because you didn't like me?" He asked with a sparkle in his eye.

"Oh, that's right," she said with a nod. "Well, I still don't like you, but at least you can dance, so it's not a total loss."

After she winked, Sam smiled, then rose from his chair. "I need to get you home before you develop a crush on me. We can't have that happening during one of the greatest comebacks in World Series history."

Brooklynn rose, then put her sweater around her shoulders. "I said it before, and I'll say it again. You're awfully optimistic."

"Yeah? About which part?"

"I'll let you figure that one out," she said with a giggle.

As they walked along the sidewalk, with Ebbets Field in the distance coming closer with every step, Sam took off his coat and draped it over Brooklynn. She smoothed it out over her shoulders, then smiled.

Sam smiled. "Thanks, Brooklyn."

"For what?" She asked as her green eyes caught the glow of the streetlight above.

Sam looked at the sidewalk, then at the lights of the houses in front of them. "Tonight. This was exactly what I needed to get away from the game for a few hours."

"I'd say I've distracted you enough for one night. Now, it's up to you," she joked.

As they continued walking, she asked, "How do you think it's going to go tomorrow?"

"Well, if we lose, the Series is over. Nobody has ever come back from a 3-0 Series deficit. But if we win, that might be the thing that gives us the momentum to sweep the rest of the games in Brooklyn. I guess we need a little luck."

Brooklynn leaned up and kissed Sam on the cheek.

"What was that for?"

"Luck."

seventeen

Johnny Podres carried the hopes of an entire borough into Game Three. With Newcombe and Loes beaten in the first two games, the Series and the season rode on his shoulders.

As the World Series moved to Ebbets Field, clouds replaced the sun. The irony of dark skies left everyone with an ominous vibe.

As Sam popped up the steps of the dugout, the first thing he saw was the stadium draped in yards of red, white, and blue bunting, banners, and balloons. The scoreboard in right field, which flew the flags of the other teams in the National League according to where they were in the standings during the regular season, flew U.S. flags in their place during the World Series.

The mood was tense through the crowd as if something was about to happen, but nobody was sure of exactly what. As was the case before a thunderstorm when all was quiet, Ebbets Field seemed to have the same anticipation moving through it.

Finally, the quiet shattered into a thunderous roar as the Dodgers raced on the field. It was as if a parent had welcomed home a troubled son.

The people who wrote the Dodgers off ate their words as the

tense struggle early turned into a rout on this cloudy day in Brooklyn. The Dodgers rolled to an 8-3 victory and placed themselves back into the 1955 World Series.

The birthday boy Johnny Podres laid to rest the bitter memories of his only other World Series appearance in 1953. He didn't get out of the first inning then, but today, he went the distance to get the victory.

The offensive heroes were catcher Roy Campanella, who was three for five with a home run and three runs batted in, and Pee Wee Reese, who drove in a pair of runs.

Brooklyn now trailed two games to one.

Game Four saw cloudy weather again, but this time the Yankees got out to the lead early, 3-1. Brooklyn sensed it could be slipping away as Erskine failed to get out of the fourth inning. But with their backs to the wall, the Dodgers rallied.

Campenella kept up his hot hitting with another home run to close the gap to 3-2. Furillo followed with a hit to give the Dodgers another base runner. The buzzing in the crowd turned to an explosion minutes later when Gil Hodges blasted Don Larsen's first pitch over the wall for a 4-3 Dodger lead.

In the next inning, Sam led off with a walk. After a pop-out, Junior Gilliam stepped up. Sam looked over to Alston, who stood in the third base coaching box, to see if he had a play on, and sure enough, Alston flashed the hit-and-run sign.

Sam took his lead, watching Larsen in case he threw over to first base. But Larsen fired home instead. The instant Larsen

A Redhead in Brooklyn

began his motion, Sam streaked for second base. After a few steps, he heard the crack of the bat and the roar of the crowd.

Gilliam drove the ball past a diving Gil McDougald at third. Sam ran as hard as he could as he saw the ball roll into the corner, knowing he could get to third base.

He concentrated as he raced around the bases. *Make sure to touch second base. Locate Alston in the crowd. Watch to see if he's waving me home.*

The ball rolled into the corner as Elston Howard raced over to retrieve it. Sam saw Alston waving him in, so he kicked it into high gear as he rounded third and headed for home.

Howard picked up the ball and fired a bullet to shortstop Phil Rizzuto, who turned and threw the ball to Yogi Berra. Sam saw Pee Wee behind home plate, shouting and motioning for him to slide.

Sam slid to the far corner of home plate as the ball arrived. Berra caught the throw, then thrust his glove down to make the tag. His leg knocked Berra over as he applied the tag, and it left both men sprawled in the dirt. When the brown cloud of dust finally disappeared, the fans saw the umpire.

"SAFE," Umpire Frank Dascoli barked, waving his arms.

Berra popped up to make sure Gilliam didn't take third on the play. Pee Wee jumped into the air in excitement, then picked Sam up from the ground. Sam responded by leaping into his arms.

"Way to run, rookie," Pee Wee smiled, hugging him.

The players met Sam in front of the dugout to congratulate him. Their excitement, mixed with the roar of the fans, left him dazed.

When he got to the bench, he wiped his sweaty face with a towel, then put his hat back on. As the game continued, and the roar intensified, he felt something on his arms, so he looked down to see goosebumps rising on his forearms. *I've never felt this way on a baseball field in my life.*

The Dodgers scored four more times, then held off the Yankees to win Game Four 8-5.

The Series stood at two games each.

Game Five dawned clear and cool in Brooklyn as the two best teams in baseball squared off for the Series lead.

In the bottom of the second with the game scoreless, Gil Hodges singled to left. With two outs, Sam walked to the plate. His bat had been quiet in the first four games, so it was now the team needed him to him to come through at this critical point of the game and Series.

The crowd roared as they sensed a rally coming. Sam put it out of his mind as he concentrated on keeping the inning alive. As he walked to the plate, he pressed on the back pocket of his uniform pants. Inside was the picture of him and Brooklynn from Coney Island.

He hadn't played a game without it since she gave it to him. It was his security blanket, the one thing that made him believe he belonged in Brooklyn. No matter what adversity he faced on the field, she was there to help him get through it. Now that he had his confidence, he summoned the Zone.

Once he dug into the batter's box, he looked out at the

pitcher, Bob Grim. As he stared, all sound drowned to an easy wave of calm. Grim's face came into focus. Sam saw the beads of sweat rolling from his cheeks. His brown eyes blazed as he looked at Yogi Berra's fingers giving the signs. Sam no longer controlled his actions. He was on autopilot as he took a few practice swings, then cocked his bat and was ready. He looked out to see everything behind Grim blurred, but the pitcher remained in focus.

Grim's first pitch was a fastball outside for ball one. Sam's mind began to think about what could be coming next, so he shuffled through Brooklynn's World Series scouting report.

When Grim begins the at-bat with a fastball, look for a curve outside.

Grim threw another pitch. This one was a curve, and it spun outside for ball two.

Two pitches, both outside. When he's behind in the count, look for a fastball.

When Grim fired the third pitch, Sam was ready. In an instant, he swung his bat. It connected with nothing but air.

Sam reset in the batter's box. His mind shuffled through what the next pitch could be. *Grim throws back-to-back fastballs 73% of the time when he's behind in the count.*

His heart beat faster. His hands gripping the bat. He sharpened his focus and swore he could read the writing on the ball as Grim held it in his hand. There was no fear. Sam welcomed the moment to unfold before him.

Sam glared out at Grim, who looked over to keep an eye on Hodges. When Gil took his lead from first base, the pitcher looked at him, then back to home plate.

Grim kicked his leg and threw home. Sure enough, it was

the same pitch. When Sam saw the white flash coming at him, instinct took over. Without thinking, his bat sliced through the crisp October air an instant quicker than last time.

Sam didn't feel anything after hearing the crack of the bat. When he looked up, he saw the ball in the creamy blue sky. As it grew smaller by the second, he knew it was going to travel a long way. He dropped the bat and ran toward first base.

The ball reached an apex, then sliced to the right, still getting smaller as it approached the scoreboard in right field. Joe Collins gave chase, but downshifted into a trot as he neared the wall and looked up. The ball dropped to the right of the Bulova clock and landed on Bedford Avenue.

The blast gave Brooklyn a 2-0 lead and sent a tremendous roar, not only in Ebbets Field but the entire Borough. Sam wasn't sure if his feet were touching the ground as he rounded the bases. After all, it wasn't every day he hit a home run in a World Series game.

When he got to home plate, his teammates congratulated him, then he trotted by the dugout and found Brooklynn standing close by, applauding. He tipped his cap to her, and she responded with a smile and wink.

The Dodgers held their lead into the bottom of the eighth inning. Sam walked to the on-deck circle and prepared to hit. As he knelt in the dirt, he gazed around Ebbets Field, much the same way he did his first day.

The cool autumn breeze roamed around the ballpark. It mixed with the sense of savoring what could be the last moments of something special. Sam breathed in the sights and sounds, knowing he was fortunate to be where he was. He knew this moment would

A Redhead in Brooklyn

never come back in his lifetime.

Could I leave this behind?

As much as he missed Kiawah, and also the opportunity to play for the Braves, Brooklyn became a second home. Chris and the Dodgers, his second family. To top it off, he met a charming woman who was a constant visitor to his thoughts from the moment they first met.

He continued looking into the crowd, as he often did, since there was no telling who could be there. Then, something caught his eye, and wouldn't let it go.

There was Brooklynn. She sat behind the Dodgers dugout, next to Pee Wee's wife and children. She laughed while playing with the kids as if they were her own. Sam fantasized she was his wife, and those were their children watching him play.

Why am I thinking these things?

The game continued into the ninth inning. The Dodgers needed three outs to become the first team in World Series history to win the middle three games after losing the first two. Whatever fear the Dodger fans had subsided as the Yankees were out of gas as they went down in order to seal the Dodgers 5-3 victory.

The advantage now shifted to the Dodgers, who would venture across town to the Bronx. All they needed was one victory in the last two games to bring home their first world championship. They left the field to a standing ovation from the Brooklyn fans.

Sam and Chris returned to the Hotel Bossert for the post-game party. They were upbeat about the last three days and the way the team played. This time Sam looked forward to the party.

As they walked inside the ballroom, Chris pointed to the food set out on the table around the ballroom. While picking through the cold cuts and cheese spread, Chris asked, "How do you think it's going to turn out tomorrow?"

"I don't know, but after the last three days, I like our chances. The Yankees are tough when they play at home though."

"They are. By the way, nice home run."

"Thanks. I owe it all to the scouting report from Brooklynn."

"If I were you, I'd say thank you n person."

Sam smiled. "You've both done a lot to get me this far. I hope we can see it all the way through."

He walked along the row of food and placed a few cheese squares and crackers on a small plate. As he looked at the other items on the table, he heard voices behind him. One he knew, and the other was familiar, but he didn't know from where.

"Hello, Chris, you son of a gun," the voice said.

"Humphrey, you old dog. How are things in Tinsel Town?"

"They keep casting me in these god-awful romantic roles. I wish I could do a gangster flick," he smiled.

Chris laughed, and said, "Once you've shown that romantic side, it's hard for them to see you as anything else."

When Sam turned, he froze in stunned silence. Standing before him was Humphrey Bogart. Chris looked at him. "Humphrey, I'd like for you to meet a good friend of mine, Sam Murdock."

Bogart switched his drink to his left hand, then extended his right. "Good God, it's Sam Murdock," he said in a flattering tone.

A Redhead in Brooklyn

"Congratulations on a great season."

Sam noticed Bogart changed a great deal from how he remembered him in *Casablanca*. His hair was grayer, there was more of his scalp visible, and the lines in his face were deeper, longer, and seemed to have doubled. He was still handsome, and his eyes were dark and powerful. He wore his traditional white dinner jacket, black bow tie, and a look of confidence. When he spoke, there was a sense of assuredness in his voice that commanded respect.

Sam groped for words. "Thank you, Mr. Bogart," was all he got out.

"Damn, this kid makes me feel like a fossil," he said, looking at Chris. "My father is Mr. Bogart. It's Humphrey to my friends."

"All right, um, Humphrey," Sam said. "Are you a Dodger fan?"

"Of course. I always pull for the underdog. Besides, Lauren likes to come to the games too. She's an even bigger Dodger fan than I am. She wanted me to ask if the Dodgers will wrap up the Series tomorrow."

"I hope so. Winning a seventh game in Yankee Stadium might be a tall order," he told him.

"You never know," he said with a smile. "Would you do me a favor and sign an autograph for Lauren? She'd love that."

Sam froze. With raised eyebrows, he asked, "For Lauren? Lauren Bacall?"

Bogart looked at Chris and smiled. "Well, that was her name the last time I checked," he said, then looked at Sam.

Sam cleared his throat, then regained his composure. "I'd be delighted. What would you like me to sign?"

Bogart patted himself, feeling for something to write on. He finally found an old claim ticket for his luggage used earlier in the week. He also pulled out a pen and handed both to Sam.

Sam took the items, then wrote on the ticket:

Lauren:

Here's looking at you, Kid.

Sam Murdock

He handed the slip of paper back to Bogart. "Do you have tickets for tomorrow?"

Bogart shook his head. "I'm afraid not. We are on break from the filming of my new movie, so we resume shooting in a few days back in Hollywood and I have to get back tomorrow morning."

They talked about various things. What it was like to hit a fastball, and what it was like working with Ingrid Bergman in *Casablanca*.

"Are you married, Sam?" He asked.

"Only to baseball," he joked.

"Well, there are plenty of ladies here tonight, so as popular as you are, you could take your pick."

As Sam thought about the words, he looked over and saw Brooklynn walking through the ballroom. She joined a group of people standing next to Walter O'Malley's table.

As she got to them, an unidentified man handed her a drink. Sam wasn't sure who it was, but he began to take note of something new gnawing at him. Jealousy.

"I see one woman already has your eye," Bogart said with a grin as he looked at Brooklynn, then back to Sam.

A Redhead in Brooklyn

As Sam looked over, he realized the man she was talking to was Bob Grim, the pitcher Sam homered off of earlier in the day. If it came to a showdown, Sam would at least have the tiebreaker.

He turned to Bogie. "If I was ever going to be with a young lady, that would be her," he said as he nodded in her direction.

Bogart looked over, then to Sam, and said, "The young woman in the purple dress?"

"Yes. That's Brooklynn Kelly. She works for the Dodgers."

"Rather fetching young lass, isn't she?"

Sam smiled, "Yes, rather."

"Well, aren't you going to ask her to dance?"

Sam's smile faded into a frown. "Nah, she looks busy. I'll do it later."

"Think about living in the moment. Later may never come."

Sam thought about the words. He wondered if Bogart was being prophetic. "I've been wondering that myself."

"Well, you know what you are doing, I suppose." Bogart extended his hand. "Sam, it was a pleasure meeting you. Knock 'em dead tomorrow, will ya?"

"I'll try," he smiled.

"Thanks for the autograph. I owe ya one."

Sam figured that would be a debt he would never collect, but he didn't mind.

"By the way," Bogart said as he turned back to Sam, "Could you help me with something?"

Sam laughed. "What did you have in mind?"

"I promised a certain young lady a dance, but I wouldn't want her to get the wrong idea, as well as get me in trouble if Lauren found out."

"Why don't you tell the girl no?"

Bogart smiled, "I couldn't do that. She seems nice, and I wouldn't want to hurt her feelings. In about ten minutes, look for me on the dance floor. When you see me, walk over, tap me on the shoulder, and cut in. All right?"

"But I don't under-"

"Do me this favor. Will you?"

How could I say no to Humphrey Bogart? "I'd be happy to," Sam told him.

After Bogart walked away, Chris asked, "I thought you'd enjoy that."

"Yes, I did. I mean, Humphrey Bogart. Alive and right in front of me. That was amazing." Sam then did a double take. "Wait. How do you know Humphrey Bogart? Did you offer him a chance to go back in time too?"

Chris smiled. "Nah, nothing like that."

Sam raised his eyebrows and looked at him. Chris smiled and said, "You wouldn't believe me if I told you." He looked out to the ballroom and saw Bogart moving through the crowd. "Too bad he's close to joining me upstairs. I wasn't sure if you knew that or not."

"He does look a little ragged compared to other times I saw him. But he still has that aura about him."

"There are some things a man never loses."

A Redhead in Brooklyn

Ten minutes later, Sam looked out to the dance floor to see if he could locate Bogart's white dinner jacket.

"What are you looking for?" Chris asked.

"I'm looking for Bogart."

"What for?"

"I am going to cut in on him and his dance partner."

"Are you crazy? He'll slug you for that."

Sam made sure it was Bogie he was looking at, then said, "I'll take the chance." He smiled, knowing Chris knew nothing of the favor he agreed to, then swaggered out to the floor, looking forward to the task at hand.

As he got closer to the couple, he couldn't see who Bogart was dancing with. He took a deep breath and tapped Bogart on the shoulder.

Bogart turned, and with a smile on his face, asked, "Yes?"

"I wondered if I-" he said, then choked on his words as he looked over and saw his dance partner was Brooklynn.

She gave him a surprised grin that eased into an impressed one.

Sam swallowed and continued, "Um, cut in?"

Bogart winked and said, "You're Sam Murdock of the Dodgers, aren't you?"

"Yes," he said, the scam coming clear now.

"Well, Mr. Murdock, I would be happy to step aside. Good luck tomorrow. Beat the Yankees."

Sam nodded as Bogart moved out of the way. "Thank you,

Mr. Bogart. We'll do our best."

He stepped closer to Brooklynn, and the two joined hands. "Hello, Miss Kelly."

She raised her eyebrows. "I have to say that was a pretty gutsy move to cut in on Humphrey Bogart. How much have you had to drink? Don't forget you have a big game tomorrow."

"Yeah, I remember something about that. We're playing the Yankees, right?"

Brooklynn shook her head and smiled. "Yeah. It was in all the papers."

As Sam took in her rosy, freckled face, the lights splashed on her at the right time. As was the case earlier when he hit his home run, he felt as if his feet were not touching the ground.

Chris and Humphrey watched from a distance with grins on their faces. "I owed him a favor," Humphrey said.

"I can see that now," Chris said. "So, you pulled the old 'cut in on my partner' scam, didn't you?"

Bogart smiled, "Yeah. I figured your boy could use a little help. For a man who is fearless on the baseball field, he sure is a lot more reserved when it comes to women."

"Yes, he is. But we're working on that."

"By the way, should I bill you for my services?"

"Of course. I can't teach him everything, so it's nice when I can get a ringer to fill in." Chris's comment got a laugh out Bogart.

Bogart finished laughing. "Bring two bottles of bourbon next time you're in Hollywood, and we'll call it even."

"As long as I get to dance with that lovely wife of yours."

A Redhead in Brooklyn

"Make it three," Bogart told him with a wink.

The party went late into the night, but Sam and Brooklynn left early so they could take a walk. The temperature dipped since they arrived at the Hotel, so once again, Sam gave Brooklynn his jacket as they walked along Flatbush Avenue.

They stopped by Gordon's Bar for a nightcap, but neither felt like calling it a night, so they took a stroll through Prospect Park.

"Do you think you'll win tomorrow?" She asked.

"I hope so. If we have to play a winner-take-all Game Seven in Yankee Stadium, I don't know how it might turn out."

"You can do it," she said, then wrapped her arm through his.

The tingles in his arms returned. He smiled and said, "I'll just call the Yankees and tell them not to bother showing up tomorrow since you said the Series is over."

Brooklynn giggled. "You do that. They know better than to mess with me."

Before Game Six, Sam located Brooklynn by the railing next to the dugout. As always, she dazzled him, this time in a royal blue dress and white hat with a royal blue bow tied around it.

"Hey, Brooklynn," he said with a smile.

"Hello, Sam. How are you feeling today?"

"Not bad. I have a feeling we're going to play well."

"Did you put your left shoe on first today?" She winked.

"You remembered."

"Of course I did. I know a lot of things about Mr. Sam Murdock of the Brooklyn Dodgers," she smiled.

Sam grinned. *She remembered. Was Chris was right about her?*

"See you after we win, all right?" Sam asked.

"I'll be here," she smiled.

There would be a Game Seven. Whitey Ford went the distance for the second time in the Series, winning 5-1.

Karl Spooner gave up five runs and didn't last an inning. Moose Skowron provided the big blast with a three-run homer, sending Spooner to the bench. The Dodger pitching staff closed the door on the Yankees from there, but it was too little, too late.

The Dodger locker room was as quiet as an elementary school cafeteria in July. The players realized their backs were to the wall once again with their old rivals. Since they had lost their last five World Series to the Yankees, it seemed as if history would repeat itself.

Sam walked through the clubhouse to get on the bus for the return trip to Brooklyn. Before getting to the door, he passed Pee Wee, who sat alone in front of his locker. His face told of the depression endured in every World Series he played in since he joined the Dodgers fifteen years ago. Another failure loomed over him.

He patted Reese on the shoulder. "Don't worry, Captain,

we'll get it done tomorrow."

Reese looked up and smiled. "You're right, Sam. We'll get it done tomorrow."

They smiled at each other as Sam continued to the exit.

"Hey Sam?"

Sam turned around. "Yes?"

"We wouldn't have made it this far without you. I wish you would have been in Brooklyn earlier. We'd have won a World Series by now."

Sam beamed. "Thank you, Pee Wee. That means a lot. More than you can imagine."

Pee Wee winked, then turned back to his locker and placed a few items in his bag.

As Sam walked out of the clubhouse, he carried something he never thought possible. His sought-after validation that he was good enough to be a major league baseball player.

After dinner at Luigi's, Sam and Brooklynn walked outside to catch a cab. Once inside, she asked, "Do you think you'll pull it off tomorrow?"

"I don't know. If we play like we did today, it won't be pretty."

"You'll do fine. And if by some miracle you don't win, I'll still be there waiting for you once it's all over."

"Really?"

"Nah, I was trying to make you feel better," she said with a laugh, then grabbed his hand.

"You're all heart," he said, then wrapped his fingers around hers. Sam looked into the night and was miles away from where he sat.

"What are you looking at?" Brooklynn asked.

Sam snapped out of his trance, then smiled and looked at her. "I was thinking. Win or lose, tomorrow is my last game."

Brooklynn smiled. "Yes, it is. But I wouldn't worry, the Dodgers will pull it off tomorrow."

"What if we don't?"

"Well, there's always next season."

Sam raised his eyebrows and looked away. "Yeah. Next season."

eighteen

Tuesday, October 4th, 1955. Brooklyn.

Sam's journey, which began in April, was almost over. Before the curtain dropped on his incredible adventure, he had two more things to do. The first was to beat the Yankees. The second was to figure out what the future held for him and for Brooklynn.

Sam lay in bed, gazing past the drapes and through the window as the sunlight crept through the cracks of the dying darkness. He enjoyed these kinds of moments, the calm before the storm. Sam was a long way from those days in Durham when he looked through the window at the sunrise and dreaded having to move a muscle for fear his body would tear apart.

Today, he rolled over in bed, staring at the light. He was sore, but not in pain. He looked forward to swinging his legs out of bed and facing the bully of the unknown. Everything he wanted lay on the other side of the sunrise. It was there for the taking. But could he reach it? And if so, could he hold on to it?

He thought about the day ahead, how things would never be the same, one way or the other, after the moment passed when the game was over. Would they be celebrating in Brooklyn tonight?

And win or lose, where would he be after the next sunrise? Would Brooklynn be there too? Or would he be waving goodbye watching her train head west?

Those questions demanded answers. As of now, he had none to give. But it didn't matter. They could wait. The question of who would win Game Seven of the 1955 World Series needed an answer first.

There was no going back to sleep since his stomach ached with nervous excitement and his mind was on a roller coaster of questions and emotions. He had no choice now but to greet the morning.

His clock read 6:44 a.m.

Sam took a cab to Ebbets Field. Before he walked inside the clubhouse, he made a detour to Brooklynn's house. As he walked past Ebbets Field, he reached into his pocket for his cell phone to see if she was home. When there was nothing inside the pocket but lint, he shook his head. *I should know this by now. Well, that's one thing I'll have to consider if I decide to stay.*

A cool, October breeze rustled the copper leaves descending to the sidewalk. As he dodged the fluttering leaves, he noted how peaceful Sullivan Place was on this golden-hued morning. Ebbets Field stood in all its glory behind him. Autumn was in front of him. And in seconds, he hoped, he would get to see the woman who made his trip to 1955 a once-in-a-lifetime moment.

When the door opened, Brooklynn's stunned smile greeted him. "Sam? What are you doing here? Don't you have a bus to catch?"

A Redhead in Brooklyn

"I do," he told her. "It's right over there," he said, pointing down Sullivan Place to the bus parked next to Ebbets Field. "I thought I'd–" he said, then stopped and raised his eyebrows.

"What?" She asked with a smile.

"Remember last night when I asked if you would be there when it was all over?"

She scrunched up her nose. "What about it?"

Sam looked to his left, then exhaled. "I...um..." he began, but stopped.

Brooklynn's eyes widened. "Is everything okay?"

Sam nodded, then looked at her. "Yes, it's fine. Look, I know you're leaving soon, so I wanted to make sure you'd be there to see what happens. I guess since we began the season together, it wouldn't be right if you weren't there for Game Seven."

Brooklynn reached for Sam's hands, and when he extended his, she grasped them. She looked up and smiled. "You're right. We started this thing. We should finish it together."

"Win or lose?"

Brooklynn smiled. "Win or lose."

"What if we don't win?" Sam asked, his eyes hopeful.

"What do you mean, if we don't win?" She asked, her eyes fierce. "I didn't watch a hundred and sixty games to watch you fall flat on your face in the last one. You know it's not smart to disappoint a redhead, don't you?"

Sam nodded. "I'm beginning to understand that."

"Well, now that we understand each other, don't forget Tommy Byrne is pitching today. So far in the Series, he's thrown first pitch fastballs on the inner half of the plate to right-handed batters sixty-seven percent of the time in the Series."

"Well, if those fastballs are high, I'll swing zero percent of the time," he smiled.

When Brooklynn looked over Sam's shoulder, she saw people exiting from the side of Ebbets Field. "You better get going."

Sam turned, and when he saw the same thing, he nodded. "Yeah. I guess I should." He leaned in and they shared a quick good luck kiss, then hugged.

Something caught Brooklynn's eye, so she looked down and saw something sticking out of Sam's jacket pocket. "What's that?"

Sam looked into his pocket, then blushed. "Um, it's nothing."

"Nothing, huh? I've seen that picture before."

Sam opened his jacket and saw the top of the picture poking out. "Yeah. It's the picture of us at Coney Island."

Brooklynn raised her eyebrows. "That was months ago. Why are you carrying it?"

Sam shook his head, then looked down Sullivan Place at a passing car. Then he looked at Brooklynn. "Aw, I don't know. I guess…I keep it for luck."

Brooklynn looked at the picture and smiled. "It looks like you haven't taken it out of your pocket since I gave it to you."

Sam looked at it. "Yeah. I've been meaning to do that. But something always seems to distract me."

"Tell ya what. Stay distracted. It's good luck."

As they smiled at each other, Sam asked, "See you after it's over?"

A Redhead in Brooklyn

"I'll be there," she assured him with a warm smile.

When Sam returned the smile and continued looking at her, she told him, "Now, get going. You have a World Series to win and all you can think about is being all sappy. Geeze."

Sam stared out of the window as the bus approached Yankee Stadium. He went over in his mind what he had to do against today's starter, Tommy Byrne, who struck him out twice in their earlier meeting.

He closed his eyes and focused on Brooklynn's scouting report. Then he visualized playing defense and what their hitters had done so far in the Series.

Once he went through what he would face for the thousandth time, he opened his eyes. Through the window in the distance, the big ballpark in the Bronx came into view. As he stared at the place where his greatest challenge waited for him, thoughts of Brooklynn's good luck kiss replaced any worries he had about the Yankees.

Everything he ever wanted as a baseball player waited for him in that big ballpark in the Bronx that grew larger with every passing mile.

As the bus pulled up to Yankee Stadium, the players filed off. Sam walked with laser focus to the player's entrance, with everything else either blurred or muted.

As he approached the door, a voice somehow slipped past the zone and got to him.

"Mr. Murdock," the young boy's voice called to him.

Sam turned and found the face it belonged to. His feet anchored on the sidewalk and wouldn't budge. When he looked at the boy, there was something in his face that was familiar, but he wasn't sure what it could be. He walked over to see if he could uncover the mystery.

Wearing a tattered Brooklyn Dodger cap, the boy handed Sam a dirty baseball and a pen. "Would you please sign this for me, Mr. Murdock?"

Sam looked at the kid. *I've seen him somewhere before. But where? Was he one of the many kids I saw during the season at Ebbets Field?*

He took the ball and asked, "How are you today?"

"Fine, Mr. Murdock."

"Please, call me Sam."

The boy grinned. "Okay, Sam."

"What's your name?"

The boy looked at Sam. "My name is Bunker."

Sam's eyes widened. "Bunker?"

"Yes. And you're my favorite player. Guess why?"

"Why?"

"My last name is Murdock too. I've been rooting for you ever since I saw we had the same last name."

Sam's mouth opened, and he stared at the boy. Finally, he spoke. "Thank you. I need all the fans I can get," he told him, then signed the ball and gave it back to him. "I hate to ask, but shouldn't you be in school?"

Bunker smiled. "Well, sort of. My dad dropped me off at the subway on his way to work. He told me not to get any crazy ideas about going to the game. I was to get on the train and go right to school. Before I could argue, he told me that for today only, the trains and routes were all reorganized in Brooklyn, so don't get on the A Train to Broadway-Nassau St. Station, then transfer to the Four Train uptown since it takes you to Yankee Stadium."

Sam gave him a wry grin. "Well, I'm sorry to hear you got on the wrong train."

"Yeah. I should have listened better," he said, with a grin, then looked away. "He also told me not to say anything to my mom. You know, in case I made a mistake with the trains. He didn't want her to worry."

Sam laughed. "Oh, I agree. By the way, do you have a ticket for the game?"

Bunker's grin waned. "No. I wanted to be here in case something good happened. The word is that usually, after the eighth inning, the ushers leave their gate and anyone can walk in. That's my plan."

"Tell ya what. If you promise not to tell your mom where you got this, you won't have to worry about sneaking in." Sam grinned and pulled out a ticket for the game. "Here ya go, kid. Burning a hole in my pocket," he said, then handed it to him.

Bunker's face lit up. "Wow. Thank you." He looked at the ticket, then up to Sam. "Promise me you won't let us down today?"

Sam's heart skipped a beat. The hopes of an entire borough came to life in the eyes and voice of a young boy. He looked at Bunker, the hope and innocence stirred something inside him.

The voice was a knife in his heart. It was the voice of everyone in Brooklyn pleading with the Dodgers not to not let them down.

Their team meant everything, and they were once again on the precipice of becoming everything they've always wanted for their team.

As Sam looked at Bunker, memories of promises made and finally making good on them came to life. *And I thought I was good on my promises. How can I promise this?*

Before Sam cautioned him that the outcome of the game was not in his hands, and all he could do was his best to help the team win, Bunker added, "Promise?"

The words stirred something inside that galvanized his will to become superhuman in the face of overwhelming odds. When it surged within him, then hit the crescendo, he patted Bunker on the head. "Promise," he said with a grin.

Bunker nodded, then waved goodbye and disappeared into the crowd.

Sam turned and walked to the player's entrance, then stopped and looked back to the spot where he saw Bunker. He smiled and shook his head. *Chris was right. He will be watching. I hope I have one last rabbit I can pull out of my hat.*

Within seconds, Sam's focus returned, and before he knew it, he was in the Dodgers clubhouse.

He saw the players placing their equipment into the lockers. Some players were dressing. Some talked amongst themselves. Others were being taped up in the trainer's room.

Sam walked towards the lockers and saw Johnny sitting alone on a stool in front of his locker. "Hey, Johnny. Alston give you the start today?"

"Yeah, he did. He called me over after the game yesterday

A Redhead in Brooklyn

and asked if I could give him at least six good innings."

"Well, can you?"

"If I can beat these guys once, I can do it again," he smiled.

"If you're pitching, we better score a bunch," Sam joked as he took a seat on his stool in front of the locker.

"I'll only need one run today, Sam. Get me one run, and I guarantee we'll win."

Sam looked over and grinned. "Fine, Johnny, one run."

At exactly two o'clock, under creamy blue skies and golden sunlight, Tommy Byrne fired a fastball to Junior Gilliam. Game Seven was underway.

Podres got the one run he asked for in the fourth inning. Roy Campenella doubled and Gil Hodges singled him in for a 1-0 Dodgers lead. It stayed that way into the sixth. Reese singled to lead off the inning, then got to second as Snider bunted him over and the throw was wide of the bag. The Dodgers now had two runners on.

Campanella followed Duke's bunt with one of his own to move the runners to second and third. After an intentional walk to load the bases, Gil Hodges blasted a fastball to deep center field. Bob Cerv caught up with the ball, but it was deep enough to score Reese with the second Brooklyn run.

With runners on second and third, Sam walked to the plate, hoping to add to the lead. Casey Stengel countered by bringing in Bob Grim from the bullpen. As Grim went through his warm-up tosses, Sam walked over to talk with Furillo, who waited on deck.

"What do you think, Carl?"

"He'll try to back you up inside since you went deep off him in the last game. He stayed away from you last time, didn't he?"

"Yep."

"Then look for the ball on the inner half of the plate."

After the last of Grim's warm-up tosses, Sam dug in and was ready to hit. Grim went into his stretch, gave a quick look to the runners, then threw to the plate. As expected, it was a fastball inside, but it veered to the right. Sam tried to get out of the way, but it struck him on his right wrist.

"Ow," he yelled as he fell to the ground, clutching his wrist in pain.

"You all right, Murdock?" Home plate umpire Frank Honochick asked, looking down at him.

"Yeah." Sam winced as he sat in the dirt.

In a matter of moments, the team doctor and a concerned Walter Alston joined him.

"Where did it get you?" The doctor asked.

"On the wrist," Sam said, wincing in pain.

The doctor looked at the wrist from both sides and frowned. When Sam grunted, the doctor shook his head.

"I can play," he assured them, despite the fact he gritted his teeth.

Alston looked at the wrist, then at Sam. "You want to play, don't you?"

Sam nodded. "Yes, Walt, I do." He picked up his hat with his good hand, then stood. "It's Game Seven. I'm not coming out."

A Redhead in Brooklyn

The doctor took the wrist in his hands to give it a closer look. When he did, Sam turned his head away and growled in pain. His swollen wrist was now purple.

Alston looked at the doctor and asked, "Can he play?"

"I can play, dammit," Sam assured them.

The doctor held Sam's wrist, then told him, "Press up against my hand."

Sam winced, then pushed his wrist up into the doctor's hand. He grimaced, then growled in pain. He couldn't move it an inch. On the verge of tears, he told them, "Don't take me out of this game."

"Doc? Can he go?" Alston asked.

"No, Walt, he's done for the day."

Sam closed his eyes and turned his head to the ground. As much as he tried to convince himself he could play, he knew he couldn't. His wrist was already numb, and since his fingers were now numb, there was no way he could even hold a bat. The disappointment of leaving the game hurt far worse than the actual injury itself.

They walked the injured rookie back to the dugout to the polite applause of the Yankee crowd. Among the people on their feet was Sam's sweetheart. She sniffled and held back tears as her eyes followed him into the dugout.

After walking up the long tunnel and into the locker room, Sam hopped onto the trainer's table. After a closer examination, the doctor determined the wrist wasn't broken, just bruised, but it was enough to end his day. "I'm sorry about this, Sam," the doctor said.

Sam looked down at the floor. The words he uttered to Bunker a second time weighed on his shoulders. *What if we lose? I made a promise and now I can't do anything about it. It's the damn New York Yankees. There's no way those two runs are going to hold up.*

They iced the wrist down, then bandaged it up and sent him back to the dugout. As he reached the steps leading up to the dugout, he heard a thunderous roar. He rushed up the steps to see why. "What happened?" He asked Carl Erskine, raising his voice over the cheering crowd.

"Johnny's in trouble. The tying runs are on."

"Who's up?" Sam asked.

"Yogi Berra. He lives for these moments."

"Who did Alston put in left field?"

Erskine looked into left field, then back to Sam. "Amoros. He'll be fine. His ankle is a hundred percent now. How's your wrist?"

"It's not broken, but it's bad enough."

Erskine looked at him with a touch of disappointment on his face. "I'm sorry, Sam."

Sam frowned as he nodded in acknowledgment.

The Yankees unleashed the rally everyone knew was coming. Both dugouts filled with tension, and it filtered into the crowd. Brooklynn fidgeted in her seat, twisting a handkerchief in her fingers.

A few seconds later, Podres fired an outside fastball to Campanella. Berra smashed the pitch to deep left field, arcing towards the corner, away from Amoros.

The Dodger players hopped up the steps of the dugout to get a better look. Brooklynn rose, watching the ball arc high and deep to left field. Sam stood on the top step of the dugout, yelling over and over, "Go foul."

A Redhead in Brooklyn

Amoros, the fleet Cuban, was off with the crack of the bat, racing towards the low gate where the fair pole meets the line. Would the ball clear the fence for a home run? Or bounce into the stands for a ground-rule double? The other possibility was it would bounce and hit the low fence and roll around in the corner.

The fate of the Dodgers hung in the air. Everything moved in slow motion. The ball continued slicing as it neared the wall.

Amoros, running full speed, reached out with his glove. As the crowd held their breath, the ball popped into it with a soft thud.

He braced himself for a split second, then wheeled and fired a strike to the infield. Pee Wee saw where the runners were before Amoros threw the ball in, so once he received the throw, he didn't hesitate to fire it to Hodges. Hodges reached for the ball, it smacked into his glove before Gil McDougald slid back to the base for a spectacular double play.

The Dodger bench let out an enormous sigh of relief. The small army of Dodger fans, who made the trip north, roared their approval. Brooklynn hugged an unidentified stranger wearing a Dodgers cap as the tension subsided on their side of the stadium.

The great defensive effort stalled the Yankee rally. The next batter was Hank Bauer, but Podres got him to ground out, so the inning was over.

Sam met Amoros at the front of the dugout and gave him a big hug. "Great play, Sandy."

Amoros smiled. "Gracias."

Sam walked over to Podres after the inning was over. "I guess Amoros saved you this time."

"Yeah, thank God he was out there instead of...well..."

He said with a smile, then they embraced.

After Sam let him go, he asked, "You think you can hold these guys for three more innings?"

Podres smiled as he wiped the sweat off his face and neck with a towel. "How many runs did I say I needed today?"

"Just one," Sam told him, repeating the line of the day.

"Well, what are you worried about?"

The tension in the dugout was incredible. Sam spent the next three innings pacing back and forth in the dugout, unable to speak. Erskine kidded Podres, yelling at him from the dugout to keep him and everyone else loose, then lost his nerve as the game entered the ninth inning.

One player they didn't have to worry about being loose was Johnny Podres, who wasn't sitting in the dugout.

He hid out in the tunnel and smoked while he gathered his thoughts. When there were two outs, one of the bat boys would tell him, then he would stub out his smoke, hop up into the dugout, and was ready for the next inning.

The game rolled into the bottom of the ninth with the Dodgers still leading 2-0. Moose Skowron walked up to the plate to the cheers of the Yankee fans, hoping to rally their team.

Skowron lined the first pitch back up the middle. Podres threw his glove down and stopped the ball as it skidded off the grass. However, the ball lodged in the webbing of his glove and stuck inside. Podres trotted over to flip the ball to Hodges, but couldn't remove it from the webbing. Finally, he tugged hard enough to loosen it, then tossed the ball to Hodges for the first out.

Bob Cerv sent a Podres fastball deep to left field, but Amoros

A Redhead in Brooklyn

raced under the ball and caught it for the second out.

Elston Howard was the next batter. Podres started him off with a fastball for strike one. The Dodgers bench erupted, and so did their fans. Podres wanted to end the game with a strikeout, so he was throwing nothing but fastballs.

Howard fouled off the next six pitches, sending everyone into a paralyzing fear with every pitch Podres threw.

Campanella once again called for a fastball. But Podres had another idea. Since he threw Howard all fastballs in the at-bat, and with the shadows cutting between home plate and the pitcher's mound making it difficult for batters to pick up the ball as it went from sunlight to shadow, he shook Campenella off and waited for him to signal for a change up. Podres knew that was the money pitch.

When Campy threw his fingers down for the change up, Podres nodded, wound up and fired home.

The off-speed pitch fooled Howard. He was out on his front foot, but managed to hold up long enough to get his bat on the ball. The weak grounder rolled to Pee Wee, which served as the ultimate irony. He waited fifteen years for this opportunity, and now he was the one to put the demon of defeat to rest.

Pee Wee fired the ball to Hodges but didn't turn it loose like usual, since he wanted to make a good throw. But the big first baseman went down to get the low throw a step ahead of a hustling Howard for the third and final out.

The Brooklyn Dodgers were the 1955 World Champions.

The players rushed out to meet Podres at the mound as he jumped into Campanella's arms. The rest of the jubilant Dodgers, as well as the Brooklyn fans who made the trip north, rushed onto the field to congratulate their heroes.

Sam was in the middle of the celebration, not feeling his damaged wrist. He hugged Podres, then followed the crowd as they all headed for the dugout. Before he got there, he raced over to the railing to find Brooklynn. He looked through the crowd, but she wasn't there.

Sam stood at the railing, weaving his eyes around the people in the seats, as well as some who were coming down the stairs to join the team on the field. A few of the fans racing on the field recognized him, so they hugged him and said congratulations. One fan kissed him on the cheek in gratitude for finally giving Brooklyn its first-ever World Series championship.

When the crush of fans finally subsided, Sam continued looking for Brooklynn. There was nobody left in the section or coming down the steps.

Maybe she left town after all. He shook his head and turned to the dugout.

As he focused on where he was going, a blur came into view. Just as on opening day, the redheaded girl appeared out of nowhere and stood before him. This time, there would be no banter. No quick exit. This would be something memorable. Through the crazy crowd and the roar of victory, she was the only person in the world he saw or heard at that moment.

"Hello, Sam. Congratulations."

He walked over and gathered her into his chest with his good arm. She used both her arms to hold him as the moment of pure joy swept through them. He somehow picked her up, and they

A Redhead in Brooklyn

twirled on top of the Yankee Stadium dirt.

Sam put her down, then leaned back and looked at her. "I worried you left town on me."

Brooklynn giggled and said, "Would you believe I took a wrong turn trying to get out of Yankee Stadium?"

Her emerald eyes and cinnamon hair held him captive, and at that moment, the reason he was there no longer mattered. What mattered was the woman who stole his heart. Nothing else. For the rest of his life.

He was about to speak when Johnny Podres rushed over, picked him up and spun him around. "Come on, Sam, let's go celebrate."

He whisked Sam away. As they rushed toward the dugout, Sam looked over Johnny's shoulder and yelled, "I'll pick you up at your house later for the party."

"Make sure you shower before you do," she yelled back, then smiled and shook her head.

Before Sam disappeared into the dugout, he yelled, "I'll be showering in champagne."

"Save me some," Brooklynn laughed, then waved.

When Johnny let him down and the pair walked up the tunnel, Sam asked, "How many runs today, Johnny?"

"Just one, Sam," he laughed, then put his arm around him.

As they walked up the corridor and into the clubhouse, a Dodger official handed each player a bottle of champagne to spray at will. Sam shook his bottle of champagne around at every player he saw. When the fizz died, and the splash of champagne dripped out of the bottle, Sam looked up and saw Chris standing in front of him with a smile.

The two shared a long embrace. When they released, Sam poured what was left of the bottle over Chris's head, as they laughed and enjoyed the moment.

"Aren't you glad you didn't know how it was going to turn out?" Chris asked.

Sam admitted without hesitation. "Yes, you were right. I haven't been this happy in a long time. I have you to thank, don't I?"

"Don't mention it. It's part of the job," Chris smiled. "Remember what I told you on the first day? I said you would thank me when it was all over."

Sam thought for a moment, then nodded. "Chris, you were right, as always. Thank you."

"Aw, no big deal," Chris said, downplaying things. "Enjoy the moment, Sam. It's yours to savor forever."

"It's yours too," Sam told him. "You didn't get to celebrate in 1941, so I hope this will suffice."

Chris smiled wide, wider than Sam could ever remember him smiling in all their time together, and looked around the clubhouse. He gazed at the scene, champagne dripping off his face, then told him, "I was wrong. I guess I have you to thank after it's all over, huh?"

"Nah, it's all part of my ballplayer gig," Sam joked. "And who thought I'd ever be helping you?"

From behind, Reese grabbed him, and they embraced. Chris watched as they congratulated each other, then tossed beer and champagne over each other's heads.

A Redhead in Brooklyn

That's my cue, Chris said to himself, then walked away from the mob of players and Dodger personnel celebrating.

In the middle of the euphoria, Sam wiped his face so he could see, then looked around for Chris. "Where did he go?"

After scanning the clubhouse, he saw his friend walking toward the exit. Through the champagne spraying and the shouts of victory, Chris turned, and their eyes met. They exchanged a long, meaningful smile and nod, saying nothing. The silence was everything they needed to hear.

nineteen

The Dodger bus pulled out of the Bronx and headed south. Through the borough of Manhattan, the streets were quiet as people walked along the sidewalk, minding their own business. It seemed like any other day.

As the bus rolled through the Battery Tunnel and onto sacred turf, it was as if they had driven into another world.

People lined the streets, cheering the bus as it went by. There were banners, signs, and a shirtless Dodger fan, who climbed a light pole, waving a Dodger pennant at the bus as it went by. The bystanders cheered him on.

The bus pulled alongside Ebbets Field to the roar of thousands of fans welcoming home their champions. Johnny slapped Sam on the back as they exited the bus and told him, "We'll savor this forever."

Sam smiled. He thought about the day and about how Brooklynn found him on the field. *Johnny was right. I will savor this forever.*

Sam hung out at Ebbets Field long after the bus dropped the team off. Most of the players didn't stick around the clubhouse since they left to begin their long awaited victory party, so the clubhouse was quiet.

He sat alone in front of his locker, looking around the place where he spent seven months of his life. It was in this space he sat alongside several hall of fame players, and now, he was there as the Brooklyn Dodgers won their first and only World Series.

Sam exhaled as a wave of awe washed over him.

It was at this moment, images of the clubhouse he left behind in Durham came to him. Sam thought about that dark day, and how he thought his life hit a brick wall with no hope of happiness ever coming to him.

He shook his head and smiled. "Chris was right. I guess miracles happen every day as long as you keep your eyes open to the possibilities."

"And you know who to thank for that," a voice said from the side of the room.

Sam looked over and saw Chris leaning on a locker. Sam smiled, then told him, "Yeah. I guess I do."

Chris walked over and pulled up a stool. "I see you're saying goodbye. Sometimes, these kinds of goodbyes are the most difficult."

"Yeah," Sam told him, then looked around at the lockers. "I don't know what's going to happen tomorrow, so in case I never get to venture back this way, I thought I would have one last moment here."

Chris looked around. "I wish I had another season here. And a few more World Series games."

Sam looked at his friend. He saw the longing in his eyes and a lost look into the past. He allowed him his moment.

Finally, Chris spoke. "Thank you, Sam."

Sam squinted. "For what?"

Chris tilted his head with a grin. "Oh, I don't know. For giving me a front-row seat to what might have been. I always wondered what it might have looked like. Felt like. Smelled like. The feeling of seeing it all come together. When you find success, especially in the face of overwhelming odds, that's the thing that lives forever."

Before Sam asked, Chris added, "No matter if it isn't in the history books. This happened, it was real, and that, my friend, will live forever. These days, that's good enough for me."

Sam smiled and nodded. "Yeah. I guess it's good enough for both of us."

They shared a nod, then Chris asked, "What are you going to do?"

Sam raised his eyebrows, then sat back. "I don't know. I wish I knew what Brooklynn was going to do."

"Have you asked her?"

Sam looked at the floor. When he didn't answer for a few seconds, Chris asked, "You haven't, have you?"

Sam's face continued staring down. "I'm afraid of her answer."

"Like I said before, it's times like this when you need courage. I sure hope you find it." Chris rose, then patted him on the shoulder. "I'll see you at the party tonight."

After Chris left the clubhouse, Sam took a last look at his locker, then performed the same duty as he did in Durham, He made sure to give Charlie DiGiovanna and all the clubhouse personnel money in appreciation for everything they did for him. He found John Griffin sweeping the floor of the manager's office, so he reached inside his pocket and gave him some money as well. "Thanks for everything, John," he told him.

"You're welcome, Sam."

Sam nodded and told him, "Go buy yourself a new hat."

"Do they make hats that can hold my beer?"

They laughed, then Sam said, "John, I need a favor."

After saying goodbye, Sam walked to the door, opened it, then turned and gave the clubhouse a last look.

He saw Pee Wee, Jackie, Duke, Gil, Campy, Erskine and the rest of his teammates sitting on their stools, enjoying the post-game conversations.

"Where did the time go?" He asked.

Sam looked at the door. He stared at it for a few seconds, then another memory came to him. There was a blur of a redheaded girl coming through, almost running into him on that first day in Brooklyn. The banter. Her cinnamon hair. The way her freckles danced on her cheeks when she smiled. "Where did the time go indeed."

He allowed the memory of her beautiful face to swallow him up, letting him have one last day of summer. The warmth. The glow. The happy optimism about what the next day brought.

As he put his hand on the cold metal door, knowing he once shared this same spot at the same time with her, he gave the past a sad smile, then let it slip away because it no longer belonged to him. It now belonged to yesterday and there was nothing he could do to bring it back. Not even time travel could recreate the innocence of that first moment when the newness of falling in love arrives, and life is never the same.

Knowing summer was over, and winter was coming, he climbed out of the warmth of what was, and braced himself for what was about to become. He took a last look at the clubhouse, and wondered, *Will I ever see this place again?*

Sam walked through the tunnel and up the steps to the dugout. He looked around, then said, "I don't know what's going to happen in the next 24 hours, but whatever it is, I loved being here with you. Farewell for now." As he thought about the words, he added, "Or maybe…Farewell forever. We'll both know in the morning."

He left Ebbets Field and walked to Brooklynn's house. On the sidewalk, he heard shouts and cheers from Dodger fans celebrating in the streets. People brought out grills, growlers of beer, and danced in celebration. Music blared from windows, while a line of cars honked their horns along the street. Convertibles with pyramids of people standing in the backseat rolled along Bedford Ave.

Most of the traffic, convertible or not, stopped in the street so people could jump out and hug strangers, then dash back to their cars. Even with cars stopping in the middle of the street, there were no reports of road rage on October 4th in Brooklyn.

Sam watched a man standing in front of a restaurant giving away free hot dogs. And also free hugs as he spun with each person walking by.

Only a block from Brooklynn's house, a heavy-set man wearing a shirt and boxer shorts yelled, "There's Sam Murdock," then rushed over in his direction. Sam saw the man moving toward him and froze. *Why is that man in his underwear?*

"Murdock, you're the best," the man said as his voice cracked.

A Redhead in Brooklyn

When tears came out of his eyes, he reached out and hugged Sam. "I've waited all my life for this day. Thank you."

Sam hugged him back. "You're welcome." Then he looked down and asked, "What happened to your pants?"

The man laughed. "I don't know. I lost them a little while ago, but I'm so happy, I don't care if I ever find them."

More of the neighborhood crowd walked over and hugged him. They expressed their gratitude, and he posed for pictures. After the last photo, he bid them farewell, then resumed his walk to Brooklynn's house.

When he arrived at the door, Margaret answered it. "Hello, Sam. Congratulations," she told him, holding a glass of lemonade.

"Thanks, Margaret. Has Brooklynn come home yet?"

She shook her head. "Not yet. She called to tell me she had to stop by Ebbets Field on her way home to finish up a few media requests for stats. But she should be home soon. Would you like to come inside and wait for her?"

"Sure. I need to hide out from that crazy crowd outside. Did you know there was a man outside walking around in his boxer shorts?"

Margaret smiled. "Must be Harold Green. He does that when the Dodgers win a big game, or when they win the National League. Since the Dodgers never won a World Series before, I'm worried it might not stop there," she joked.

"The way things are going, he'll lose everything by tonight."

Margaret laughed. "I know. It's crazy out there. Luckily, Brooklynn told me where she was before the phone went out. I guess the flood of calls must have knocked out the circuits."

"I'm surprised the telephone poles are still standing," Sam joked.

Margaret led him to the living room. "Can I get you anything? Lemonade?"

"No thank you," he said, then sat on the couch. After she sat in a gray chair across from him, he told her, "Did you see the game?"

She nodded, then pointed at a wide box with a gray glass screen. "Yes. I watched it on television." Then she looked at his arm. "How's your wrist? The guys on TV were sure it was broken."

Sam looked at his arm, then back at her. "Luckily, it's only a bruise. But it hurts."

"I'm sure it does."

"You know the funny thing? As soon as Pee Wee got the last out, it stopped hurting. Isn't that crazy?"

Margret laughed. "You're a miracle of modern medicine."

After they stopped laughing, Sam asked, "Forgive me if this is rude, but did Brooklynn mention anything about leaving town once the Series was over?"

Margaret's laughter vanished. She shrugged and told him, "Well, yeah. She mentioned it."

"She did?" He asked. "If you don't mind me asking, what did she decide?"

"Well, she has something in Los Angeles. Something she's excited about."

Margaret's words sent a shiver down his spine. *Excited. That means a man. No wonder she's been evasive about the future.* Sam sucked up the fear and icy slivers of doubt with a smile. "Wow. I'm happy for her. But is she okay with leaving her job with the Dodgers? I

A Redhead in Brooklyn

thought she loved that job?"

Margaret raised an eyebrow. "I have a hunch she's in love."

Oh boy. She's in love with someone in Los Angeles. No wonder why she was distant when we first met and said she didn't date ballplayers. This all makes sense now. "Love? What do you mean?" Sam watched as Margaret's face became guarded, then she uttered a quick laugh and reached for her glass of lemonade.

She took a sip to mask her glowing cheeks. Then they heard the door open. "Margaret? Are you home? Has Sam come by yet?"

They both rose and turned to the hallway. "We're in here," Margaret told her.

Sam stood and saw Brooklynn's face. It smiled the same as it had ever since they met. Her eyes still sparkled. The same glow he always saw when she walked into a room was there. But somehow, things were different. *Be careful, Sam. Baseball did the same thing to you. Don't let her steal your heart too.*

But he knew it was too late.

The Hotel Bossert was ground zero for the Brooklyn Dodgers victory party.

Search lights rolled back and forth as a crush of fans bellied up to the police barricades surrounding the entrance to the hotel. Never had Brooklyn seen something this crazy.

"New Year's Eve is a walk in the park compared to all this," a policeman said as he monitored the barricades around the entrance to the hotel.

Sam and Brooklynn took a cab to the Hotel. They exited the

cab to the roar of the crowd lined up at the barricades. He signed a few autographs, and paused for a couple of pictures, then joined Brooklynn at the entrance.

Two policemen walked them inside to a large ballroom, where they found couples dancing to the sounds of an orchestra on stage. Tables lined the room as people sat and watched the festivities.

As Sam and Brooklynn sat and talked about Game Seven, Chris appeared from the crowd. "How ya feeling, Sam?"

Sam raised his bandaged arm and with a smile said, "Never better."

"How does it feel to be on a championship team?"

Sam smiled. "So far, it is everything I thought it would be."

"You earned it," Chris told him.

"Would you excuse me?" Brooklynn asked. "I need to powder my nose."

While they waited for Brooklynn to return, Chris asked, "Have you made your decision yet? Don't forget, when the sun rises tomorrow, I'll need to know one way or the other."

"I know," he told him, then reached into his coat pocket, pulled out a well-worn black-and-white picture, and placed it on the table.

Chris looked at it. "What's this?"

"Look at it." Chris picked it up, squinting his eyes. Finally, he said, "I remember that day. That's the autograph session at Coney Island, right?"

"Yeah. Seems like it was years ago, doesn't it?"

Chris gazed at it for a few seconds. "Looks like this thing has been through the wringer. I would have thought you'd have taken better care of it."

"I did. It never left my side from the first day she gave it to me. I put it in my pocket during games for luck. I also carry it with me, so after she leaves, I'll have something to remember her by."

"But only if you stay. Remember the first morning we spoke?"

Sam thought about it, then nodded. "Yeah. I guess I forgot I can't bring anything back from Brooklyn, can I?" He looked at the picture again, then placed it in his coat pocket. "I thought I'd at least have this to hold on to."

He looked into the flashing colored lights over the dance floor, then back to Chris. "I made up my mind earlier. I'm not staying. So I'm okay with knowing I don't deserve to have anything left of her except the memories."

"You're not going to fight for her?"

Sam looked into the multicolored hue of the room, then shook his head. "It doesn't matter. She is in love with someone in Los Angeles. Why else would she be so excited about going there?"

Chris stared at him for a few seconds, then said, "It can't be. I saw the way she looks at you. I don't believe that for a second."

"Well, it's true."

"How do you know?" Chris asked.

"Her roommate Margaret told me. She said something about Brooklynn being in love with something out in L.A."

"Something? Or someone? You know there's a big difference." As Chris allowed Sam to digest the words, he added, "Did you ever think about asking her what's in Los Angeles that she's so damn excited about?"

Sam thought for a few seconds. He shrugged. "No."

"Well, I'd start there."

"It doesn't matter."

"Doesn't matter? It means everything," Chris told him, his eyes fierce and locked on Sam's. "Damn it, you love that girl. Fight for her. For God's sake, fight for what you have together. Because I guarantee that one day, you'll look back at this moment, and you'll regret not standing up for something you love."

Sam looked at him, the resignation on his face evident. Chris continued. "All you have to do is tell her you love her, and that you don't want her to go. As long as you do that, no matter what happens, you'll live the rest of your life without regret. Whether it's here, or in Kiawah."

Sam took a deep breath. "I'll have to live with regret. There's nothing left for me in Brooklyn."

Chris nodded, then rose. "Fine. I said what I had to say. Once the sun comes up, I'm taking you back to Kiawah."

Sam nodded. "I'm ready." When he saw the lost look on Chris' face, he told him, "I'm sorry, Chris. "For what it's worth, I loved your speech. It almost made me stay."

Chris raised his eyebrows and frowned. "I see. Well, I gave it my best shot."

Sam plastered a smile on his face and said, "We had a helluva run though. Didn't we?"

"Yeah. We did."

"Since I've made my decision, and there's no going back, let's celebrate our friendship and also winning the World Series."

Chris rose, then looked at Sam. "I need to take care of a few things before tomorrow so I can wrap up your case. But don't worry, I'll see you in the morning so we can have an official goodbye."

"You're not going to celebrate with us?"

"Nah, this is your party. Besides, I hate being the third wheel."

"You've never been the third wheel," Sam assured him.

"Thanks, but I learned my lesson at Luigis," he said with a smile.

As they looked at each other, an unidentified man walked up and extended his hand. "Sam Murdock, thanks for a helluva season." Sam looked at the man, then shook his hand. Chris smiled and said, "Have fun."

Brooklynn returned to the ballroom and joined Sam. While they watched the couples on the dance floor, Sam looked at her and asked, "I know this might not be the best time to mention this, but, are you looking forward to getting out to Los Angeles?"

Brooklynn frowned, then placed her glass of champagne, on the nearest table. She turned and smiled at him. "Margaret told you, didn't she?" After Sam nodded, she continued. "Yeah. I guess so. I have some things out there I need to do. Things I've told myself that I would regret not taking a chance on."

The icy spears that slit him when he spoke to Margaret returned. He smiled, which took effort, but he had played hurt before. Now, he was doing it again, but this time, instead of being on a baseball field, he was doing it in front of the woman he tried to convince himself he didn't love. "Well, I am happy for you. I am sure you will find what you're looking for in Los Angeles."

"Sam, I have to–"

"Brooklynn, you don't need to explain. Besides, we told each other that this was only a friendship and once October came, we would go our separate ways."

She gave him a sad stare, then looked down. Finally, she said, "You're right. We made a promise to each other and now that October is here, we have to stick to it."

She looked away, and Sam detected a sniffle. Sensing the insincerity in her voice, he was about to ask a question, but she turned back to him. "Hey, how about we have a last dance? You know, we were always good at that."

Sam was on autopilot as he gave her his best smile. "I would love that," he told her, then reached for her hand.

As the walked on the dance floor, an older man in a tuxedo walked to the microphone. "A special guest is here to congratulate the Dodgers, as well as perform a song for his upcoming album."

Brooklynn looked at Sam. "Who could it be?"

The man looked to the side of the stage, nodded, then looked back to the crowd. "Here is a gentleman who needs no introduction. Put your hands together for Mr. Nat King Cole."

A few gasps, then a hush came over the room. Then polite applause.

Sam smiled. "Wow. Nat King Cole."

Brooklynn stared at the stage, clapping with the crowd.

The handsome singer walked to the microphone, adjusted it, then waved to the crowd. "First, I'd like to congratulate the Dodgers for their first World Series Championship."

A Redhead in Brooklyn

The crowd roared.

He waited for the cheering to die down, then spoke. "I'd like to do a song that my friend, Doris Day, sang a few years ago. She gave her blessing to add it to my upcoming album, so here it goes."

He looked back at the band, said something, then turned back and adjusted the microphone as the music began. As the music echoed through the ballroom with an easy rhythm, the crowd wondered what it could be. Finally, he crooned, "When I fall in love, it will be forever."

The stunned crowd stood in awe as his silky smooth voice flowed through the room.

Sam turned to Brooklynn. She was already staring at him. He didn't want any part of a romantic moment, since he was already beginning plans for the long days ahead without her. "You know I'm hungry. Would you like to get something to eat?"

Brooklynn shook her head, then reached for his hand. "No. I'd like to dance." When Sam hesitated, she gripped his hand tighter, then pulled him toward her. "Please?"

Sam thought about her words, Margaret's words, and his decision. *Why am I doing this? I'm going down in flames and there's nothing I can do about it.*

He allowed the softness of her hand to warm the icy tingles of pain to melt within him. They put their arms around each other, and as they swayed to the music, their bodies came together.

Brooklynn closed what little space there was between them and placed her cheek next to his. Sam wanted to back away, but his heart wouldn't allow him to retreat. With no escape, he closed his eyes and breathed her in.

Her sweet smell allowed him to see her clearly in the darkness of his uncertainty. As her soft cheek touched his, it weakened whatever walls he built to keep her out. He knew this would be one of those moments that would survive time and place and would live on within him forever.

When the music ended, Nat King Cole bowed, and the crowd gave him a rousing ovation.

After the applause died down, Brooklynn looked up. "Sam...I..." but she stopped when she saw a woman over Sam's shoulder staring at her. The woman pointed at the door, then headed toward it.

From the bar, Chris watched as Brooklynn followed the woman out of the ballroom, then squinted. *I've seen her somewhere before. But where?*

Chris thought for a few seconds, and when no answers came, he turned and walked out of the Hotel.

twenty

When they arrived at the end of a side hallway, far away from the party, Brooklynn asked, "What are you doing here?"

Margaret looked at her. "I'm sorry. You need to leave for Los Angeles now."

Brooklynn's face went pale. "You told me I'd have until the season was over. Can't you do anything about that?"

"The season ended with the last out of the game today. I delayed things as long as I could but you have to be on the next train west."

When Brooklynn's eyes filled with tears, Margaret looked her over. "You love him, don't you."

She looked away, then sniffled and wiped her cheek with her gloved hand. "Yes. I do."

The words gripped Margaret as she looked at the carpet, then up the hallway, not sure what to do next. Finally, she looked at Brooklynn. "I told you not to fall in love with him. You know what's about to happen."

Brooklynn sniffled. "I know. And I hate myself for what I've done. I never meant to hurt him."

Margaret shook her head. "I know. But Brooklynn, it's too late."

"I thought you–"

"You better tell him goodbye."

Brooklynn sniffled. "Margaret, is there anything you can do?" When Margaret exhaled, Brooklynn told her, "Let me stay until morning. If you can't change things by then, I'll head to L.A. Without complaint."

Margaret was about to speak, but Brooklynn beat her to it. "Please. One last favor. For old time's sake?"

Margaret looked at her, then exhaled. "Fine. You have until morning. But if I were you, I'd pray for a miracle."

"Well, if a miracle is all there is, I'll take it." "We'll meet back at the house in the morning. Don't forget, when I say morning, it better be first thing. Understand?"

Brooklynn nodded. "Yes. I understand."

Margaret nodded, then they hugged and kissed goodbye.

Chris arrived on the fourth floor of the Lost Causes Section, ready to close up the Murdock case. He took the same walk down the long hall as he had for years, then opened the door and walked in.

He walked to the end of the large space and found a light on in the corner office. He popped his head inside the door and found St. Jude at his desk, looking inside a manila folder.

Chris walked inside with the usual jovial greeting. "Hi, Boss.

I wanted to donate to the cause this morning, but I heard they were all lost, so I'll have to wait until the next payday."

St. Jude looked up. Without expression, he pointed at a chair across from his desk. "Hello, Chris. Have a seat." Then he returned to reading the file.

Chris' smile vanished as he sat in the chair Jude pointed to. "I've seen happier faces at a car crash. What's up?"

"How are things with the Murdock case?"

"Well, he's going back. I tried to talk some sense to the kid since he is going to regret not fighting for the girl, but hey, I'm in no position to tell anyone how to live. I spoke my peace so there's not much more I can do."

Jude closed the file and stared at the desk.

Chris sat forward. "Me and St. Bernard have a bet going. I put twenty on Sam staying. Talk about adding insult to injury."

Jude didn't smile.

"I know that look. What's wrong?"

"We have a problem."

Chris squinted "What do you mean, a problem?"

"You need to find Murdock. And find him fast."

Chris shifted in his chair. "Jude, be straight with me. What's going on?"

"Do you know where he is?"

"He could be anywhere. There's a over a million people in Brooklyn right now, celebrating the Dodgers winning the World Series."

Jude stared a hole through him. "Find him. Now."

The celebration in Brooklyn continued past midnight, and Sam and Brooklynn were in the middle of it all. As the party continued, Sam leaned over and whispered, "I have a surprise for you."

"Surprise?"

"Yes. Follow me." Sam took her hand and led her through a back door of the Hotel Bossert, avoiding the crazy Brooklyn crowd.

They found a cab, and within minutes, they were away. "Ebbets Field," Sam told the driver.

"Isn't the party back there?"

"Yep. But it won't be as fun as the one we're going to."

The driver squinted his eyes, then put the car in drive and they were on their way. "With the way the streets are, it might take a while to get there."

Sam looked at Brooklynn, then told the driver, "No problem. We have time."

The darkness disguised Sam from detection as the driver honored the request. Brooklynn curled up into him, being careful to not bump his bandaged arm. "How is your wrist? Does it still hurt?"

"Yes, it does. But it's a good kind of hurt."

Brooklynn smiled and asked, "Why are we going to Ebbets Field?"

"I told you it was a surprise."

It took longer than usual, but they made it to Ebbets Field.

A Redhead in Brooklyn

They walked around the brick building, dodging a mass of people celebrating in the streets and around the ballpark. When Sam stopped. Brooklynn asked, "What's this?"

"You'll see."

He knocked on the metal door and after a few seconds, it opened with a loud grinding ache. "Get those hinges some oil," Sam joked as the door creaked open.

John Griffin stood in the doorway. With a cigar in the corner of his mouth, and wearing a fez with a black tassel hanging off of it, he greeted them holding a bottle of half-drunk champagne. "Hello, Sam," he said with a goofy grin and slight slur. "I wondered where you were."

"Hello, John." He looked at Griffin's headgear and told him, "Love the hat."

"I wore it just for you," he replied with a laugh.

"Sorry we're late. It's a little crazy out here."

Griffin looked out of the door at the crowd. "Tell me about it. I was drinking with these crazies earlier. It's a wonder I still have all my fingers and toes," he joked, then wobbled before steadying himself.

Sam asked, "Is everything set?"

Griffin nodded. "Yes, it is. Here's a flashlight so you can find your way. Have fun"

"Thanks," Sam told him, then watched his friend stagger, then right himself as he made his way through the bowels of the park.

"What are we doing?" Brooklynn asked.

"I'll show you," he said as he led Brooklynn underneath the bleachers. After a few steps, the round, bouncing light coming from the flashlight illuminated a door.

Sam stopped at the wide rectangular door, finding the handle by flashing his light on it. He reached for the handle, then saw the bandage and stopped. Not wanting to injure himself further, he reached down with his good hand and pulled. The aluminum wall rolled up with a loud, creaking echo.

As the wall opened, Brooklynn looked out and saw the field before them. Shrouded in darkness, the only lights came from the grandstand and the neighborhood behind the scoreboard.

They stepped out to the crunchy warning track. Once they walked through the gate, Brooklynn saw a blanket lying on the grass. "Why is that blanket there?"

"Griffin put it there for me. It cost an extra ten bucks, but it was worth it."

Brooklynn smiled. "Is this the surprise?"

Sam nodded. "Well, you surprised me at the Botanical Garden, so I thought I'd return the favor."

Brooklynn looked around in the darkness. "It's perfect."

They sat on the blanket, staring up at the stars. They could hear the sounds of cars honking, loud music, and people shouting as the borough was in the middle of the wildest celebration in its history.

When a stream of sparkles ascended into the sky, then burst into a wide giant panorama of fireworks, they watched as the glow from the multi-colored lights illuminated the field.

As they stared into the colorful sky, Sam waited for a loud

burst to subside. When it was quiet, he asked, "I don't want to put a damper on our night, but since the season is over, I have to know something."

"What?"

"I'm sorry if I intruded into something that was already established before we met in April. I didn't know you had someone in Los Angeles."

Brooklyn looked up at him. "Someone in Los Angeles? What do you mean?"

Sam looked at her. "Margaret said there was something in Los Angeles you were looking forward to seeing. I thought it must be...well, you know."

Brooklynn shook her head and smiled. "Oh Sam, she giggled. "That's not it. Not at all."

Sam exhaled as the weight of the world lifted from his shoulders. "It's not?"

Brooklynn nodded. "I have a job opportunity in Los Angeles. Something that I've wanted to do all my life. That's what I was trying to explain earlier at the party." She paused, then put her head on his chest. "But now, I'm not so sure I want it."

"What do you mean? If this is something you've wanted to do all your life, then why aren't you sure about it?"

Brooklynn paused, then told him, "I would have to say goodbye to Brooklyn, and that will be difficult. But it would be more difficult to say goodbye to you."

Sam smiled. "Me?"

"Yes. I grew up a baseball girl. The game means everything

to me. But, as time passed, and the season wore on, I realized that," she said, then stopped, and reached up and caressed his cheek with her hand. "You mean more to me than the game."

Sam's heartbeat accelerated. He gazed at her freckled face, illuminated by another round of fireworks. He looked away and shook his head. "This isn't what I thought would happen when I came here." His gaze continued looking out to the night.

"What do you mean?"

Sam broke out of his trance. He smiled and told her, "I never told you this. Heck, I never told anyone this, but I made a promise to someone a long time ago about being a major league baseball player."

"You did? Who did you promise?"

Sam pursed his lips and stayed silent for a few seconds. Finally, he said, "My father."

"Your father?"

Sam nodded. "Yeah. He was the biggest Brooklyn Dodgers fan, and growing up he told me stories about the team and how he used to watch games at Ebbets Field. He loved baseball in general, and the Dodgers in particular, so I promised him that one day, I would make the major leagues. Well," he said, then shrugged, "I guess I made it. But if I leave Brooklyn now, then I will have let him down all over again."

"If you stay in Brooklyn?" She asked. "What do you mean? You aren't getting traded are you?"

Sam thought about the words, then said, "I meant...Oh, I'm just talking crazy. Maybe it's all the champagne." He exhaled, then said, "I have everything I've always wanted here. Why would I leave?"

"Leave? You can't leave now. Especially after winning the World Series."

Multicolored sparkles filled the sky, and when the boom subsided, Sam asked, "When do you know if you have to leave Brooklyn?"

"I need to see Margaret. I'll know for sure after I speak with her."

"What does she have to do with this?"

"She set up some things for me here and also in Los Angeles. Once I speak with her, I'll know where I'll be."

Sam swallowed hard and gave her a sad smile. She saw the look on his face and told him, "No matter what happens, I hope you know you've given me every reason to stay."

He placed his cheek on the top of her head. Brooklynn looked into the sparkling sky, the fireworks splashing colors on her face. She asked, "Do you ever think about what brought us together?"

Sam immediately thought of everything since the first morning he met Chris. *I wish I could tell her the truth, but she wouldn't believe any of it. Besides, where would I begin?* He thought for a few seconds. "Sometimes, it's better not to ask, but to revel in the beauty of two people overcoming incredible odds to be together. I suppose that's the way life works."

Brooklynn nodded. "It's romantic not to know how it happened, or why it happened, but that it happened," she told him.

"You're right. All that matters is that we are both here. Well, at least for the moment," he said with a smile. "I'll take that for now."

Brooklynn held him tighter. "I want you to know the last few months have been very special to me. No matter where we go after tonight, I'll cherish the summer we shared."

"I'm flattered you would say such a thing," Sam said. "But if you have to leave, I'll miss you."

A small tear leaked out of her eye and when Sam heard her sniffle, he asked, "Brooklynn? What's wrong?"

She wiped her cheek, then looked up at him. "Nothing. I...I love you."

Their eyes met, and he smiled. "I love you too, Brooklynn."

As they embraced, she looked up and said, "If something happens, and we end up apart, I..."

"People who love each other carry something of that person wherever they go, so they are never apart. But if you figure out a way to stay, I'll be here. I promise I'll never leave. So we'll never have to worry about being apart."

A gentle breeze blew through her hair, and Sam smelled her in the wind. He closed his eyes and at that moment, he thought, *To hell with the Braves and everything else in Kiawah. This is where my life is.* Sam opened his eyes and looked down at her. When she looked up, all he thought about as how much he looked forward to kissing her.

But as he moved to her, a tiny sliver of sunlight illuminated her emerald eyes. He squinted, then turned and looked out to the scoreboard. The steel blackness of the sky cracked around the edges as the sun began its glorious breakthrough to the new day. A dark, azure sky lurked behind the puffy, low-lying white clouds. As they gazed over the scoreboard, the ascending orange turned some of the choppy clouds into cotton candy pink and blueberry purple. It was a striking contrast to the black clouds above, still not yet touched by the sunlight. Specs of pink, purple, and orange were now visible on some clouds, and it looked as if a paintbrush flicked color into them. The stadium still lay in darkness, but it wouldn't stay that way for much longer.

Sam saw the darkness turning. As he marveled at the colors, he heard a voice. *Once the sun come up, I'm taking you back to Kiawah.* When the words faded, paralyzing fear gripped him. He leaned forward and told her, "Brooklynn, I need to find Chris. Right now."

She looked up at the light changing. "Oh no. I need to get home and see Margaret.

Sam rose and when Brooklynn joined him, he grabbed her hand and the pair sprinted across the wet grass. As the glow seeped through the cracks in the clouds, he looked at her and exclaimed, "We have to hurry."

They left a trail of footprints behind as they headed across the field As they got closer, a glow splashed on the advertisements painted on the left field wall. Brooklyn saw the glow coming off the metal sign, then let go of Sam's hand and stopped. With a grin, she looked at him. "Sam, it's okay. I don't need to see Margaret. I'm staying in Brooklyn."

Sam stopped, then turned. His smile matched hers. "You are?"

Brooklynn's eyes sparkled as she nodded. Sam's face lit up, then he rushed over and scooped her up in his arms. When they released, he said, "Now all I have to do is find Chris," he told her as the glow intensified.

From the portal, Chris rushed into the grandstand and looked around the darkened stadium. Through a sliver of sunlight, he saw Sam and Brooklynn on the outfield grass, only steps from the warning track. He rushed through the grandstand and onto the field. As he ran across the infield, he called out, "Sam?"

Sam stopped and looked over "Chris?" Then he turned to Brooklynn and smiled. "This is going to work out."

Before he said another word, an orange light blinded him. He turned to his left and looked at where it came from. "Wow, that sun is bright," Sam said as he shielded his eyes. "It's a lot like—"

As the light blinded him, a sick feeling splashed into his stomach and his knees buckled. He reached for Brooklynn, but all he grasped was the stiff breeze. "Brooklyn?" He shouted, but the glow drowned him and his voice went unheard.

A rush of wind blew through him and he no longer felt his feet on the grass. When the light subsided and the wind calmed to a gentle breeze, he opened his eyes and looked around. *Oh my God. I'm home.*

twenty-one

Sam took a look around his high school baseball field. As he stood alone, watching the sun rise over the ocean, a wave of resignation gripped him. "I'm out of options now," he said as the sun illuminated his face.

The glow left him numb but the numbness wouldn't last. As he took his first steps, the familiar spear of pain sliced through both knees. It caused him to stop and brace himself. "Oh yeah. I guess I'm home now," he said as he welcomed back the pain after it returned from its seven-month vacation.

As he hobbled off the field in stunned amazement, the next thing he noticed was his wrist. It wasn't dipped in purple, or swollen beyond recognition.

"I guess I'm safe now," he said sarcastically. "There's nothing left to connect me to 1955."

Sam spent the first week back wondering what happened. The questions rolled over in his mind, one after the other, every hour, interrupting his attempts to have peace. He knew he missed his window, and the last minute change of heart was his fault. *Why didn't I tell Chris I wanted to stay during the victory party? I have nobody to blame but myself.*

As the days unfolded, he spent time walking the beach, watching the waves crash to the shore. He remembered the same ritual before he left for Brooklyn, but this time was different. This time, it was not a career, but it was a girl who he lost.

Brooklynn was gone, and she was never coming back. The life he loved was also gone. He came to terms with the fact he was back to being a nobody. There were no requests for autographs, no cheering, and no feeling of fulfillment that being a baseball player brought.

Sam didn't know what to deal with first. Life in the world he was a citizen in, or trying to beat back the memory of the world he was no longer a citizen of. Those feelings were still a work in progress as the guilt piled high on his shoulders.

He walked along the beach, hoping the crashing waves would bring peace. As he walked over the cool ocean water, his footprints eroding in the saturated sand, he looked into the sunrise. "Well, at least I fulfilled a promise to my father."

When the pain of losing the girl he loved got to be too much, he searched online for every picture he could find of the 1955 Dodgers. He hoped he'd see Brooklynn in one of them.

Strike One.

Sam logged on to the *New York Daily News* website where he looked at every newspaper from April to October 1955. He knew he wouldn't find any stories about Sam Murdock, but he hoped there

A Redhead in Brooklyn

might be a picture of Brooklynn. Maybe at Ebbets Field? Maybe during the celebration at the Hotel Bossert?

Strike Two.

Not giving up, Sam thought of another place to look.

Sam owned a copy of the *Baseball Documentary* by Ken Burns. He watched the episode on 1950s baseball in New York, hoping against hope he would see Brooklynn somewhere.

When he watched the video for the fourth time, and he didn't find what he was looking for, he heard the umpire growl, "Strike three. You're out."

Since he couldn't find Brooklynn, he hoped to find Chris instead. He woke up early every morning and walked to Kiawah High School, hoping to get a do-over.

Sam sat in the dugout, hoping Chris would appear as he did before. He would begin by asking him what happened on that last morning in Ebbets Field. And if there was anything he could do to find Brooklynn.

But after a month of mornings of sitting alone, waiting for a miracle to appear in the sunrise, none ever came.

On the last day of October, in the middle of a chilly rain that numbed the tips of his fingers and toes, Sam sat back and closed his eyes. As memories of Brooklynn flooded his mind, he thought about the picture of them at Coney Island. As he thought about it, he heard Chris tell him, *You can't bring anything from the past back with you.*

He looked out to the field and located the exact place where he first heard those words. They echoed in his head and rolled on an infinite loop. He accepted his fate, and once he did, it was a reality he would have to deal with.

The last hope of surviving the wave of the past now overcame him. Sam disappeared below the water and would not be coming up for air. He opened his eyes, stood and left the dugout. As he walked home in the cold autumn rain, he thought about where he'd been.

Sam's baseball career didn't pan out as he expected, but he could live with it. His dream of becoming a professional baseball player came true, although it took a path that no other major league player ever traveled. Although he'd be the only person who knew it happened, it didn't matter. He was proud of the fact he kept his promise to his father.

As winter arrived, he decided enough was enough. He once again pulled out the *Baseball Documentary* and found the footage of Ebbets Field's demise by the wrecker's ball. With the remains of the place that was home to the greatest days of his life lying in a heap of twisted steel and rubble, he savored the irony.

Sam watched the screen go black, then he stopped the video. "Well, they demolished Ebbets Field. I'll never see Chris or Brooklynn again, so that leaves only one thing I need to say goodbye to."

He pulled out his cell phone and made a call. "Hey. It's Sam. Tell the Braves thanks. I appreciate their interest, but I'm retired. Give my spot to some kid who deserves his chance to begin his career."

After he finished the call, he made another. This one to an old friend. "Hello, Coach Wilson? It's Sam Murdock."

A Redhead in Brooklyn

Spring brought renewed life and color back to the Clemson campus. It brought the same to Sam Murdock.

Being back in a place that held wonderful memories made him feel safe. Safety bloomed into confidence. Eventually, the black cloud hanging over him eventually floated away.

Sam took comfort in knowing he didn't have to worry about his knees, or major league pitching, or the pressure of playing in a World Series. He also didn't need to worry about falling in love. All he had to do was mentor young ballplayers, and he knew he could do that. He welcomed the opportunity to give back to those who were learning the game.

One aspect of the job he looked forward to was recruiting. He enjoyed being able to go places and see others playing the game. His territory was the Atlantic coast since he spent several years in Durham and knew that part of the country well. People would recognize him, and that helped with meeting recruits.

Sam sat in his office, gazing through the window at the ground crew taking care of the field. As he watched them raking and smoothing out the dirt around home plate, his desk phone buzzed.

"Hey, Coach. What? Sure. I'll be down in a few."

Sam walked down the hallway to head coach Steve Wilson's office. Wilson was an old-school coach who grew up in rural South Carolina. His southern colloquialisms had players and coaches throwing their hands up in bewilderment.

He knocked on the door, then walked in. "Hey Coach. How are you doing?"

Steve looked up, then shook his head with a frown. "Aw damn it, Sam. This team keeps peein' down my back and then tellin' me it's raining."

"I don't...Um..."

"Hell, son. If idiots could fly, this place would be an airport. And we're favored to win the conference this year. I'm gonna have to do a come to Jesus meetin' before long."

"You have a way with words."

Wilson got to the business at hand. "Aw, damn it, Sam," he told him in his southern twang. "I heard from Scanlon today. He's taking a job with the Red Sox, so we need someone to cover the northeast territory until I can get a replacement. I want you to go up there and see a few players we have our eye on."

Wilson spit into his cup. "I hope these boys wanna come south since our best players are either graduating or being drafted. Unless we get some stallions in the paddock, there ain't gonna be any grits in our cupboard once the rooster wakes us up."

I have no idea what the hell he's talking about.

"There's a couple of boys I want you to see. One's in Roanoke. Then I want you to check out a boy in Baltimore, then head up to New Haven. Oh, and there's a boy in New York City we got a tip about. His name is Alex Gordon and they say he would be perfect in our outfield."

Sam raised his eyebrows. "New York?"

"Yeah. We're getting reports that this kid is something special."

"Where in New York?"

A Redhead in Brooklyn

"Brooklyn. Ever heard of it?"

Sam looked over prospects in the three cities and came away impressed. He hoped rain would cut his trip to the fourth place short. Unfortunately, it was a perfect afternoon for a baseball game at Brooklyn Prep.

He took a seat in the metal bleachers and looked out to the field. With the Verrazano-Narrows Bridge in the background, he soaked in the ivy-clad stone buildings and immaculate athletic facilities.

Alex Gordon was everything Steve Wilson said he was. Sam watched him slug two home runs, and throw out a runner from left field. Sam fell in love with the kid.

He reminds me of another Brooklyn ballplayer.

After the game, the athletic director led Sam back to the coach's office so Sam could talk with Gordon and sell him on coming to Clemson.

Sam was more impressed with the player off the field. Gordon was respectful, attentive and showed genuine interest. But what got Sam's attention was when Gordon asked him about his days at Clemson. *The kid did his homework.*

After a half hour, Sam gave Gordon his card and told him he would love to have him at Clemson for a weekend series during the season.

The kid's eyes lit up. "I'd like that."

Sam won round one.

After telling Gordon he would be in touch, he walked out of the building, then pulled out his phone to order an Uber. As he swiped his phone to get to the app, a text alert popped up.

Flight 994 - Delayed - Mechanical Issue - New Depart time 10:19 pm.

"Great," Sam said. "And I thought I was going to get out of here unscathed."

He found the Uber app and scheduled a pick up. But, with time on his hands, he wasn't going to the airport immediately.

Sam asked the driver to take him to 124 Sullivan Place. The driver looked at him in the rear view mirror, and after exchanging small talk, allowed him peace as the car rolled along Fort Hamilton Parkway.

After passing Prospect Park, Sam knew he was getting close. As they passed the apartment buildings, some were recognizable, although they looked updated.

His eyes widened when they crossed the intersection where he had to pull Brooklynn away from the speeding car. The trees had grown taller and fuller, and the stoplight looked different, but the feeling of that night was alive and powerful within him.

When the car came to the intersection of Sullivan and McKeever, Sam tricked himself into thinking he'd see Ebbets Field. But when they came upon the intersection, instead of a ballpark looking down on him, in its place was a tall apartment complex soaring into the sky.

Sam stared at the buildings. *That's a tragedy.*

A Redhead in Brooklyn

The car stopped on the curb outside 124 Sullivan Place. Except for two trees on opposite sides of the driveway, the house hadn't changed much since the last time he saw it.

"Can I have a second?" Sam asked the driver.

When the driver nodded, Sam got out of the car, shut the door and walked on to the sidewalk. He stood in front of the house and soaked it all in. The house looked back at him in all its amorous glory.

Sam was no longer in the present. He was back in 1955. He didn't feel the pain in his knees, or the pain of a broken heart. He was in the moment, and it was as if he never left Brooklyn..

As he looked at the house, before his eyes came the image of a man and woman standing in front of it, laughing. Then the man leaned in and kissed her on the cheek.

Sam watched the man walk away from the house, then along the sidewalk. He was full of optimism as he walked with a spring in his step.

When the night swallowed up the man, the feeling of being back in time eroded, and Sam was back to the present.

He looked at the house, then nodded. *Time to go.*

Sam walked back to the car, opened the rear door, and slid inside. "I have one more place I need to visit, then you can take me to the airport."

Sam walked under the rose-covered pavilion, then down the steps to the stone floor. The girl he came to see had her back to him, so he walked around to see her face.

She hadn't changed since the first time he saw her. The look of longing at the bouquet of roses rocked him harder this time, because he understood what that look was about.

The first time he saw her, the sun was warm, his heart full, and standing next to him was an alluring woman who taught him about the beauty of the world. But now, as the sun dipped into the horizon, all that stood was the breezy cold of spring, and a heartbroken woman staring into a bouquet of bronze roses.

He approached the statue. "Hello Rose Maiden," he said, as he stood before her. "I guess we have something in common now."

The statue continued looking down.

"I'm sure you're asking why. Well, a long time ago, there was this girl. She brought me here and introduced us."

Sam smiled as his mind drifted back to the past. "She was the girl with the cinnamon hair and freckles. Kinda sassy. You remember her, right? She drank beer from a bottle and liked to dance in these dive bars. Between you and me, I liked that about her."

The Maiden never moved.

"She was smart too. Much smarter than me. She knew things about the world. About how things make you feel. How they give you a moment that lives forever." Sam shook his head. "Everything reminds me of her. How brief our time was together. Time we'll never get back." He exhaled. "Yeah. She was something."

A woman from behind watched the exchange.

Sam continued. "Guess what? I lost her. That's why it's only me here." He looked into the distance, shook his head, then looked at the Rose Maiden. "I don't know if she ever came back here after I left, but if she did, I hope she told you about me and what happened at Ebbets Field." He looked away, then shook his head. "Aw, that was a long time ago. It doesn't matter now."

He stared at the statue, then told her, "I hope one day you find your lost love." He paused, then with a sad smile told her, "I lost mine and she's never coming back."

The woman approached. "Excuse me?"

Sam saw an older woman with glasses held by a silver chain around her neck, and her reddish gray hair pulled back in a bun. He looked at her for a few seconds, seeing the wrinkles around her eyelids and cheeks, but her emerald eyes captivated him. He shook his head, then asked, "I know this might sound a little strange, but... have we met?"

The woman smiled, then shook her head. "I don't think so. If we had, I'm sure I'd remember," she said with a smile.

Sam nodded, then told her, "Yeah, I suppose you're right." He paused, then looked at the Rose Maiden again. "I've always wondered who she's waiting for."

The woman looked at the statue. "Yeah. Me too. I'd like to think she fell in love. But something happened, and she had to say goodbye. She must have promised that no matter how far apart they would be, she'd always be there."

Sam listened to her words, and when they came together in his head, his eyes squinted.

Where have I heard that before?

As he continued looking at the statue, his brain threw up a video of him and Brooklynn on their last morning at Ebbets Field. He heard her voice tell him that no matter what, they would always be together, no matter how far apart they might be. He turned to the woman and gave her a long look. "Are you Brooklynn?"

The woman smiled and gave him a long look. Then she spoke. "No. I'm sorry, I wish I was. But I live in Brooklyn. My name is Annabelle. Annabelle Thomas. I am a horticulture specialist here at the Botanical Garden."

Sam's initial excitement faded, and it landed with a thud in the pit of his stomach. "Oh, I'm sorry. You reminded me of someone I used to…Well, it's not important."

Annabelle smiled, then told him, "I enjoyed your conversation with the Rose Maiden. It's funny, but I rarely hear such beauty in someone's words. Thank you. This was a privilege."

Sam nodded. "You're welcome."

"I would love to ask you more about who this girl was, but I'm afraid we don't have time. The Garden is closing."

"Oh, I'm sorry. I was just leaving."

"It's okay," she assured him. "I have to know. Who was she?"

Sam raised his eyebrows and smiled. "Um…She was a girl. A girl that a boy fell in love with. But I wasn't smart enough to hold on to her."

The woman's smile faded. "I'm sorry you lost your girl. Do you think you'll ever find her?"

"Nah. She's gone forever, so she'll have to live on in here," he said, then tapped his chest.

The woman frowned, then told him, "I'll stall the guys at the gate. Take as long as you like."

Sam gave her a sad smile. "I won't be long."

A Redhead in Brooklyn

The woman nodded, then walked away.

Sam returned to the Maiden. "I wanted to say thank you for bringing beauty into the world. These days, I appreciate those kinds of things more than I used to. I hope one day your longing ends. For me, I'll never be that lucky."

He touched her bronze arm, feeling the cold of the spring in it, then turned and walked away.

twenty-two

After Sam returned to Clemson, he gave Coach Wilson his assessment of the players on his recruiting trip.

"What about the kid from Brooklyn?"

Sam remembered what he saw on Sullivan Place and at the Botanical Garden. *That guy didn't survive the trip. He's dead.* Then he answered, "He's as good as advertised."

After Sam pulled out the reports from a folder, he looked them over and gave them to Coach Wilson. "You can see the ratings for each player."

Coach Wilson looked over the sheets. "If we can get these boys, we'll be livin' in the tall cotton."

Sam pulled out a few more folders and looked through them. "Do we have an analytics person on staff? We need to modernize these forms to have more succinct data on our recruits. I also would like to have some specialized stats on our current players. I want to see how they're hitting in certain situations, and evaluate their at-bats in game."

"If the creek don't rise, we can get you what you need.

A Redhead in Brooklyn

Analytics hired a girl who can turn goat piss into gasoline."

"That's great, Coach. She'll be useful when we need someone to fill up the team bus for away games. But I need someone who can crunch some numbers."

Wilson spit into a paper cup. "Aw damn it, Sam. I meant this girl is slicker than owl shit. She can give you a reason for every outcome on the field."

For a moment, Sam thought of someone who was way better than anyone they had at Clemson. But as the image of Brooklynn's face materialized, he waved it away. Sam stared at the pages inside the folder for a few seconds, then returned to the present. "Great. Do you know where I could find her?"

"She got here a few weeks ago. But she's busier than a one-legged man at a butt-kickin' contest, so go easy on her."

"I will," he promised.

A few minutes later, Sam found himself along a long hallway. As he got to the last door, his eyes focused on the purple and white nameplate with an orange paw print in the top right corner. The top of the nameplate was blank, but underneath he read, 'Baseball Analytics.' Sam stared at it, and with no name above, he grinned. *The ghost of baseball's past. Oh, how I love a cliffhanger.*

He leaned his head around the corner and looked into the office. The woman standing with her back to him at the whiteboard wasn't a redhead. She was a brunette.

Sam exhaled.

"Excuse me, I'm Sam Murdock, the new batting coach. Coach Wilson told me you put numbers together to help with charting player performance?"

The woman turned, and when she focused on his face, smiled. "Well, you're in the right place. Nice to meet you, Coach Murdock."

The woman pulled the cap off the back of the marker, clicked it over the top, and placed it on the tray. "I can help you with that. Did you have an idea of what you wanted?"

"I'd like to create a new form for recruits so we can analyze their performance. Then I'd like something to track our current player's output, and do it in-game as well."

"Something like what pitches the batter sees? The result of the at-bat? And the percentage of swings that result in contact?"

The woman looked nothing like Brooklynn, but sounded like her. Sam ignored the comparison and nodded. "That would be perfect. Would it be possible to pull the forms up on my iPad during games?"

"Yes. We have an application that will do that. We are working with the video team to track every pitch for both home and away games that will update each at bat live. When would you like to have it?"

"Would later this week be too soon?"

"I can have a mock-up for you by then. The other analyst is at lunch right now, but we can put something together for you. Once we create a few mock-ups, you can let me know which one works best."

Sam walked over and extended his hand. "Thank you for your help. Welcome to Clemson."

The woman extended her hand and gave Sam a warm smile. "Nice to meet you too. I'm sure we'll see each on the field."

Her smile wasn't lost on Sam. "I'm sure we will."

A Redhead in Brooklyn

As he walked back to his office, he thought, *I've heard that line before. I hope this time we aren't out there at sunrise.*

With the rest of the afternoon free, and the team having the day off before a series at Georgia Tech, Sam had the field all to himself.

He wanted to get lost for a few hours in something he loved, and taking batting practice was the thing that would take him where he wanted to go.

Since the team had the day off, Sam had the clubhouse to himself. He sat on a stool, and while he changed clothes, looked around the large room. All he saw were the lockers from Ebbets Field and the players he played with here.

He shook his head, exhaled, then brushed the memory aside. *I thought I told you never to come back?* He told himself, then smiled as the clubhouse turned from black and white 50s to present-day orange and purple.

After changing into his workout clothes, he walked out to the field. Waiting for him was the cool spring sunshine, which hinted at warmer weather in the days to come. In the trees around the field, the sound of birds serenaded him as he walked to the pitcher's mound.

He loaded the pitching machine with a bucket of balls, then walked back to home plate. Sam looked down at his feet and placed them in the batter's box. Instinctively, he moved his back foot away from home plate and took a couple of practice swings. When he looked at the pitcher's mound, he saw Ebbets Field behind it. Then the scoreboard resting in right field, and the sound of Hilda Chester's cowbell. *Stop it. This isn't Brooklyn.*

When the machine spit out the first ball, Sam heard the cheers of the Dodger fans. BAM.

There was Brooklynn's face smiling at him. BAM.

Sliding past Yogi Berra to score a crucial run in Game Four of the World Series. BAM.

The home run he hit in Game Five. BAM.

The wild celebration in Brooklyn. BAM.

The victory party at the Hotel Bossert. BAM.

Talking with Chris. Dancing with Brooklynn. BAM. BAM.

The sunrise in Ebbets Field. BAM.

Seeing Brooklynn's house a few days ago. BAM.

Memories of the first time he met Chris. BAM.

He took swing after swing, and before he knew it, the pitching machine was empty and the only sound was the motor. Sam stared at it, the sweat pouring off his face, bat cocked, waiting for the next ball that never came.

When the haze lifted, and he saw the machine empty, he dropped the bat, and walked out to turn it off. He wheeled it to the dugout railing and placed the cord on top of it.

After gathering up the baseballs, he grasped the handle and, ignoring the pain in his knees and palm, placed it next to the pitching machine.

Sam walked into the dugout and sat on the green padded bench. He stared into the sunset, thinking about the last hour of his life and how the memories attacked him. He felt something painful coming from his chest, so he brought his hand up to feel where the pain came from.

A Redhead in Brooklyn

It was his heart. Pumping hard and deep, it brought back a familiar ache.

It was more powerful than the ones coming from his knees. But for this one, he cursed himself, since this was self-inflicted. He knew better than to backtrack around corners he'd turned. The wrecker's ball from his days in Brooklyn found him, and it demolished everything he'd rebuilt in Clemson.

Sam wiped the remaining sweat off his face, then leaned back and placed the back of his head against the dugout wall. A haze of hurt, anger, and confusion engulfed him. As he tumbled into a pitch-black abyss with no floor, a voice grabbed him and pulled him back to the surface.

"Hello, Sam."

twenty-three

Sam looked down the long row of the dugout. The voice was familiar. The glare was new. "If it isn't the man in the fedora. What are you doing here? You take a wrong turn leaving Brooklyn?" He asked, his voice terse.

Chris stood at the railing in front of the dugout. "I've been looking for you. You're a hard man to find."

"Apparently not hard enough."

Chris nodded, his face unsure of what would happen next. "I see you're taking batting practice. You know, this reminds me of the first time we met."

"A day that will live in infamy," Sam quipped as he picked up a towel.

Chris ignored the indifferent response. "How are the knees?"

"Great. Never felt better."

Chris gave him a small grin. "It's good to see you."

Sam wiped his face with the towel and dropped it on the bench. "Yeah. I wish I felt the same." When the awkward silence grew tense, Sam asked, "I'll ask you again. What are you doing here?"

"We have unfinished business."

"Unfinished business? Last time I checked, and I've checked every day for the last six months, our business was concluded. I'm sorry you wasted your time and the resources of your crack research team to track me down. Next time, save yourself a trip and leave me the hell alone."

Chris said nothing as he stared at the dugout floor.

Sam broke the silence. "If you're here to take me on another magical mystery tour, I have better things to do with my time. Besides, you're a rotten tour guide."

Chris smiled. "You have a way with words."

"And you have a way of making my life hell. I didn't pay for that upgrade. Oh, and when they ask how my customer experience was, I'm not giving you five stars."

He stood, and after a brief wobble, got his legs under him. "What brings you to the only place in the world that you haven't ruined?" Sam looked skyward and sniffed a couple of times. "What's that smell? Oh, yeah. I've smelled it before. It usually arrives after one of your little speeches."

Chris shook his head. "Look, I'm here since we have to talk."

"Fine. Talk."

"Sam, I–"

Sam cut him off. "On second thought, there's nothing to talk about. I was late. I own that. But you were the one who said I needed to fight for her. Well, I was ready to start swinging. I thought you'd be in my corner when the bell rang."

"I've always been in your corner."

"Yeah, right. Where were you when I needed an extra ten seconds to tell you I was staying?"

"Let me explain."

"I wouldn't believe you now no matter what you told me." He looked at Chris, then snarled, "Get the hell out of here."

"You don't know the truth, Sam. I'm here to tell you exactly what happened."

"Give it your best shot. Maybe the ending will come as you go along."

Before Chris spoke, Sam beat him to it. "Tell ya what. Save the song and dance. I'd rather not spend my night getting all warm and fuzzy with old memories." As Sam took a step toward the door to the clubhouse, he turned and told Chris, "By the way, you told me I couldn't bring anything back from Brooklyn. Well you go that wrong too."

"I did? What do you mean?"

"The one thing I brought back with me was a broken heart." He paused then shook his head. "Thanks again for the wonderful parting gift. I'll cherish it forever."

"If you are bitter, then fine," Chris said, his voice rising. "But there's an explanation for what happened that morning at Ebbets Field."

"I wouldn't bring up Ebbets Field again. It's lousy salesmanship."

"I have an idea where we're going with this conversation," Chris told him.

"Good. And you know where you can go once this

conversation is over. How about you save us both the trouble and head that way now?"

Chris stared at Sam. He never moved.

Finally, Sam spoke. "Are your legs broken? I said leave."

"I have my reasons for being here."

Sam smiled. "Oh great. The plot thins."

"Sam there are reasons for everything that happened. Just give me a chance to explain."

"You've had six months to explain what happened. Wow, you're attention to detail is as sharp as ever."

Chris looked at Sam and smiled. "You said it."

Sam squinted. "Said what?"

"Wow."

From his left Sam heard footsteps approaching on the crunchy dirt in front of the dugout. A woman approached and stopped at the railing.

Sam looked over. After a few seconds his face became mired in twisted wonder. Then it came to him. "Wait a second. I know you."

The woman smiled. "I look a little different than I did in Brooklyn."

Sam focused on the woman, then asked. "Margaret?"

Margaret nodded.

Sam turned to Chris and smirked. "Again with your brilliant attention to detail. Right house. Wrong girl. Mine was the redhead." He shook his head. "Can't you do anything right?"

Ivan Scott

Margaret shook her head. "Chris didn't bring me here."

"Excuse me?" Sam asked.

"I said he didn't bring me here. I brought myself."

twenty-four

Sam asked, "You brought yourself?"

As he gazed at her, Margaret nodded. When he looked at Chris, he got the same nod. Sam shook his head and sat. "What's this about?"

Chris stepped forward. "I'll explain my part and then let Margaret take it from there."

"Okay," Sam said as he leaned forward on the bench and looked at Chris. "Give it your best shot."

Chris walked in front of him. "I was responsible for bringing you back to Brooklyn so you could live out your fantasy of playing baseball. Along the way," he said, then looked at Margaret, "You encountered a certain redhead and her roommate."

Sam looked at Margaret, who raised her eyebrows and smiled.

Chris continued. "I didn't know about Margaret, since she was new in the Lost Causes section."

Sam's face went white. "Wait. Lost Causes section?" He asked as he looked at Chris. "You mean she's a Saint too? This has to be a joke."

Chris shook his head. "Notice I'm not laughing. By the time I found out who she was and what she was doing there, it was too late. I went back to the hotel, and when you didn't show up, I thought about what you loved about Brooklyn, I knew then it had to be Ebbets Field. I rushed over there and saw you and Brooklynn in left field. I yelled for you, but when the sunrise came, the process had already begun, and I couldn't stop it."

Sam's eyes drifted to the floor of the dugout. His mind replayed every event from that day. Then he looked at Margaret. "You aren't from 1955?"

She shook her head.

Sam stared at her for a few seconds. Then he asked, "What were you doing there?"

Margaret walked into the dugout. "I was with Brooklynn to help her rectify something that happened with her family. Did she tell you about her mother?"

Sam thought for a moment, scanning the past with Brooklynn to see if something clicked. His eyes widened, and the answer came. "She told me her mom grew up without a father. A drunk driver hit him while walking home in Brooklyn. But what does that have to do with you? And with her?"

Margaret smiled. "Yes. She was there to help her mother and grandfather. But she left after the season was over."

"Yeah, to Los Angeles. I know all about that."

Margaret shook hr head. "No, Sam. She wasn't from 1955."

Sam's mouth opened, but nothing came out. He shook his head, his face twisted in confusion. "What?"

A Redhead in Brooklyn

"Sam, she is not from 1955. She is from the present."

Sam gulped, then shook his head. "You mean..." he said, trying to make sure he understood what she was telling him.

Margaret nodded.

Sam shook his head. "I can't believe it."

"Why not?" Chris asked. "You were from the present."

"She was helping her mother and grandfather?" Sam asked. "Where do you fit into this?"

"I helped arrange for Brooklynn to be in the right place at the right time so she could speak with her grandfather. She gave him tickets to the World Series so he would be at Ebbets Field instead of being on the street. That's why she was working with the Dodgers, so she would have access to tickets. Having a baseball background in analytics made it an easy fit. Especially when the Dodgers saw the results."

Sam squinted. "She gave him tickets to the games?" He then looked away as the pieces fell into place. "She said something about if he was at the game, then he... That's why she helped me during my slump. She told me it was critical the Dodgers made it to the World Series." He looked down and shook his head. "Now it makes sense." He looked at Margaret. "How did she pull it off?"

"She had to wait until her mother was born and her grandfather came to the hospital to see his new daughter. It was there Brooklynn gave him tickets to the Series so he wouldn't be on the street. She was supposed to leave after that, but things got complicated."

"Complicated?"

"Yes. She worked for the Brooklyn Dodgers in 1955. That was her cover for why she was there. But she also had an offer from the Los Angeles Dodgers in the present. She was doing analytics for her alma mater, the College of Charleston, when the Dodgers offered her a job. It was always her dream to work for a pro baseball team, and since it was the team her family followed, it was a dream come true. She was going to be the V.P. of Analytics."

"Did she take the job?"

"Yes, she did. But the night before she was due to move to Los Angeles, I offered her the opportunity to change history and have her mother grow up with a father. Once she took care of things in Brooklyn, she was supposed to head to L.A. to fulfill her dream."

"So that was what she was in love with in L.A," Sam told them.

"Well," Margaret told him, "She fell in love with something else in Brooklyn. What happened that morning in Ebbets Field?"

"She was ready to stay in 1955 with me. We were leaving Ebbets Field to find you and Chris, then the sunrise came and the next thing I knew, I was standing in my old baseball field in Kiawah."

Margaret nodded. "You two met the same fate."

"What do you mean?" Sam asked.

"At the victory party, I spoke with Brooklynn and she told me she wanted to stay in 1955 to be with you. Since I was new, I wasn't sure if we did things like that, so I told her I would check, but not to get her hopes up. I began researching our time travel case files to see if anyone from the present wanted to stay in the past. During my search, your name popped up in a list of current time travel cases, and Chris was your escort."

A Redhead in Brooklyn

"Wow," Sam told her. "What happened next?"

"I explained it to St. Jude, he green-lighted the request, so I waited for her to come home since that's where we said we'd meet, and tell me in person. When I saw the sunrise, I thought the same thing as Chris, so I rushed out of the house and over to Ebbets Field. I ran into the portal behind him, but by the time I got there, you two were already gone."

"So, she's in Los Angeles? Like, right now?" Sam asked, his eyes hopeful.

Margaret looked at Chris and raised her eyebrows. Chris told him, "We don't know where she is. Margaret and I looked for her all over L.A., but she's not there."

"She's not?" Sam asked.

Margaret shook her head. "I'm sorry, Sam. We thought she was at Dodger Stadium, but they told us she turned down the job." She looked at Chris, then back at him. "We were hoping you might have an idea, since, well, we're fresh out of them at the moment."

Sam looked at them. A small smile came to his lips. The first one he'd had since the last morning at Ebbets Field. "I might."

Chris looked at Sam. "Where are you going to look for her?"

Sam looked into the distance for a few seconds. Finally, he snapped out of it. "Charleston."

"Why there?" Chris asked.

"Whenever you're hurting, you go home. Home is the place where you heal. Where you feel safe. Home is where you find peace." When Chris and Margaret nodded, Sam told them, "I came back to Clemson since it was home."

With newfound energy and a look of optimism on his face, Sam hopped off the bench. "I have a redheaded to find." He moved to the door leading to the clubhouse, then stopped and turned to Chris. "I'm sorry. I was wrong to be angry with you."

"It's not a problem," he assured him. "I'm glad I came back so we could work things out. Remember what I told you back in Brooklyn?"

"What?"

"There was a reason for me taking you back there."

Sam smiled. "Oh, I know. And I appreciate the fact you let me live out my dream of being a professional baseball player."

Chris raised his eyebrows. "Well, not exactly."

"Not exactly? What do you mean?"

"The first night when we had dinner in Brooklyn, you asked me why you were there. I told you it was so you could find something."

Sam nodded. "I did. I found out what it was like to be a professional baseball player. I was able to fulfill a promise, as well as make a dream come true"

"That's true, Sam. But you were there to find something much more meaningful than being a ballplayer. You were there to find true love. You were there to find Brooklynn."

Sam stared at him, then looked at Margaret. "Is this true?"

Margaret smiled and gave him a gentle nod.

Sam shook his head. "Well, the jury is still out on that."

"No matter," Chris told him. "You found the girl you are supposed to be with. No matter the time, distance, or incredible circumstances, you overcame it all. In life, we all deserve that. No matter how long you got to spend together. You found yours, and nothing can take it away. Now, will you do me a favor?"

"Anything."

"Remember when I told you she will need to be there after all the wins and losses are over and it's time for all the wins and losses of life to begin?"

Sam nodded.

"Well, the clock is ticking so stop wasting time and go find her."

Sam nodded. "I'm on it." He took a step, then stopped and turned to Chris. They looked at each other, then embraced. "Thank you for everything."

"No charge," Chris assured him.

Sam hugged Margaret, then moved to the door so he could get on the road to Charleston.

As he went to open the dugout door leading to the clubhouse, it came open, and Sam stopped in his tracks. His eyes widened, and he groped for words. It was a familiar feeling.

twenty-five

Sam stared at the redheaded girl sporting cheeks full of freckles. He froze in a hazy glow.

The girl smiled. "Hello, Fred."

Sam smiled, letting the moment unfold in a slow panorama of emotion. His eyes focused only on her. Finally, he said, "Hello, Ginger."

The pair stared at each other with confused, but optimistic smiles on their faces. Their focus was so intense, they forgot about Chris and Margaret, who vanished to avoid being a distraction. But they stuck around to see how this love story would play out.

A slight smile came to Sam's lips. Brooklynn continued staring. As Sam tried to make sense of what was happening, he finally spoke. "You're here."

Brooklynn nodded. "I am." She stared at him with sparkling eyes. "What are you doing here?"

"I live here."

Brooklynn's eyes widened. "You do?"

Sam nodded.

Brooklynn's knees buckled. Sam rushed over and wrapped his arms around her before she wobbled and fell into the dugout wall. He held her as she buried her face in his chest. Muffled sobs led to a soggy patch on his shirt.

Sam comforted her. "Don't cry, Brooklynn. It's okay. I'm here now."

She raised her head. "I'm not crying." Sam had been down this road before. He wouldn't contradict her this time. "I thought I lost you forever," she said through the tears.

"I thought the same thing," he told her.

When the sobbing continued, he felt her arms around his back. They wrapped him in a warm embrace and they stayed there for a long time.

Eventually, they released. Sam reached for Brooklynn's hand, and her fingers wrapped around his. He felt them on the back of his hand and it brought tingles that raced up his arm and roared into the rest of his body.

He led her to the bench so they could sit. "Nobody knew where you were. Margaret told me she was late in getting to you before the sunrise, and when it came, it took you back to the present."

Brooklynn's eyes widened. "You know about Margaret?"

Sam nodded. "I do. And I'll do you one better. Chris and Margaret work together. He brought me to Brooklyn in 1955, like Margaret did for you."

Brooklynn paused, then asked, "You are from the present? I...you were...What were you doing in 1955?"

"Chris brought me back to fulfill a promise I made to my father to play major league baseball. Remember I told you about that on our last morning at Ebbets Field?"

Brooklynn nodded. "Yes. How could I forget that day?"

"I haven't," he assured her. But all that matters now is we are here, inches apart, and now there's no time limit on where we are. We can stay here as long as we like."

Brooklynn smiled, then asked, "What are you doing in Clemson?"

"I took a job with the baseball team. I'm the new hitting coach." He paused, then asked, "What are you doing here?"

Brooklynn's puffy eyes looked up at him. She wiped her cheeks, then spoke. "Remember, we said after the season was over, you'd show me Clemson?"

Sam nodded. "I remember."

"I thought I lost you forever, so I had to figure out a way to be close to you. I called a friend of mine at Clemson and asked about the baseball team. Turns out, they were looking for an analytics person. Even though I knew I'd never see you again, I figured it would be okay since I would at least have your spirit here with me. Knowing you once existed here, that was good enough. I guess when we take a chance, it's better than never risking everything for the things you love."

Sam's eyes widened. "Love?"

Brooklynn shrugged, then looked away. "Did I say that?"

"Yep," he said with a nod.

Brooklynn shrugged her shoulders. "I guess your optimism rubbed off on me."

"Oh, well. There's that optimism popping up again. I hate

A Redhead in Brooklyn

when that happens."

As they shared a small laugh, Brooklynn continued. "That morning at Ebbets Field, I was trying to get back to my house to ask Margaret if I could stay. But when the sunrise came, and I was still standing in Ebbets Field, I knew I was okay, and she must have arranged it so I could stay there with you. But the sun blinded me, so I reached for you, but there was nothing but the breeze. As soon as the light subsided, I was standing in my apartment in Charleston."

Sam nodded, "I know. Chris and Margaret told me all about why you were there."

After a moment of silence, Sam moved closer and breathed her in. It was a simple pleasure he promised himself he would never take for granted if he ever got a second chance to be with her a second time. "So you were in 1955 to give tickets to your grandfather?"

"Yes, I was. How did you know that?"

Sam exhaled. "Margaret told me. So that's why you were trying to help me that day in Ebbets Field."

Brooklynn looked up at him. "What day?"

"When I was in a slump and you suggested I move my back foot back in the batter's box. You mentioned something about making sure the Dodgers were in the World Series, so he wouldn't be on the street, didn't you?"

Brooklynn looked at him, then nodded. "I was the one who put your bio together. When you got off to a hot start, I knew that as long as you kept hitting, the Dodgers had a chance to be in the Series. If not, then I would have to come up with something, anything, to keep my grandfather off the street."

"He still would have been on the street?"

Brooklynn nodded. "He and his friends never missed a World Series game, even when the Dodgers weren't playing. Chances are he would have been in that bar, watching whoever was playing, and would have met the same fate."

"Where did you find him?"

"At the hospital after my mother was born. I knew he'd be there, so Margaret drove over there in a cab with me. She stayed in the cab, since it was something I had to do by myself. I walked in, found the maternity ward, made some excuse about it being his lucky day and he had won tickets in a hospital raffle, and gave them to him. Then I walked by a window where all the babies were, and I found my mom. I told her everything was going to be okay. She would grow up with her father."

Sam gazed at her in awe. He exhaled, then shook his head. "You're something, you know that?"

"Aw, what can I say? I had an opportunity to do something for my mother." After a pause, she asked, "You were there because of the promise you made to your father?"

"Yeah. I spent years in the minors, then they released me, so I failed to make good on my promise. Then Chris comes along. He offers me a chance to play for my father's favorite baseball team, the Brooklyn Dodgers, during their championship season in 1955."

"So we did all this for our parents, huh?"

"Yeah, I guess so. Now, I'll never have to live with the regret of a broken promise. But Chris told me there was another reason I was there. He told me I was supposed to find something."

"Find something? What were you supposed to find?"

Sam explained, "Chris told me that after the wins and losses end, it's time to find someone to share all the wins and losses of life with." He looked at her with a sparkle in his eye.

Brooklynn's eyebrows rose and she smiled. "Well, did you find what you were looking for?"

Sam grinned. "It was looking a little bleak only a few hours ago. But I think it's finally within reach."

Brooklynn blushed. "You were always the optimistic one. Good to see success hasn't changed you." Then Brooklynn folded her arms in front of her chest. "Well, Mr. Optimism. Are you going to do something or sit there and wait for the sunrise to take me away from you a second time?"

Before he knew it, they rushed into each other's arms and shared their first real kiss.

This was well worth the wait, Sam thought.

As the kiss ended, he told her, "I'll never let you go."

She grinned and told him, "You'll never have to."

After their second kiss ended, Brooklynn asked, "What do we do now?"

"Well, since we can't have lasagna at Luigi's, how about a few beers at the Esso Club?"

"No glasses, right?" She asked. "You know that's an instant deal breaker for me."

Sam grinned. "Right. And maybe we'll find some Nat King Cole on the jukebox."

Brooklynn beamed. "I'll hope for the best. After that, who knows where it could lead?"

Sam reached for her hand. When she grasped it, they grinned

at each other. He led her out of the dugout and into the navy blue sheet that became the sky. He paused, then looked up.

"What are you looking at?" She asked.

"I wanted to make sure it was the right time. You know what happened the last time we walked across a ball field?"

Brooklynn laughed. "We're good. At least until the morning."

"Yeah. So we better leave now."

With the sunset in front of them, the sunrises from the past were long gone. They found each other, and now, time nor place could ever keep them apart.

Chris and Margaret watched them walk across the field and eventually leave the stadium.

"Ain't love something?" She asked.

"It's where miracles come from," he agreed.

Margaret turned and said, "Our work here is done." After Chris nodded, she asked, "By the way, are you going to the All Saints Dance next week?"

He looked at her, then smiled. "Well, I might be in the neighborhood. What did you have in mind?"

"I was thinking on our way back to the office, we could have a drink and discuss what time you'd like to pick me up."

Chris smiled, then extended his arm. When Margaret pulled hers through, they gave each other a flirtatious grin. With the crickets serenading them, they walked out of the dugout and vanished into the South Carolina night.

Acknowledgments

This book could not have been written without a lot of help from my friends and the writing community.

Many thanks to Karen Crawford and Katie Cunningham for their patience and giving the story suggestions and thoughts I never considered. And to my Bama buddy, Ashlie Bowman, I cannot thank you enough for your extra set of eyes and getting this book ready to go out into the world. Special thanks to Peter Trunk for help with the Ebbets Field Picture!

To my friends in the writing community on social media, thank you for your constant encouragement, When things gets tough, you all are always there to help me get through it, I am blessed to have you all in my corner.

And to Red, thank you for always being there!

Find Ivan Scott

For more information on Ivan Scott, please find him on the following social media sites @ Author Ivan Scott:

Instagram
Twitter
Facebook
YouTube
Goodreads
Pinterest
TikTok

Are you curious as to what Ivan saw when he created the characters and settings? Visit his Pinterest page for videos and photos of each character and setting so you can be taken to the exact places the characters were, and visualize what they looked like while they were there.

Printed in Great Britain
by Amazon